THE WIRE RECORDER

THOMAS A. LEVITT

THE
WIRE
RECORDER

A NOVEL

THOMAS A. LEVITT

THE WIRE RECORDER

Cover design by Monica Haynes / The Thatchery
Book design by Morgana Gallaway

For Megan, Sarah, Mary Lou, Phil Sr., Phil Jr.,
Naomi Sr., Naomi Jr., Anthony, Stacey, Alex, Stefan, Celeste,
Elise, Olivia and Sadie

and

In loving memory of my wife
Janeth Auer Levitt
(1939-2014)

my mother
Helen Slote Levitt
(1916-1993)

my father
Alfred Lewis Levitt
(1916-2002)

and my sister
Ann Lois Levitt
(1950-2016)

ACKNOWLEDGMENTS

I am most grateful to Peter Gelfan, Doug Wagner, Karinya Funsett-Topping, Monica Haynes, Norma Barzman, Freddie Hannan, Sarah Starr-Levitt and Pattie McDonald for the honest feedback they provided—some in their professional capacities and others on a personal level—which helped me bring this book to where I felt ready to "put it out there."

I would also like to acknowledge the countless suggestions and words of support my late and beloved wife, Janeth Auer Levitt, gave me over the many years it took for this story to morph into its present form.

TABLE OF CONTENTS

Webster • Chicago Model 80 is a self-contained, general purpose, portable magnetic wire recorder and player. It comes complete—ready to use—with microphone and three spools of wire. It can be readily carried and takes up no more space than an overnight bag.

Voice and music can be recorded and played with clear, life-like fidelity. Recordings can be replayed thousands of times or stored for future play with no appreciable loss of volume or tone quality. Programs can be erased in favor of new recordings, these in turn may be played back as many times as desired.

Model 80 is equally useful in the home, in business, and in the professions.

Instruction Manual
Webster Chicago Model 80 Wire Recorder
1947

CHAPTER 1

A Boy and His Toy

1947

Larry Hearn was a sucker for gadgets.

Most of the time he was a man of restraint and common sense, but brand-new mechanical and electrical devices turned him into a child. He exasperated his wife by buying things they couldn't afford, things that often became obsolete soon after he bought them. Such a purchase was the wire recorder.

It was on one of those crisp Southern California January days, when you could stand in your shirtsleeves on any street corner in Los Angeles and see the snow blanketing the San Gabriel Mountains, that Larry stepped into the little radio shop on Hollywood Boulevard intending only to buy some replacement tubes for an old Philco radio. He sneered at the enthralled crowd gazing through the display window at one new gadget that didn't interest him: television. But a seasoned salesman quickly guessed what device would hook Larry Hearn.

"Not ready for television yet?" the salesman asked him.

"Nope," Larry said. "Stupid overpriced gimmick. Give me a good radio drama any day. I'll see the pictures in my head—in Technicolor."

"Come over here, then. Bet this is right up your alley."

Larry had seen wire recorders in the Army. Nifty things, they recorded sound on spools of metal wire as thin as human hair. You could speak, sing or play music into the hefty metal microphone and instantly play back what you'd recorded. If you didn't like it, you could erase it and use the same wire spool to record something else.

"The first model for the consumer market," the salesman said. "A hundred and fifty dollars. One fifty-three, to be exact, since we're west of the Rockies."

Larry sighed. "I'd love to own that thing, but I can't afford it. Got a pregnant wife at home."

"You could record your baby's first words."

"I'm barely on my feet since I got back from the war. We're trying to buy a house."

"Where?"

"Van Nuys."

"Van Nuys. It's beautiful out there. What do you do?"

"I'm a screenwriter."

"A screenwriter! Surely you must be making good money."

"Not really . . . I was just starting out before the war."

"But you *will* make good money once you get established. I can tell. You have the look of success about you."

The salesman told Larry he could have the wire recorder for the east-of-the-Rockies price, and he'd throw in a box of blank wire spools and a special cord you could use to record sound directly from a radio or phonograph.

Larry forgot all about the radio tubes and walked out of the store the proud new owner of a Webster Chicago Model 80 Wire Recorder.

"How could you do this?" Ruth Hearn's face was fuming red. "We're expecting a baby, we're buying a house . . . Of all the times to throw away a hundred and fifty bucks on one of your stupid, frivolous *things*. A *wire recorder*! Jesus Christ! What on earth do you need a thing like that for?"

"There'll be lots of uses for it. I can record you playing the piano. I can record the baby's first words."

"Remember that expensive movie camera you bought just before the war and never used?"

"I'll use it now. For the baby."

"I'll bet you don't even know where it is. It'll be the same with that thing. A *wire recorder*! I didn't even know there was such a thing. Take it back, Larry. Take it back to the store and get your money back. Save the money for the house. And the baby."

"I don't want to take it back."

They went back and forth like this for several minutes. Finally, Ruth broke down. "For Christ's sake! Keep the damn thing if it means that much to you. But God help you if we come up a hundred and fifty short on the down payment."

Though Ruth lost that argument, time vindicated her. Larry's initial excitement notwithstanding, the machine saw little use. For a time, he carried the twenty-eight-pound device around their new house in Van Nuys, looking for something to record. He tried to get Ruth to let him record her playing the piano, but she refused. She was a graduate of Juilliard and had played live concerts before hundreds of people—she'd even performed on the radio once—but making a recording that she would then hear played back made her self-conscious.

Larry did make a few recordings of their little daughter, Sophie, as her early babbling evolved into words, words into sentences. But by the time Sophie was three, he had tired of the machine. It didn't seem quite so nifty anymore; the newer tape recorders, with their superior sound quality, had rendered his pricey plaything obsolete. It sat unused, gathering dust on the floor of his study.

CHAPTER 2

Black-Blistered

1951-1955

When Sophie Hearn was four, her two best friends were Stevie and Laura. Stevie was a year younger than Sophie, Laura a year older. Each was an only child, and since their parents were friends, they saw each other often. The parents would get together at one of their houses and the kids would play together. The friendship among them filled the void each had for want of a sibling. Their play often revolved around dolls, of which the girls had large collections. Though Stevie had no dolls of his own, it was obvious that he enjoyed playing with Sophie's and Laura's, joining in the elaborate fantasies they acted out with them.

Being the oldest, Laura usually directed the doll action—and did so in the studied manner of a film director. She'd seen one of those in action once, when her father brought her to the set of a movie for which he had written the screenplay. One Saturday afternoon when Stevie and Laura were visiting Sophie's house, while the six grown-ups sat in the living room absorbed in a conversation in which they repeatedly used a strange term that sounded like "black-blistered," the three children sat on the floor in Sophie's room organizing a group of dolls Laura had designated as a wedding party. A prince and princess were about to get married and in so doing be promoted to king and queen.

"Lights! Action! Camera!" Laura called out. Standing facing Sophie and Stevie, who knelt on the floor propelling the entourage forward, she walked backward and directed them out the door of Sophie's room, down the short hallway and into the kitchen.

"*Cut!*" she yelled when they got to the kitchen, prompting her two subordinates to freeze the dolls in place. "You walked too slow," she said with playful anger, scolding not her two friends but the dolls.

"We did not!" Sophie said, speaking for the bride.

"We did not!" Stevie said, giving voice to the bridegroom.

"You did, too!" Laura said. "We're going to do it over."

The two underlings groaned, but they cooperated. They gathered up the dolls and carried them back to Sophie's room, setting them in position once again.

"*Lights! Action! Camera!*" Laura shouted for the second time, with all the authority and arrogance of a director. This time the wedding party went flying down the hall into the kitchen, Laura chasing after them.

"*Cut!*" she yelled. "That was too fast. Do it again."

"We will not!" Sophie said.

"We will not!" Stevie said.

"You will too!" Laura said. "Or I'll make you black-blistered!"

Stevie and Sophie looked at each other, puzzled.

"What does *black-blistered* mean?" Sophie said, her tone suddenly serious.

"My mommy said it's something bad that happens to people even if they didn't do anything wrong," Laura said as she sat down on the floor, momentarily abandoning her directorial role. "She said it isn't fair and I'll understand when I grow up."

"Do you get black blisters on you?" Sophie said, cringing.

"I don't know. My mommy said don't worry about it, 'cause it can't happen to kids."

Stevie said nothing, but with eyes wide, he was clearly taking it all in.

While Laura was talking, Sophie noticed that the door to her father's study was open. All three of the children, knowing one another's homes intimately, were well aware of which rooms they were allowed to go into at each house and which were forbidden. One room that was off-limits at all three houses was Daddy's study.

Stevie's, Sophie's and Laura's fathers were all writers, and all three had studies where they did their work. The dark, cluttered room off the kitchen where Sophie's father did his writing had originally been a garage; the previous owner had converted it to a den and built a new garage in the back. The door was almost always shut, whether he was in there or not, but today for some reason it had been left open.

The room was dark and forbidding, the sun shut out by the venetian blinds that were usually closed.

"Let's go in," Sophie whispered.

"Let's go in!" Stevie said out loud.

"You're not supposed to," Laura whispered back.

Without another word, Sophie tiptoed in. The others followed, leaving the dolls behind in the kitchen.

On the floor, half hidden by a pile of books, was her father's wire recorder. She approached the machine and stared at it for a moment, and then she leaned over and reached for one of the knobs.

"Don't touch it, Sophie," Laura said.

But Sophie did. She touched some knobs and a lever, as she'd seen her father do, and a spool began spinning. What came loudly out of the machine's speaker startled her. It was her own voice. Not the way it was now, but the way it had sounded a year earlier.

"That's you!" Stevie said.

When Sophie tried to turn the machine off, the voice stopped but the wire spool spun faster. She grabbed Stevie and Laura and yanked them toward the door, but the parents in the living room had heard the sound coming from the machine, and the minutes that followed were a blur of scolding grown-up voices and angry faces. Stevie's and Laura's parents had been about to leave anyway, but all three sets of parents pretended that the children's visit with each other was being cut short as punishment for their romp into verboten territory. All three wept inconsolably.

After that day, Sophie saw Stevie only a few more times before he and his parents inexplicably disappeared from the joint family get-togethers. Sophie and Laura remained best friends and still played with their dolls when their parents got together, missing Stevie at first but quickly forgetting him as the endless days and months of childhood drifted by.

Things had gone well for Larry Hearn after the war. His screen-writing career had taken off faster than he'd expected, and by 1951 Hollywood seemed to be smiling on him. But trouble was in the air. The House Un-American Activities Committee was on its way to Los Angeles to identify Communists in the film industry, and one by one, the subpoenas flew out and found their marks.

"This is it," Larry said. "They're really going to get us now."

Yes, he and Ruth had been in the Party along with many of their friends. They'd both joined as college students in New York City, she at Juilliard, he at the Columbia School of Journalism. It was the middle of the Great Depression, and it had seemed obvious to them, and to countless other young intellectuals, that capitalism was a failed system that had collapsed under the weight of its collective greed. They had continued as members after moving to Hollywood, but by then the revolutionary fervor of the 'thirties had begun to dissipate. None of the leftist groups Larry and Ruth had been involved with after the war were more than discussion forums, little collections of armchair idealists no more likely to influence the content of motion pictures than to overthrow the United States government.

Well before the start of the HUAC hearings, the Hearns had begun to drift away.

"I'm sick of all this idealization of the Soviet Union," Larry said one night as they drove home from a meeting. "I can guarantee you the Soviet Union is no utopia, no matter what they want us to think. No country can be that perfect. Especially if it's run by rigid ideologues like those guys tonight."

"I know," Ruth said. "But I'm not going to quit. Are you?"

"I don't know."

"Look, there are some jerks in the Party, like those guys tonight, but where would we be today without it? No unions in Hollywood . . . the Sleepy Lagoon boys would still be in prison . . . "

"You know what? You know what makes *me* want to stay in? It's all this shit that's going on right now. All the pressure."

"I know. I feel the same way."

"*Nobody's* going to strong-arm me into changing my politics. Not HUAC, not McCarthy, not the studios . . . and not the goddamn guilds that are marching in step with the studios like a bunch of fucking sheep."

Two weeks later, Larry got his subpoena.

Larry had, of course, no intention of cooperating with the House Un-American Activities Committee. Along with his friends, he planned to invoke the Fifth Amendment and refuse to disclose his "subversive" affiliations, denying the committee grounds to make him bear witness against others. But though there was never any doubt as to that choice, his gut tightened as his appearance date drew near and the reality of standing up to a panel of U.S. congressmen loomed large. Excellent writer though he was, Larry was neither skilled nor schooled in the art of public speaking, and his worry centered more on his possible ineloquence under pressure than on the virtual certainty that the studios would blacklist him. As he listened to the radio newscasts of the HUAC hearings, he paid close attention to the unyielding words of the other "unfriendly witnesses"—many of them close friends of his—and measured their effect, asking himself if he could be as articulate as the best of them in the face of authority at its most hostile and frightening. Whatever the scenario, he intended to emerge with his dignity intact.

Then he got a brilliant idea.

He dug the now-little-used wire recorder out from the clutter of his study and carried it into the living room, cleared away some knickknacks from the table next to the old Philco radio (for which he'd finally bought the replacement tubes) and set the machine beside it. He found the special cord the salesman had given him and, carefully following the instructions that had come with it, soldered the stripped-and-tinned nibs at one end to the radio's innards. After inserting the plug at the other end into the record-er's microphone receptacle, he was ready to record his compatriots' words of resistance as they came over the radio waves each day.

He recorded all of them, resisters and cooperators alike, applaud-ing the defiant ones and spitting curses at the name-naming syco-phants. Again and again he replayed the oratory of the better-spo-ken non-cooperators, taking notes, studying every nuance of rheto-ric, ruminating over how his own voice of protest might emerge when it came time to make his stand.

The night before his appearance, Larry decided he wanted his own testimony to be recorded as well. Ruth had planned on attend-ing the hearing to lend him moral support, but Sophie was home from nursery school with a sore throat.

"Why do you want to record yourself?" Ruth said.

"To play it for Sophie when she's old enough to understand. Of course, that's assuming I do well. If I don't do well . . . if I sound timid . . . stumble over my words . . . I'll erase the recording."

"You'll do just fine. But I can't imagine wanting to hear yourself talk. No matter how well you do. And I have no idea how to oper-ate that damn thing."

"It's simple. I'll have it all set up. All you have to do is turn a lever when you hear them call me."

Larry's careful preparation paid off. He did well.

After he had declined to answer the first two questions about his political affiliations, one of the questioning congressmen said to him: "Mr. Hearn, as I am sure you are aware, it is the purpose of this committee to investigate and expose Communist influence in the motion picture industry. I should think that a person with your distinguished and valorous record of service to your country would wish to help this committee defend those same ideals which you and so many others fought to preserve. Am I correct in making this assumption?"

Larry's voice was strong and clear as he spoke, trying not to look at all the cameras and microphones pointed at him. "I am indeed interested in defending the ideals on which this country was founded . . . and therefore am vigorously opposed to, and deeply repelled by, the activities of this committee—"

"Mr. Hearn," the congressman said, trying to cut him off.

". . . which have made a mockery of the United States Constitution and the American tradition"—feeling his voice start to quaver, he took a mid-sentence breath—"of freedom of speech and freedom of thought . . . and attempted to stifle those freedoms—"

"Mr. Hearn—" The congressman rapped his gavel three times.

". . . by creating a climate of fear and hysteria"—he took another deep breath as the cameramen's flashbulbs popped around him— "which is what this committee plainly thrives on."

"Mr. Hearn," the congressman said, "you are entitled, in this great and free nation of ours, to hold whatever opinion you will with regard to this committee and its work. If, however, you *are* truly interested in preserving the right of free political expression in this country, then I should think you would want to help us expose those individuals who are bent on destroying that freedom."

Larry took another breath. "I believe the greatest threat to freedom in this country today is the House Committee on

Un-American Activities and the self-glorifying, publicity-seeking witch hunt it's carrying on in the guise of a legitimate investigation."

Ignoring Larry's denunciation, the congressman asked him about his membership in the Communist Party. Another quizzed him about his involvement with organizations, committees and causes suspected of being Communist fronts. Listening at home as the reels of the wire recorder spun, Ruth heard him repeatedly invoke the Fifth Amendment, refusing to answer one after another of their queries.

She had tried to get Sophie to stay in her room, but her daughter came out into the kitchen just in time to be confused by the sound of her father's voice.

"Is that Daddy?"

"Yes, sweetie, that's your daddy."

"Why is he on the radio?"

"Someday you'll be old enough to understand . . . and you'll be *very* proud of him."

"I don't like this," Sophie whined. She had eaten only a few bites of her mashed potatoes.

She was now seven, and mashed potatoes were one of the foods she had never learned to like. But the rule now was that you had to finish what was on your plate, like or not, before you could have dessert or a second helping of something you liked.

During their daughter's early years, Ruth and Larry, along with many of their liberal peers, had looked to Benjamin Spock as their guiding light of child care. Dr. Spock preached liberation from the strictures of old-school child-rearing, with its emphasis on rigid routines and corporal punishment, and urged parents to give their children love and affirmation. But his book was widely misinterpreted as a gospel of permissiveness, and thus had Sophie been allowed for her first seven years to eat what she wanted, sleep when she wanted and play where she wanted, the family's life revolving around her wants and needs. By the time she turned seven, she was sufficiently spoiled that her parents had seen the error of their ways and reversed course.

Sophie took another bite of the mashed potatoes and almost gagged. "Is that enough?" she said, frowning with disgust.

"No," Ruth said. "You know what the rule is."

Sophie gradually learned to obey the limits her parents set down. Along with the new food rules, she had to practice the piano for half an hour each day, she had to keep her room straightened up, bedtime was bedtime and tantrums were a no-no. It took about a year of newly learned firmness on her parents' part, but in the end she emerged as a winsome, well-behaved and musically talented girl. She was smart and perceptive, excelled in school and adjusted well socially.

Larry and Ruth felt confident that they were providing Sophie with the opportunities she deserved, shielding her as best they could from the harsh reality of the blacklist, as she grew from early to middle childhood in the warmth and comfort of the little ranch-style house in Van Nuys.

Everyone knew the blacklist was real—though the studios denied its existence—but always there was the nagging if irrational question for those affected by it: *Is it really just because of the blacklist that I'm no longer getting work? If I were the writer I thought I was, wouldn't they still want me, blacklist or no blacklist?*

For the first few months after the studio work dried up, Larry tried to see his unemployment as a gift of time, time to work on the projects he'd been toying with since his pre-Hollywood days: plays, short stories, perhaps even a novel. But all he could think about was his present situation, which might someday be a rich source of material but was too immediate to write about now. He spent hour after hour slumped at his desk, alternately looking at the light filtering in through the blinds and staring at the blank sheet of paper in the typewriter.

When the reality hit that he could no longer support his family as a writer, Larry sought other employment. He worked as a part-time assistant in a film lab, sold encyclopedias, graded papers for correspondence courses. He tried his hand at commercial photography, using a Rolleiflex camera he'd bought before the blacklist, but he lacked a "good eye" and failed at it.

Ruth's contribution, besides giving her husband the emotional support he was desperate for, was to teach private piano lessons. Early in the blacklist period she had contemplated applying for a position teaching music in the Los Angeles public schools, but dropped the idea when she heard that teachers were being fired because their husbands had been tarred by the HUAC investigations.

Larry and Ruth worked together in every way they could to keep the family from going under. They scrimped each month to keep up the mortgage payments so that there would be a house for Sophie to grow up in. They struggled, and they survived.

Barely.

CHAPTER 3

The Elwoods

1952-1958

Arthur and Rosemary Elwood didn't understand what had happened to their son.

Everything had gone well at first. Stevie was obviously a very bright child. He was aware beyond his years; he had passed all the developmental stages ahead of schedule and, while slightly shy, had interacted well even with kids who were a year or two older. He'd had a particularly close relationship with two little girls, Sophie and Laura.

Though the two girls disappeared from Stevie's life when he was three, he made other friends in the neighborhood and at nursery school. He seemed happy. He delighted everyone with his vocabulary and expressiveness.

Then, when he was four, his development seemed to stop. His precocious verbalism disappeared; almost overnight, he began limiting himself to terse statements and one-word answers. He withdrew from other children and became a target of teasing by his nursery-school classmates, crying at every punch, every shove, every unkind word.

When Stevie started kindergarten at a highly regarded, progressive private school, things became worse. The other boys hectored him without mercy and subjected him to cruel practical jokes, on one occasion locking him in a utility closet. The teachers, in keeping with the school's philosophy, did little to comfort Stevie or stop the bullying. Instead they showered attention and affection on his worst tormentors, on the theory that deep insecurity lay behind their behavior.

It was around this time that Stevie began to have quirky, obsessive interests. The first was electricity. With components his father bought him at the hardware store and the hobby shop, he built amazing devices with motors that whirred and lights that flashed; he showed little interest in anything else.

When he was six, he abandoned his electrical hobby in favor of horned animals. Any animal with horns or antlers fascinated him. He leafed through the family dictionary for pictures of animals with horns; at school he made paintings of elk and mountain goats, molded clay figures of gazelles and water buffalo. His classmates ridiculed his fixation and drew portraits of a horned Stevie.

At seven, he committed to memory the call letters of every radio and TV station in Los Angeles and could soon recite stations from all over the United States. "The ones in the west begin with *K* and the ones in the east begin with *W*," Stevie would announce to complete strangers.

His parents took him to a therapist—a European-trained female psychiatrist—who viewed Stevie's maladjustment through the classical Freudian lens, making him describe his dreams in detail and linking his odd behaviors to far-fetched sexual causalities. After a year's worth of costly sessions, she admitted to being utterly baffled by Stevie and having no idea what to do with him. Shortly afterward, he was expelled from the private school, the directors saying they could no longer protect him from the abuse of the other kids. They recommended he be sent to a much more expensive private school where every child was assigned an on-site psychotherapist.

Fed up with psychotherapy and private schools, the Elwoods discontinued their sad little boy's analysis sessions and enrolled him in the local public school. Though initially picked on there as well—he now wore glasses, attracting the inevitable "four-eyes" taunts—he soon distinguished himself academically, pulling way ahead of the other children in reading, spelling and arithmetic. His obviously superior intelligence won him admiration from his teachers and a measure of respect from most of his classmates as well. Though still shy, he began to speak more. The teasing diminished, and by the end of third grade, only the tough, hard boys still harassed him.

In October of 1957, the Soviet Union launched Sputnik 1, the world's first artificial satellite, and America went feverish with the space race. Astronomy and space travel became everyday topics. Steve Elwood, now nine and in fourth grade, got caught up in the fervor, and it became his new obsession.

He tacked star charts and moon maps to the walls of his room. He read adult-level science fiction. He built intricate model spacecraft from Revell kits, meticulously following the instructions as he fastened the little plastic parts together with foul-smelling glue. He dragged his father to the Griffith Observatory whenever there was a new planetarium show, subscribed to *Sky and Telescope* and begged his parents to buy him one of the pricey scopes on the magazine's ad pages—which they did.

About this time Steve also began to put on weight. He enjoyed eating more than anything else—more even than building his models, watching planetarium shows or gazing through his telescope at the moon's craters, Saturn's rings or the tiny pinpoints of Jupiter's four largest moons.

"Whatsa matter, big Stevie? Afraid of us?"

Terry Mackey, a tough kid from his class who habitually mocked him for his weight, bookishness and disinterest in sports, had cornered him on the playground with two other tough-looking boys Steve didn't know. One of them was a short boy with a mean-looking face; the other was a tall boy who looked older, maybe junior-high age. In his arms Steve carried a big cardboard box, open at the top, holding several of his most prized satellite and spaceship models. He had brought them for show-and-tell, but he'd been awkward in front of the class and his presentation hadn't gone well. After school, he'd stayed late talking to the teacher about his models and his passion for astronomy. It was after four o'clock now and the playground was nearly deserted.

He edged slowly away from the boys, placing himself between them and his box of models.

"Whatsa matter, Spaceship Stevie?" Terry said. "Afraid we're gonna break your Sputniks?"

Steve edged away faster. The boys edged closer.

"*Nawwww*," the older boy said. "We wouldn't do a thing like that. Would we, Terry?"

"Nawwww, I just wanna see 'em. Didn't get a good enough look when you showed 'em in class."

"Yeah, we just wanna see 'em," the short, mean-looking boy said.

Steve stopped edging and started walking fast toward home.

"Hey," the older boy said. "You're not being very nice. Why don't you wanna show us your Sputniks?"

"Come on," Terry said. "Show us."

Steve walked faster, but the boys quickly overtook him. The older boy grabbed the edge of the box and yanked it away. The models, which Steve had packed in carefully, shook and rattled. The boys began taking them out of the box.

"Hey," the short boy said, "these are nice rockets. You're a pretty good model builder." He held up a rocket. "What kinda Sputnik is this?"

"It's not a Sputnik," Steve said, his voice trembling. "It's a Vanguard."

"A *Vanguard!* I've never seen one of those before. But then, I guess I don't know too much about rockets."

Terry grabbed the Vanguard and set it gently on the ground. "Now, be careful with these," he said, almost sounding sincere. "We don't wanna break them."

The short boy took out a large, complex spaceship. "What's this one here?"

"That's an XSL-01," Steve said in a more relaxed tone. "It's a four-stage moon rocket."

"That's really somethin'. You got some pretty tough models in there."

The older boy picked up the XSL-01 and threw it down on the asphalt. It bounced once and several small pieces broke off.

"*Don't*," Steve said.

"You hurt my feelings when you wouldn't let me look at 'em."

"Yeah," the short boy said, picking up the Vanguard. "All we wanted to do was look at 'em. We weren't gonna break 'em." He carefully set the Vanguard back down on the ground and then stepped on it hard.

Steve cried. One by one, the boys took all the models out of the box and stomped on them, shattering them into fragments. Then they turned to walk away.

"Have fun putting 'em back together, Spaceship Stevie," Terry said.

"Yeah, you four-eyed fatso," the short boy said. "Next time don't be so rude. You're lucky we didn't break your glasses, too."

"Spaceship Stevie," Terry said. "Smart in the classroom, stupid everywhere else."

Steve sobbed as he slowly picked up the plastic shards and dropped them in the box.

Steve wanted to go to the principal, but his parents talked him out of it.

"Nobody likes a snitch," his father said. "If you tell on them, they'll just pick on you more."

"They're probably very unhappy boys," his mother said.

They gave him the money to replace his broken models, and first thing Saturday morning he rode his bike to the hobby shop and bought new kits for all of them except the Vanguard, which had been discontinued. It took two trips on his bike to get all the kits home. He rebuilt them more carefully than before, making each one perfect, with no stray glops of glue, uneven paint edges or badly-centered decals.

He didn't bring his models to school again, and he walked straight home every day so he'd never again be caught on the empty playground alone.

CHAPTER 4

A Better and Fairer Country

1958

Clouds were gathering. It was late afternoon and near time for Mexico City's daily summer rain. Larry, Ruth and Sophie were picnicking in Chapultepec Park for the first time, though they had lived less than a mile from it for the past two years.

The Hearns had rented out their Van Nuys house and moved to Mexico City in 1956 in the hope that Larry would find work in the film industry there, as a few of the other blacklisted writers had done. At first there had been a little work and the promise of more, but the big opportunities had failed to materialize, and in the end they found themselves stranded in a strange country without financial resources. Knowing only a bare minimum of Spanish, Larry couldn't even work at low-paying odd jobs, nor could Ruth teach piano; the income from the rental of their house barely covered the mortgage payments. To survive they'd had to borrow money from Ruth's parents, an intense humiliation for Larry.

The picnic was a celebration of their decision to move back to Los Angeles.

"Who were the 'Niños Héroes'?" Sophie asked her parents. Now eleven, she pronounced the words with the native accuracy she'd acquired in just two years. They'd taken the tour of Chapultepec Castle and heard a lecture about the Niños Héroes in English, but it had rolled off her.

"Don't you remember what the guide said?" Ruth said. "He told the whole story."

"I wasn't paying attention."

"Why not?"

"I was thinking about going home."

"Excited?"

"Yeah . . . but scared, too."

"Why scared?"

"I dunno. Seeing all my old friends."

"I can understand that, but there's absolutely nothing to be scared of. All your old friends will be just as excited to see you."

"Tell me about the Niños Héroes. I'm sorry I wasn't paying attention."

"They were the boy heroes of Chapultepec—the teenage boys who tried to defend the castle against the American invaders—and they all died. Remember the plaques inside the castle that showed where each one died? And the last one who wrapped himself in the Mexican flag and jumped from that tower?" Ruth pointed at the castle, now shadowy and sinister against the darkening sky.

"The Americans were invaders?"

"Yes."

"Then they were the bad guys?"

"Yes, from the Mexicans' point of view we were the bad guys.

We stole their land. The whole southwestern part of the United States—including California—used to be part of Mexico."

"Including Van Nuys?"

"Yes."

"You mean our house used to be in Mexico?"

"The house wasn't there yet, but yes. The land where our house is now was once part of Mexico."

"So America stole that land?"

"Yes."

"And that was bad."

"Yes, it was."

"Does that mean America is bad?"

"No, it doesn't mean America is bad. This happened over a hundred years ago. The people who were responsible are all dead now."

"Every country in the world has done bad things at some time in its history," Larry said. "It doesn't mean those countries are bad or that the people of those countries are bad. It's just that evil men sometimes get in power and do evil deeds. Like Hitler."

"And the people who blacklisted your father," Ruth said.

"Do you love America?" Sophie asked her mother.

"Yes, I love America. I want to make it a better and fairer country."

"How do you want to do that?"

"Well . . . to begin with, I'd like to end racial discrimination once and for all. I want Negroes to have all the same rights as white people."

"What else?"

"I would like for there not to be a blacklist, of course. What else, Larry?"

"We should end poverty," Larry said. "Everyone should have a good job and a decent standard of living."

"We should end all war," Ruth said, "and get rid of the atomic bombs."

"Do you think you can do all those things?" Sophie said.

"No," Larry said. "No one person can do it. But I have hope that maybe over time, with a lot of people working together . . ."

Sophie stared silently at the castle.

"I'm glad we're going home," she said.

As the first drops of rain fell, the Hearns gathered up their picnic blanket and made their way to the old Studebaker they'd driven from Van Nuys to Mexico City and would soon be driving back.

CHAPTER 5

Mr. Barton

1958-1961

Coming home was a nightmare.

Ruth and Sophie wept when they saw the condition of their house. They'd expected some wear and tear, but what they found was a catastrophe beyond belief: carpets stained and torn, drapes ripped down, hardwood floors horribly scratched, furniture damaged or missing and, for some unknown reason, holes knocked in some of the walls. Larry's study—excluded from the rental agreement and left locked—had been broken into and ransacked, his private papers strewn about, many of his books missing. Ruth's heirloom Steinway, which they'd covered up and also excluded from the rental, had been uncovered and damaged, the finish scratched, drinks spilled on the keys.

In Sophie's bedroom, large swaths of her feminine wallpaper had been haphazardly torn down, cowboy and sports posters glued to the walls in its place. Fortunately, though, her most prized belongings—including her doll collection—had been stored in boxes in the garage, which, by some miracle, had been left undisturbed.

The destructive family the Hearns had rented their house to had disappeared with no forwarding address. It took more than two months to get the house functional again while they lived in an apartment, and they had to borrow still more money from Ruth's parents. Meanwhile, the blacklist was still on. Larry had no work prospects, and it would take a year or more for Ruth to rebuild her piano-student clientele. They had absolutely no idea how they were going to survive.

But at least they were home.

Sophie enrolled in the sixth grade at her old elementary school. She readjusted well and resumed her old friendships. By the time she started at Millikan Junior High the following year, her parents had begun to regain their financial footing. Through an old friend, Larry had managed to land some TV writing assignments under a pseudonym he'd made up by inverting his first name (Lawrence) and middle name (Henry), and though the content was vacuous and the pay far below his pre-blacklist standard, it gave him no small amount of pride to be once again making money writing.

The biggest price of the name ruse was the constant fear of being found out. There'd been a close call involving a schoolmate of Sophie's whose staunchly anticommunist father worked in TV and knew Larry at the studio as "Hank Lawrence," but his cover had remained intact, and Sophie abided by her parents' command not to tell anyone at school even that her father was a writer.

As for Ruth, happily, the blacklist of teachers had eased enough for her to get a position as an elementary-school music instructor.

Though not a prodigy, Sophie had music in her blood. She was a very good pianist—Ruth had seen to it, during their time in Mexico and throughout the blacklist years, that her daughter kept up her practice—and had a beautiful singing voice as well. In sixth grade, soon after her family's return to the United States, she had also taken up the flute. She had sung in the elementary-school chorus, given piano concerts at school assemblies and, by the start of junior high, become good enough on the flute to play in the beginning-level band.

Though her parents had admonished her to be cautious about discussing politics, Sophie spoke out in the band room and on the lunch benches against war and capital punishment, for racial equality and social justice, for treatment instead of jail for drug addicts, for Kennedy in the 1960 presidential election. She was the star pupil in her academic classes, and the liberal-themed essays she composed were so well-written that even her conservative seventh-grade social studies teacher gave her A-pluses.

She made A's in her homemaking classes as well, but they bored her to death. The sights and smells she caught while walking past the doors of the wood, ceramics, metal and electric shops, the interesting things the boys showed off after making them in their shop classes, intrigued her and sparked resentment that those classes were for boys only. It frustrated her even more that none of the other girls seemed to feel any injustice in that. The time or two that she had brought it up, they'd looked at her as if she'd said something loony.

"No," her mother said, "it isn't fair. Our society is unfair to women in many, many ways. Did you know that women in America weren't allowed to vote until 1920? Just forty years ago?"

"Really?"

"Yes, and they had to fight very hard for a very long time in order to get that right. Maybe someday you'll be the one to right the injustices that still remain. Maybe you'll be the one to win the right for girls to take shop classes."

By the beginning of her eighth-grade year, Sophie had become the top flutist at school. For her "A-8" semester—the upper term of the eighth grade—the instrumental music director practically begged her to sign up for both band and orchestra. Flattered, she agreed. But with both those class periods occupied, there was only one A-8 social studies class that didn't conflict: Mr. Barton's.

Mr. Barton was notorious for his far-right political views, which he didn't hesitate to express in class, and for his brutal attitude toward any student who dared contradict him. Rumor had it that Mr. Barton was an officer in the local chapter of the John Birch Society.

"Just keep quiet," her father told her. "Do your homework. Study hard and do well on his tests. Your family's politics are none of his business. Keep your mouth shut about them."

"But that's wrong," Sophie said. "It's a free country. If Mr. Barton can talk about his politics, I should have the right to talk about mine."

"But you're a child," Larry said. "You're thirteen years old. He's a grown-up. He's going to be your teacher, and he's the one in authority."

*

At first things weren't as bad as Sophie had expected. Mr. Barton was a good history teacher; his lectures were entertaining and sprinkled with humor. Sophie spoke often in class, but only about uncontroversial topics pertinent to the era of history they were studying. She got A's on all her tests and assignments and an A on the mid-term report card. But then, one day soon after the mid-semester point, Ed Sarmington—one of Barton's favored students—gave a current-events report on a Los Angeles *Times* article describing how Dalton Trumbo, the best-known of all the blacklisted writers, had begun receiving screen credits in his own name once again. Dalton Trumbo and his family were friends of the Hearns'. Sophie had been to parties at their home in Highland Park.

"Communism is all around us," Mr. Barton said in response to the boy's report, "and now that Senator McCarthy is gone, there doesn't seem to be much effort toward fighting it. There are Communists right here in our community, living amongst us, plotting against us. Look at the movie industry. Communists and their fellow travelers are making movies again, just like they were in the forties."

Sophie cringed.

"People are going to those movies," Mr. Barton continued, "enjoying them, soaking in the propaganda. *Spartacus*—have any of you seen *Spartacus*? Pure propaganda, written by one of the worst of the Communist writers, the man Mr. Sarmington just reported on, Mr. Dalton Trumbo. Watch out for him. Before you go to see a movie, find out who wrote it. Everyone knows who directed a film, the actors, but how often do people ask who wrote the script?"

Sophie nervously clicked and re-clicked the button on her ball-point pen.

"The most important figure of all, the one who wrote the lines the actors speak, and his name is way down in the fine print. It isn't fair. The people who create the scripts for the pictures ought to get more recognition, and then it wouldn't be so easy for Communist writers to sneak their propaganda into those scripts unnoticed."

Sophie raised her hand.

"Yes, Miss Hearn?"

"Mr. Barton, I don't mean to be disrespectful, but I don't think I agree with what you're saying about those writers."

"Very well, Miss Hearn. All views are respected here. Would you care to elaborate?"

"The blacklist wasn't fair. It was a witch hunt."

That was all the elaboration she could manage. She wished right away that she could un-say the words, un-raise her hand.

"Well, Miss Hearn," Mr. Barton said, "you've just used two very strong terms that we need to analyze. You used the terms *blacklist* and *witch hunt*. A legitimate investigation into subversive activities can hardly be called a witch hunt, and as for *blacklist*—those writers were given the chance to clear themselves before a congressional committee. Some were honest—they admitted to past flirtations with Communism, atoned for it and were allowed to continue writing for the pictures. But others of them, unfortunately, chose to employ our Constitution's Fifth Amendment as a shield. They refused to answer the committee's questions or help with its investigations. Why do you think they refused to answer the questions of a committee investigating Communism in America, Mr. Sarmington?"

The boy was stymied. Sophie could tell that he hadn't really understood the article he'd reported on, though he was obviously glad Mr. Barton had seemed pleased with his report.

"I dunno," Ed Sarmington said.

"Miss Varney?" Mary Varney was another of Barton's pets.

"Because they had something to hide," she said.

"And what might they have had to hide, Miss Varney?"

"That they *were* Communists . . . and they wanted to keep putting their propaganda into the movies."

"Well said, Miss Varney," Barton said, his voice heating up. "Shouldn't that be obvious? It was dishonest and hypocritical of them to hide behind the very Constitution they were determined to destroy. Does anyone think there would be a Fifth Amendment under Communism? Does anyone know what happens to someone in Russia if he doesn't respond to political questioning? If he's lucky he gets a one-way ticket to Siberia. If he's not so lucky, he gets a bullet in the back of the head. If anyone wants to call it a blacklist when those who want to turn our country into the Soviet States of America are denied access to the mass media, where they could brainwash people like you and me into thinking that might be a good idea, that person should buy himself a one-way ticket to Moscow."

As he spoke, Sophie sat in silence, on the verge of tears. For all the righteous passion within her, she had managed only the feeblest of responses to Mr. Barton's canards. Yet she knew that even with those few timid words she had crossed the line, that Mr. Barton would not be nice to her anymore. And he wasn't.

She still got A's on tests of simple facts, but he picked apart her essay answers and gave her C's and D's on her written assignments. On the final report card, she received a C for the class, spoiling the straight-A record she'd maintained for the first half of junior high. She asked her father to intervene and complain to the principal.

"It wouldn't do any good," he said. "The principal would defend Mr. Barton and might even poison your other teachers against you."

"It could also be dangerous," her mother said. "It would call attention to your father. Someone at school might investigate and find out who 'Hank Lawrence' really is, and then your father would lose his living all over again."

Sophie clenched her fists.

"But you've learned an important lesson," Ruth said. "You've learned what it feels like to be denied fair treatment because you had the courage to speak out about your beliefs."

Though Sophie recovered from the unpleasantness with Mr. Barton, it wasn't long afterward that episodes of darkness began to steal some of her days. Usually, she would be her ebullient, optimistic self, but on certain days she would walk around in a morbid black cloud, convinced that she was never going to amount to anything and that her death, or that of one of her parents, was imminent.

CHAPTER 6

The Report on Hitler

1962

At a table in the North Hollywood Library, Steve Elwood sat researching the oral report he was to give in his social studies class. It was nearly five o'clock, time to get on his bike and ride the two miles home. He was going on fourteen now and in the A-8 grade at Walter Reed Junior High.

He had a stack of books before him and was taking careful notes on index cards the way his teacher, Mrs. Bowman, had taught the class to do. He was doing a term project on the history topic he'd chosen: "Hitler and the Nazis." Mrs. Bowman's class was an "honor" class; all the kids in it had high IQs. The term project was a college-level paper and had to be typed in college format, with footnotes—using abbreviations like *op. cit.* and *ibid.*—and bibliography.

Steve had long been fascinated by Adolf Hitler, by the pure evil the man had embodied. The term paper wasn't due until the end of May, almost three months away, but each student was required to give a preliminary oral report. To give the students practice in memorization and oral delivery, Mrs. Bowman required that the reports be given without notes.

He called his parents from the pay phone and got permission to stay at the library for another half hour. He worked feverishly and nervously until that time was up, and then he gathered his notes, checked out the new books he'd found and headed off on his bike.

He pedaled hard down Tujunga Avenue toward Studio City and home. The load of books in his front basket was so heavy that it took extra effort to control the bike. As he rode, with the early-March wind ballooning his jacket and burning his face, he wished he'd chosen a different topic. Just about any other would have been fine—in particular, any that didn't involve Jews.

Steve had a thing about Jews. He thought they were special. There were a lot of Jewish kids at his school, and his parents had Jewish friends. They all seemed so smart, so sophisticated. Even though he was near the top of his class—he would have been a straight-A student but for the C's and D's he got in P.E.—he always felt inferior to the Jewish kids. They just seemed to have something he didn't.

When he'd first chosen the subject for his term paper, he had stupidly thought it would make him a hero among the Jewish kids to report about Hitler, to repeat over and over what a monster the man was. But now he saw what a fool he'd been. He realized how self-conscious he would be, how crimson he would blush, every time he used the word *Jews* or *Jewish*, every time he mentioned how Hitler had hated them and wanted to exterminate them, with Jewish kids sitting right in front of him. It occurred to him that they might not even think it proper that he should report on Hitler, because it was their people, not his, who had suffered under the dictator.

There was one Jewish kid in particular whose displeasure Steve feared more than any other's. Her name was Cindy Wiser.

Cindy Wiser had been in Steve's class since the beginning of seventh grade, when her family had moved to Los Angeles from the east, and he'd immediately become aware of her presence. He'd been paying close attention to her ever since.

Cindy was petite, with almost-blond hair and green eyes—unusual for a Jewish girl—and was the smartest girl in the class, regularly tying Steve's test scores. And she was nice to him, nicer than most of the other kids. She spoke sweetly to him in the cadences of her New York accent, complimenting him when he got the highest grade on a test, not noticing (or pretending not to notice) when he turned away to hide the reddening face his classmates often teased him about.

Steve had felt a powerful drive to find out as much as he could about Cindy. A member of the Science Club, he'd decided to make a scientific study of her high intelligence. So he watched for opportunities to gather data on her.

One day during their seventh-grade year, the English teacher had carelessly left several students' school record folders—including Cindy's—in full view on his desk. With little effort, and without anyone noticing, Steve had managed to see and memorize her complete name (Cynthia Rebecca Wiser), birth date (October 15, 1948), birthplace (Brooklyn, New York), parents' names (Herschel and Esther Wiser) and parents' birthplace (Poland). Cindy's address and phone number were there, too, and Steve had committed them to memory along with all her other personal information. Not that he would ever have dared to call her, or ride his bike past her house; he'd just wanted to find out as much about her as he could.

A scientific study.

Steve would have sooner died than have anyone know about his special interest in Cindy—even his parents, in whom he confided nearly everything. The mere thought of the vocabulary his parents might have used, perhaps calling it a "crush," humiliated him. So his covert study of her had continued, without interruption, into the eighth grade. A *top-secret* study, duration indefinite, findings to be disclosed to nobody.

But how, now, could he even think of being able to speak in front of the class about Hitler's loathing of the Jews, of his desire to eliminate them, of the hideous death camps and piles of emaciated corpses, with her sitting there?

He confided his fear to his parents. Not about Cindy in particular, of course, but about the Jewish kids in general.

"Don't be silly," his mother said. "You've grown up with Jewish kids. There's nothing wrong with your giving a report on Hitler."

"Just make it a good report," his father said. "List all the horrible things Hitler did. Delve into the psychology of his evil mind."

After making meticulous notes on the research he'd done, Steve wrote his report exactly as he was going to give it, word for word. Then he rehearsed. And rehearsed. And rehearsed. For the five days before he was to present the report, he rehearsed the whole thing out loud twice a night, making notes and changes with each rehearsal. Several times he practiced it with his parents as the audience, and each time they assured him it was excellent.

The night before his presentation, Steve stayed up until two in the morning doing final rehearsals and revisions. He went to school in a fog. When he stood before the class, none of the practice, none of his parents' reassurances, made any difference. He froze for a few seconds and then closed his eyes and began, his voice tremulous and barely above a whisper:

"Adolf Hitler was born on April 20, 1889, in Braunau am Inn, Austria. His father . . ."

"Speak up, please," Mrs. Bowman said. "We can barely hear you."

Steve forced his voice up, but he trembled more, rattled by the interruption. He felt the warm blood rush to his face as the much-rehearsed words of his memorized presentation slipped away, replaced by the very scary realization that he was going to have to ad-lib.

He recovered quickly and hit his stride, recounting what he could remember of the highlights of Hitler's childhood and adolescence. For a minute or two he thought he was doing well, and felt proud of his successful extemporization, but then he realized that he was dwelling far too much on the man's personal history. The topic of the report was the Nazis—their philosophy of the "master race," their invasion of other countries leading up to World War II, and, yes, their persecution of the Jews—not the minutiae of Hitler's life story. He knew he was stretching out the early portion of the biography to postpone getting into the Jewish thing.

Steve looked out at the audience. Cindy was on the far right side of the room, and as long as he looked straight ahead, he couldn't see her. But Judy Gold, Mark Kottler and Lynn Saperstein sat directly in his line of sight, listening politely along with the gentile kids. He tiptoed nervously into the topic he'd been avoiding:

"As a young man living in Vienna, Hitler became . . . anti-Semitic. He soon came to hate . . . to hate the Jews because . . . he believed that they were enemies of Germany, and that they were an inferior race. Of course, that wasn't true. Hitler just thought that because of his sick, insane mind . . . "

"Steven, you're dropping your voice again," Mrs. Bowman said.

Steve blinked, reddened and glanced for the briefest moment at the three Jewish kids in front of him. He saw—or thought he saw—Lynn Saperstein flinch slightly.

As he neared the end of what he could recall about Hitler's young manhood, he tried to fix his gaze straight ahead on the treetops outside the classroom's second-story window instead of on the class, which was growing fidgety. When he realized that he'd been speaking the whole time in a slow, droning monotone, he cranked up his voice and, with an abrupt burst of bravado, leaped across the crucial decades of Hitler's political development, skipping the Beer Hall Putsch and the Reichstag fire, jumping straightaway into the flames of what would one day come to be known as the Holocaust.

"Because he believed that they were inferior, Hitler decided . . . that all the Jews had to be killed . . . so he built concentration camps."

He glanced at the Jewish kids again, and a sudden new wave of shyness engulfed him, but still he strained to push the words out as he continued to stare through the window at the trees and the red-tiled ceiling of the gym building across the courtyard. He knew his presentation was awkward and full of gaps, and that Mrs. Bowman's judgment was likely to be harsh, but he soldiered on and managed, finally, to stumble to the report's conclusion with the suicide of Hitler and the collapse of the Third Reich. He felt himself flush and hung his head as he walked to his seat.

As she called the next student, Mrs. Bowman handed Steve a

slip of paper with his grade. It was a C plus. *Your delivery could have been stronger and you omitted a number of important events in the rise of the Nazi party and Hitler's ascent to power*, she'd written. *Please see me to discuss this before you do any further work on your term project.*

After class, Cindy approached him. "That was a good report, Steve. I'm glad you told about all the terrible things Hitler did. A lot of people don't know."

"Thanks," he said, blushing.

"The Nazis killed some of my family."

He thought he should say something both profound and sympathetic, but all he could manage was a dumb-sounding "Really?"

"Yes. My parents came here from Poland to escape from the Nazis."

"Really?"

"Yes, and they barely made it out in time. They were lucky. If they'd waited any longer I wouldn't be here right now."

"Really?"

"Yes. My grandparents stayed behind in Poland, and they got sent to a concentration camp, and the Nazis killed them with poison gas. It makes me so sad that I never met them."

"Really?"

Over dinner, Steve told his parents how badly he had done with the report.

"You were too nervous," his father said.

"You were too afraid of what the Jewish kids were going to think," his mother said.

"This one girl"—he hesitated—"this one girl . . . her name is Cindy Wiser . . . came up to me and said my report was good. I don't think she meant it, though."

"Why don't you think she meant it?" his mother said.

"Because I . . . I think she was just trying to be nice."

"You've mentioned Cindy Wiser before. She sounds like a very sweet girl."

"She said her grandparents were killed by the Nazis."

"How *terrible*."

"She's very intelligent," Steve said. "She's from New York."

In bed that night, Steve realized he'd said far too much about Cindy, and he thought about what wonderful parents he had, that they'd known better than to comment.

CHAPTER 7

The Hootenanny

1963

During her first year at Grant High School, Sophie Hearn was drawn to folk music, a genre that had of late become popular with her peers. She took up the guitar and learned it quickly, adding that very social instrument to the list of those she had already mastered.

In the spring of her tenth-grade year, Sophie and her folk-music-loving boyfriend, Phil Hertzman, invited some of their friends to her house for a "hootenanny." That word, in their circle of friends, meant a gathering for the purpose of singing folk songs, listening to folk songs on records and talking about the comparative merits of this or that folk song, folk singer or folk group.

"So who's coming?" Phil asked Sophie as they sat eating their sack lunches on a bench off the Grant Quad.

"Okay . . . Jeff Weissbrot . . ."

"Good," Phil said. "He needs to have more of a social life. Who else?"

"Dave Mandell."

"Let's hope he's not in one of his obnoxious moods. Who else?"

"Julie Berman."

"That's good. Julie needs to have a social life, too. Maybe she and Jeff will finally—"

"*Phil.* I told you not to try to match up Julie and Jeff. Everyone's tried, and neither one of them is the least bit interested in the other. It just embarrasses them when people keep trying to push them together."

"What a shame. They're so perfect for each other."

"Why? Just because they're both shy? They don't even *like* each other. And even if they did, Julie's parents would never let her go out with Jeff. They eat kosher food and all that, and Jeff's family doesn't even go to temple."

"Your dad isn't even Jewish and your mom married him."

"Yes, and both their families disapproved. But they were older. They didn't have to obey their parents. Anyway, that's not the point. The point is that Jeff and Julie aren't interested in each other."

"Okay, okay," Phil said, putting his hand up as if fending off a punch. "I get the point. I will not try to match Jeff and Julie. Who else is coming?"

"That's all."

"What about Laura Gelman?"

"Are you serious?"

"She likes folk music. I was just talking to her about it the other day."

"I haven't talked to her in months."

"But you grew up together."

"I know—but I don't like what she's become."

"What? You mean, a socialite?"

"Yes."

"So what? You get along okay with the soshes."

"Yes, for some strange reason they seem to like me. But I hate what they stand for, and I hate it that Laura's become one of them."

"Aren't you being a little snobbish?"

"Snobbish? You're calling *me* snobbish? Compared to the soshy crowd? Can you imagine how they'd treat Julie or Jeff?"

"It's backwards snobbishness. You're looking down on them because of who they are. Is that any better than the way they look down on us?"

"Okay, you've made your point. I'll invite Laura. Or even better, *you* invite her. You're the one who sees her in class."

"Didn't mean to pressure you. It's your house, it's your decision who to invite."

"No, go ahead. Invite her. But be sure to tell her who else is coming. If she'll come to a get-together where Jeff Weissbrot and Julie Berman are going to be, that'll be to her credit."

Sophie thought about Laura—how shallow her childhood best friend had become since falling in with the popular crowd. She thought about Julie and Jeff—how lonely and isolated they both were. And the next thing she knew she was falling into a depression. Just thinking about little things like that could do it; she never understood why.

Suddenly *everything* was depressing. That was how it always went. The music they were rehearsing in band and orchestra, pieces Sophie liked, turned morbid and melancholic. She kept seeing Laura's phony, pasted-on smile and wished she hadn't given Phil the go-ahead to invite her. That nameless dread—the feeling that something terrible was about to happen—swirled about her as it had so many times in the past two years.

But nothing terrible happened, and by the night of the hootenanny she was up again. Laura did come, and though she came with her affected smile and far too much makeup, Sophie was pleased to see the way she greeted meek, bespectacled Jeff and shy, plain-faced Julie without any trace of superciliousness. Perhaps she had been too quick to pass judgment on the girl whose dolls she'd once played with.

Dave Mandell, the brash, dominating guitarist, immediately began to flirt with Laura. As he and Sophie strummed out "Man Come Into Egypt," from the latest Peter, Paul and Mary album, he made frequent eye contact with her. Sophie had studied guitar for only a few months but sounded as if she'd been playing for years. Laura sang along with gusto as she reciprocated Dave's glances.

The group sang for over an hour: "Michael, Row the Boat Ashore," "This Land Is Your Land," "Four Strong Winds" and more. When their energy began to lag, Sophie put the new Bob Dylan album—his second—on the phonograph, and they all listened intently to the new songs. Laura, who had never heard of Bob Dylan before, liked "Blowin' in the Wind" and "Don't Think Twice, It's All Right" so much she asked to hear them again.

After that night, Sophie and Laura rekindled their friendship. Laura also began dating Dave Mandell, who became and remained her boyfriend for almost a year. Sophie and Phil went together for two more years, until the middle of senior year, when she decided to end it; besides his increasingly aggressive attempts to pressure her into sex—she just didn't feel ready yet—their impending separation would have made it difficult to continue the relationship. Sophie had already applied to Berkeley, while Phil was planning to stay behind and attend L.A. Valley College, the junior college next door to Grant High (some joker had dubbed it "Grant with ashtrays"). But the biggest factor driving her decision to break up with him was her realization that he simply wasn't her intellectual equal.

Yes, she realized with chagrin, she was a snob.

CHAPTER 8

A Painful Subject

1964

Steve finished his lunch quickly and spread his book open on the cafeteria table. He was reading Upton Sinclair's *The Jungle* for Mr. Hirschenfeld's tenth-grade English class at Hollywood High. He was about halfway through and eager to continue. Its main character, the poor Lithuanian immigrant Jurgis Rudkus, had beaten up his boss upon finding out that the boss had seduced his wife. After serving his jail term, Jurgis found himself unemployable in the Chicago stockyards.

> Out in the saloons the men could tell him all about the meaning of it; they gazed at him with pitying eyes—poor devil, he was blacklisted! What had he done? they asked—knocked down his boss? Good heavens, then he might have known! Why, he stood as much chance of getting a job in Packingtown as of being chosen mayor of Chicago.

The word *blacklisted* rang a bell with Steve. It came from some very distant memory he couldn't quite get a handle on.

Mr. Hirschenfeld's class was fifth period, right after lunch. During that day's class they discussed *The Jungle*, and by chance a conversation ensued about the section of the book Steve had just been reading and the word that had caught his attention.

"Blacklisted," Mr. Hirschenfeld said, "means that you are on a secret list of people who cannot be employed. At the turn of the century, employers were afraid of unionism, and they kept a list of people who were suspected of union organizing."

He paused for several seconds, giving his students time to absorb the definition.

"There was a blacklist here in Hollywood not long ago. A list of writers, actors and directors the studios would not employ because they were suspected of Communist sympathies. I had friends who were affected by it."

A Hollywood blacklist. Steve had never heard of it. His parents had never mentioned it. His father was a screenwriter, and while Steve didn't think he had ever been a Communist, he was certainly a liberal. He voted Democratic; he favored nuclear disarmament and decried racial prejudice. He had cried when President Kennedy was assassinated. Did he perhaps know anyone who had been affected by the blacklist in Hollywood? Might *he* have been affected by it?

After class he mulled over the word, trying to figure out why it was familiar to him. *Blacklisted*. It was tied to something deep in the past, something from early childhood. Then, suddenly, it came to him: those two little girls he used to play with. They'd heard the grown-ups use a word that sounded like "black-blistered." They'd thought it was a funny word and wondered what it meant. His parents had been among that group of grown-ups, and it would have been the early '50s—the time when, according to Mr. Hirschenfeld, the Hollywood blacklist had begun.

Now he most certainly had to ask his father about it.

"Yes," Arthur Elwood said, shifting uncomfortably in his chair, when his son questioned him over dinner. "I was affected by it."

"You were blacklisted?"

"I'd rather not discuss it."

Steve gave a slight start. There had never been any forbidden topics in the Elwood household.

"It's a painful subject," Rosemary Elwood said. "It was a very painful time for your father and me."

Steve let it drop, but he was excited. The next day, before class, Steve told Mr. Hirschenfeld that his father had been affected by the Hollywood blacklist. Mr. Hirschenfeld seemed to be impressed.

Open house was three weeks later. As Arthur Elwood sat at his son's desk in Mr. Hirschenfeld's classroom, the teacher approached him.

"Steve is doing beautifully," Mr. Hirschenfeld said. "In fact, he's top of the class."

"He's always been a good student," Arthur said.

"He's a little shy about speaking up in class."

"Yes, I know. He's always been shy."

Then Mr. Hirschenfeld leaned in and whispered, "I hear tell that you were blacklisted."

Arthur pulled back and cleared his throat, feeling his face warm.

"I'm sorry," Mr. Hirschenfeld said. "That was very indiscreet of me. You don't have to say anything . . . I just wanted you to know that I'm on your side. And I sympathize with the *very* rough time you and your family must have had." Without giving Arthur a chance to respond, Mr. Hirschenfeld moved on to the next parent.

When he got home, Arthur chastised his son. "You are not to discuss this again with *anyone.*"

"I'm sorry," Steve said. "I was just so proud—"

"No one else. Am I clear?"

"Yes."

The following summer, Arthur Elwood moved his family to Newport Beach.

CHAPTER 9

UCSC

1965-1966

In September of 1965, when the founding cadre of 650 students descended on the University of California's new campus on the hillside above Santa Cruz, the dorms were a year away from completion. The group, all freshmen save for a smattering of junior transfers, was housed in clusters of trailers set in the middle of a former cow pasture destined to become an athletic field.

Sophie Hearn was part of that group. She had always assumed she would go to Berkeley, and at the beginning of her senior year in high school, she had applied there. But as graduation neared, she read an article about the new campus. The idea of being a groundbreaker appealed to her sense of adventure, so she changed her application and was accepted as a member of UC Santa Cruz's first freshman class.

Sophie loved UCSC. She loved the camaraderie among the pioneering students, the intimate setting of the trailers and the Field House where their life was centered, the boundless woods and pastures of the erstwhile cattle ranch on whose two thousand acres the initial array of buildings formed but a speck.

Sadly, the down moods that had plagued her since junior high school did not diminish in Santa Cruz; in fact, they became worse. Her psychologist back home had warned her that this might happen, no matter how well things went, as an unconscious reaction to living away from home for the first time.

The normal Sophie was fully engaged with her new environment, making smart contributions to class discussions, presiding over animated gab sessions at the dining table and sharing confidences with the girls in her trailer. But when she slipped into one of her episodes and the darkness engulfed her, she became so listless that she could hardly carry on a conversation. On really bad days, she would minimize human contact, sitting alone to escape mealtime talk and keeping late hours in the library to avoid her trailermates; on the worst days, she would skip class, grab her guitar and hike deep into the verdant wilds of the new campus's undeveloped parts, where she would sit herself down in some hidden meadow and sing, unheard, into the redwood forest until the black mood ebbed away. Sometimes it took a few hours, sometimes the better part of a day. Occasionally, the rustic retreat failed to work at all, and she would drag herself back to the trailers feeling no better than when she'd left. All she could do then was wait however long it might take until, for no particular reason, she would suddenly feel better again.

"We can't just get out," Dianne Hausmann, Sophie's trailer-mate from Palo Alto, said.

"Why not?" Sophie said.

"Because our country has made a commitment."

"A commitment to what?"

"Stopping the Communists from taking over all of Vietnam."

"So what if they take over? It's their business."

"It's ours, too. Communism *is* a threat to us. It's not like I'm a Bircher or anything. You know me—I'm a liberal Democrat. But I'm against Communism."

"How are the Communists in Vietnam a threat to us?"

"If Vietnam goes Communist, then so will the countries around it. I believe in the domino theory."

While they were arguing, Bob Kelsey, a close friend of Sophie's, rode up on his ten-speed bike and ground to a halt in the dirt in front of the trailer door. He jumped the wooden steps and popped into the girls' trailer, breaking the rule against "intervisitation."

"What's going on?" he said. He was a diminutive boy with tousled hair whose home was San Francisco. He was in his usual outfit, a striped T-shirt, baseball jacket and white Levi's with no belt.

"We're having an argument," Sophie said.

"What about?"

"Whether we should get out of Vietnam."

"Of course we should. How can anyone think otherwise?"

"Dianne does."

"So, Dianne . . . you think we should be dropping napalm on babies?" Bob liked to make blunt statements and then sit back and watch their effect.

"No," Dianne said. "I don't like that part of it. But I *do* think we should drive the Communists out of South Vietnam."

"What's so terrible about Communists?"

"Dianne," Sophie said, "tell Bob why you're against Communism."

"Communists commit atrocities and kill innocent people, and they're brutal dictators when they get into power."

"Did you know," Bob said, "that South Vietnamese agents have dressed up as Viet Cong and committed atrocities? And killed innocent people? Just to make people like you believe all that crap you just said?"

"Really?" Sophie said. "I hadn't heard that."

"I don't believe it," Dianne said.

"It's true. Also, did you know that the declaration of independence Ho Chi Minh wrote for North Vietnam was based on *our* Declaration of Independence?"

"I don't believe that, either."

"This is pointless," Sophie said. "We're not going to change each other's minds. Let's just accept that we're not going to agree. Can we still be friends even though we don't agree on politics?"

"Of course," Dianne said.

"How about sex and religion?" Bob said.

"We disagree on both of those, too," Sophie said. "She's against premarital sex; I think it's okay if two people care for each other. She believes in God; I don't."

"It's not like I'm a religious fanatic or anything," Dianne said. "I'm a Reform Jew. But yes, I do believe there's a God, and it's comforting sometimes."

"I'm half Jewish and half Catholic," Sophie said, "so if I wanted to believe in a God, I'd have to choose which one."

"I'm an atheist, too," Bob said. "And I believe very strongly in premarital sex."

Dianne reddened slightly. "I just think a person should wait till they're married."

"Why?"

"Let's drop it," Dianne said. "I've had enough arguing for today . . . and I've got an essay to write for my World Civ seminar."

"I need to get to work, too," Sophie said. "I have to write a paper for Spanish Lit."

"You're so lucky you've already met the language requirement," Bob said. "I'm terrible at languages. I'm afraid I'm gonna fail my French class."

"They're not going to fail anybody here," Dianne said. "That's the trouble. Everything's too easy. It's pass-fail grading, and nobody's afraid of failing, so nobody studies."

"*I* study," Bob said. "I'm gonna go study now." He jumped directly from the trailer door to the ground, ignoring the two wooden steps, and pedaled away on his bike.

"Was your dad really a Communist?" Dianne said.

"Yes," Sophie said.

"And your mom, too?"

"Yes."

The blacklist was over. Once-banned writers were writing again under their real names. Though Larry Hearn, having made a modest name for himself during the dark years as "Hank Lawrence," had gone on using that moniker in his still-sporadic TV work, it no longer mattered if people knew his true identity. Sophie no longer had to keep it secret that her father was a writer; she could, in fact, talk openly about the blacklist and how it had impacted her family.

"I hope you weren't offended by what I said about Communists," Dianne said.

"Not at all," Sophie said.

"Your parents aren't Communists *now*, are they?"

"No."

They were interrupted by their trailer-mate Liz Evanson, who suddenly stepped up into the trailer crying. She wore a blouse with a chaste round collar, a wool sweater and a pleated flannel skirt. She was the only girl in the trailer who regularly wore a skirt and makeup.

"What's the matter, Liz?" Sophie said.

It turned out she had seen the boy she thought was her boyfriend with his real girlfriend. The other girls in the trailer had known what was going on and tried to warn Liz, but she'd refused to believe it.

"It's all right, Lizzy," Dianne said. "You'll find someone better than that two-timing rat fink. You'll find a boy who really cares for you."

"No," Liz whimpered, "I'll never find anyone. I'm too ugly."

"You are *not* ugly," Sophie said.

They comforted her as best they could for nearly half an hour, and by then it was time for dinner. Liz pulled herself together and fixed her makeup, and the three girls strolled over to the Field House together and got in the dinner line.

On a Saturday night five months later, Sophie was at her desk typing a sociology paper when Bob Kelsey came to the trailer door.

"Come with me," he said.

"Where?

"Outside."

"Why?"

"Just come."

"It's cold out."

"Put on a warm coat."

"I have to work on this paper."

"Come on . . . It's Saturday night. I'm taking you out on a date."

"Okay," Sophie said, laughing. "I'll go out on a date with you, but just for a little while. Where are you taking me?"

"You'll see."

She put on her quilted ski jacket and followed Bob into the nippy April night. He led her away from the trailer clusters and to the dark at the edge of the grassy field, where he sat down cross-legged on the ground and motioned her to do the same.

"What are we doing?"

"I got some pot."

"Some what?"

"Marijuana." He reached into his shirt pocket and held up the hand-rolled cigarette. "Wanna smoke it with me?"

"Are you serious?"

"Sure."

"Have you done it before?"

"No."

"Where'd you get it?"

"Can't tell you that."

"You're really going to smoke it?"

"Yeah."

"You're not scared?"

"Why should I be? It's harmless. You can't get addicted to it."

"But it's illegal. We could go to jail."

"That's why we're out here in the dark."

"Well . . ." Sophie knew how useless it was to try to talk Bob Kelsey out of anything. "Why don't you go ahead and I'll watch the effect it has on you."

"Okay."

After pulling a cigarette lighter from the pocket of his jeans, he lit the joint and puffed hard on it.

"Here goes," he said. "Wish me well." The tip of the reefer glowed bright as he drew a deep breath. He held it for about five seconds and then coughed the pungent smoke toward Sophie.

"You all right?" she said, turning her face away.

He nodded.

"What does it feel like?"

"Nothing yet."

He inhaled more deeply this time and held it twice as long before coughing it out again.

"Anything yet?"

"Little dizziness, that's all." He took another long draw, then another.

"How do you feel?"

He didn't answer. Sophie waited while he took several more hits. Then his eyes and mouth opened wide. "Oh, my God," he said.

"What?"

"Just oh, my God."

"Tell me."

"I can't. I'm falling."

"Falling?"

"Oh, shit."

"What is it? You feel like you're falling?"

"Not feel like. *Am* falling."

"You okay?"

"No. Scary. Very scary."

"Can I help?"

"Just stay here."

"I'm not going anywhere."

"Hold my hand."

"Okay."

She held Bob's hand for several minutes while he described elaborate phantasmagorical images he was seeing behind his closed eyelids. Then he suddenly opened his eyes and released her hand. "Now it isn't scary anymore. It's beautiful."

"Beautiful how?"

"I can't describe it. I just can't describe it at all."

"Can you *try*?"

"No. Just come join me." He held out the joint to her.

"Uh . . ." She hesitated and thought for a minute.

"Come join me," he said again.

"Uh . . . I don't think so."

"Why not?"

"It was scary for you."

"But now it's beautiful."

"But you had to go through the scary part to get to the beautiful part."

"It was worth it," he said. "Just do it. Come on."

"Well . . . okay. Just a little, and just this once. If you promise not to tell anyone."

"You serious? You really think I'm gonna tell anyone?"

She took the glowing joint out of Bob's hand and drew deeply on it but lost it in a coughing fit. "Oh, shit," she said. "That burns."

"Try again."

She did. This time she managed to hold it in.

"I don't feel anything so far except a sore throat."

"Course not. You haven't smoked enough."

She took another drag.

"Ooooh, I feel it now . . . but it's not real pleasant."

"Are you falling?"

"No, not falling. Just kind of an unpleasant all-around sensation."

"Smoke some more."

"No, I don't think I want to. Not yet."

"You gotta get to where I am."

"Just give me a few minutes to get used to where *I* am." After half a minute, she tried again. And again. "Okay, now it's kind of pleasant."

"Just pleasant?"

"Yeah, but it's fine. I like it."

"No, keep going. Smoke a little more. Come to where I am."

"I don't want to smoke any more. My throat's too sore."

"Please?"

"No." It wasn't easy to say no to Bob, but her refusal was firm and final.

"Okay, then. I wish you could join me, though."

"Maybe some other time."

"Let's walk."

"Where to?"

"Around. I want to see what everything looks like when I'm like this."

They walked around the perimeter of the field, keeping their distance from the trailers and the Field House to avoid contact with people. Bob said he couldn't cope with talking to anyone. When they reached the road, they began walking downhill, toward the cow pastures, away from the populated part of the campus.

"Are you still feeling the effects?" Sophie said after they'd walked about ten minutes.

"Starting to come down a little. Maybe. I guess."

"Let's start walking back up. I want to go back to my trailer now."

"Why?"

"I need to get to work on that paper."

"You can't work now. You're high."

"I'm not high anymore. I wasn't that high to begin with."

"But we're out on a date."

"It's not a real date. We're just platonic friends."

"I know. I was kidding. But still, it's Saturday night."

"I've barely started that paper and it's due Monday."

"You got all day tomorrow to work on it."

"I don't want to leave it till the last minute."

"You're so virtuous."

"No, I'm not virtuous. I just don't want to screw up this assignment. I was late on the last one because I got depressed."

"But it's pass-fail and you know you're not gonna fail. What difference does it make?"

"I want to impress my professors and make them tell me how brilliant I am."

"I didn't know you were that insecure."

"I'm not insecure. I just have certain needs. Don't you ever feel the need to be praised?"

"Not since I was about eight years old."

"I'll bet you're lying. There must be someone whose opinion you care about."

"Just my own."

"How did you get to be so secure?"

"I don't know."

"Well . . . if you ever figure it out, tell me."

"I'll smoke more pot, then maybe I'll know. They say it gives you insight into yourself."

They walked in silence for a while.

"Will you smoke with me again?" Bob said when they were almost back to the trailers.

"I don't know . . . Probably not."

"Why not?

"I don't know, it just wasn't that exciting. And it's illegal."

"You gotta take some risks in life."

"Not this one. I don't want to go to jail—or get expelled."

When they came near the trailers, Bob stopped.

"Aren't you coming?" Sophie said.

"No. I'm just gonna walk around a while. I'm not ready to face people."

"Be careful. Don't get lost."

"I won't."

When she got back to her trailer, Sophie told Dianne what had happened.

"You shouldn't have done that," Dianne said. "It's against the law and it's dangerous."

"I know it's against the law," Sophie said, "but I don't think it's all that dangerous."

"Of course it's dangerous. You can get addicted."

"They say you can't."

"Who says you can't?"

"I don't know . . . everyone I've talked to about it."

"I don't believe that. I wouldn't try it again if I were you."

"I don't plan to."

CHAPTER 10

Rick and Craig

1967

For their junior year, Sophie and Dianne moved off campus together. Dianne had loosened up considerably since their freshman days in the trailer and was now, along with Sophie and most of their friends, smoking pot on a regular basis. Some in their crowd did it for the visions of enlightenment they believed the drug brought them, others for plain hedonistic fun. No matter the reason, and despite the risk of arrest, it had become the norm. LSD was widely available as well, and many of their friends had taken it at least once (Bob Kelsey had done it four times), but there Sophie drew the line. She'd heard too many frightening tales of people having "bad trips."

It was the fall of 1967, the fall after the "Summer of Love." The character of the Santa Cruz student community had changed radically in less than a year. Nearly all of Sophie's friends had moved down off the campus into town, having finally found the hillside dorms too confining, the close-knit academic community—an essential part of the UCSC concept—too stiflingly familial. There was an abundance of bargain rentals in the beach resort town, whose landlords were only too happy to have long-term tenants in the off-season. Sophie and Dianne found a two-bedroom apartment in an old stucco duplex, a few blocks from the beach, for sixty-five dollars a month, utilities included.

As Santa Cruz morphed into a college town, the inevitable bohemian student culture took root. People dropped in on each other without calling first, and open-to-all parties were a common thing. On a Saturday night about a month into the school year, Sophie went to such a party.

A particularly nasty depression had descended on her that day, one that neither walking on the beach nor playing soulful ballads on her guitar could banish. She was restless and unhappy at school; she had changed her major twice—from Spanish lit to philosophy, then to history—but still she felt lost and aimless. At such times in the past she had usually avoided social contact, but when she heard about the party, she thought that being around people just might distract and cheer her.

The party was within walking distance of her apartment, in a grand old Victorian mansion rented by several students. When she arrived, there were twenty-five or thirty people already gathered in the living room. She sat on a couch alone and took in the scene, and as she'd hoped, she felt her mood start to improve.

She had been there for only a few minutes when she saw a group of people at a table across the room bending over something, and she knew someone was about to roll a joint. She made a quick decision not to partake. It could sometimes help bring her out of a depression, but the last few times she'd smoked for that purpose it had made her feel worse. She decided to make this an experiment:

to see if she could enjoy being in a place where everyone else was stoned without being under the influence herself. She watched the familiar scene unfold: the rolling and licking of the joint by the person who had brought the pot; the lighting; the handing off to the closest guest, the provider graciously declining a hit until the others had taken theirs; the passing around; the sharp, deep breaths held in, the occasional cough; the compliments to the provider on the quality of the weed.

The Doors' first album was playing on the stereo, somebody's high-quality component system instead of the usual portable record player. A boy with a goatee sat down next to Sophie. When the joint came around to him, he took his puff and passed it on to her as he held the smoke in his lungs. She declined it and handed it over to the next person.

"You don't smoke grass?" the boy said after he exhaled.

"Sometimes I do," she said. "I'm just not in the mood tonight."

"I'm always in the mood. But it's cool if you don't want to. You can get a contact high."

"Maybe I'll do that."

"What's your name?"

"Sophie."

"Glad to meet you, Sophie. I'm Rick."

"Nice to meet you."

"Where do you live?"

"Couple of blocks from here. On Second Street. And you?"

"I live here."

"You live in this house?"

"Yeah."

"You're lucky. It's a beautiful house."

"Yep. Can't deny it. It's pretty groovy."

On the stereo the Doors' "Light My Fire"—the full seven minutes of their best-known song, not the truncated version that had climbed the pop charts earlier that year—began to play. On its second tour of the room, the now-much-shorter joint came around to Rick again, and after taking another deep drag, he handed it to Sophie to give to the next person. Jim Morrison's voice boomed from the two big stereo speakers. When the initial vocal part of the song ended and the long instrumental interlude began, Rick threw his head back, closed his eyes and "grooved" to the music, his head bobbing in time. Amused, Sophie sat and surveyed the room, watching others bob their heads as the glowing joint continued to circulate.

By the time "Light My Fire" concluded with its climactic reca-pitulation of the opening lyrics, Sophie was ready to go home. It had been a mistake for her to come. For a brief time she had felt better, but now she was just bored.

"Wanna see my room?" Rick said.

She should have said, *No, thank you, I'm feeling a little tired and I think I'll go home.* But he was kind of sweet, and she didn't want to hurt his feelings. So she climbed the stairs with him and went in to look at his room.

"It's really nice," she said.

It really was a charming room, with dark wood paneling and an angled ceiling. It was on the second floor and commanded a view of the beach and the long, seedy expanse of the Santa Cruz boardwalk. Through the open window she could hear the screams of the people on the roller coaster. Though the room was small, it had a full-size bed.

"Yeah," Rick said. "I think it's pretty bitchin'."

While Sophie pondered how long it had been since she'd last heard the expression "bitchin'"— a quaint relic of the earlier sixties—Rick walked over and stood uncomfortably close to her. Now she knew she'd made a mistake.

"It's a far-out room to make love in," he said, taking hold of her shoulders. As he pulled her toward him and kissed her, she was too startled to resist at first, but then she gently pushed him away.

"Come on," he said, undeterred, as he started to remove his belt. "Take off your clothes and let's ball."

"Keep your clothes on," Sophie said.

"What's the matter?"

"What's the matter is that that I've known you about fifteen minutes."

"So what? Aren't you liberated?"

"Being liberated has nothing to do with it. Did you really bring me up here thinking I was going to jump into bed with you?"

"What's the matter, don't you dig sex? You're not a virgin, are you?"

"Yes, I dig sex, and no, I'm not a virgin. But I have to at least get to know a guy before I'll sleep with him."

Sophie had impulsively lost her virginity one night near the end of freshman year with Bob Kelsey—the second time they smoked pot together—and in spite of that one lapse, they'd continued being platonic friends. A second sexual experience sophomore year had almost led to a serious relationship, but the boy had pulled away.

"So, you'll get to know me now," Rick said. "What are you so uptight about?"

"I'm not uptight! I just wasn't prepared for you to assume I wanted to make love with you just because I came up here to look at your room!" She felt a sudden attack of guilt and contrition, certain it was her fault. "I'm really sorry if I misled you."

"I'm sorry, too," Rick said. "I guess I misread your vibes. I thought you were a liberated chick, but obviously you're not. I can see you're really hung up."

"Well . . . I guess maybe I am," she said, no longer feeling apologetic. "If not wanting to ball someone I just met makes me hung up, then I guess I'm hung up. I don't mean to be rude, but I'm going to leave now." She moved toward the door, afraid he might try to block her way, but he didn't.

Angry at herself for having stupidly placed herself in that situation, she hurried down the stairs and back into the party. Her depression was coming back and she wanted to leave right away, but she had to pee and didn't know if she could make it home. So she made her way to the only downstairs bathroom, which was occupied and had two people waiting.

"You look bummed," said the boy who was second in line.

He wasn't handsome but had a pleasant air about him. His expression of concern seemed genuine, not just a pickup ploy, and something made her want to tell him what had just happened.

"Who was it?" the boy said. "I'll bet it was Rick."

"Yes. It was."

"I know Rick. He's a nice guy, but he sometimes acts like an asshole around girls."

"Well, he sure did tonight."

"What's your name?"

"Sophie."

"I'm Craig." As he reached out to shake her hand, the girl who had been in front of him in line emerged from the bathroom. He motioned toward the door. "You go first."

"Thank you."

After Sophie came out, Craig asked her to wait for him and went in. She waited.

"I'm going to go home now," she said.

"Me, too. Need a ride?"

"No, I walked here and I can walk back. I'm just a few blocks away."

"You sure?"

"Well . . . okay. I'm pretty tired."

They walked to Craig's car.

"You have a VW," Sophie said. "So do I."

"Yeah. I love my Vee-Dub. What year's yours?"

"Sixty-two. Yours is a lot newer."

"Yeah, it's a '66. High-school graduation present from my parents."

When they got to her place, she invited Craig in for coffee. Dianne was away for the weekend visiting her parents in Palo Alto.

As they talked, she found they had much in common. Within twenty minutes they were bantering playfully, poking fun at all that was fatuous and foolish about the hip student scene they were part of.

An hour later they were in bed.

CHAPTER 11

A Visit Up North

1968

In his Mustang convertible, with the top down, Steve drove slowly along a street of new, look-alike Irvine houses and apartment buildings. He recognized the building the party was in by the number of cars in front of it.

Steve was in his second year at one of the three new UC campuses—Irvine, Santa Cruz and San Diego—that had opened the year before he started as a freshman. His parents had decided that UC Irvine would be the ideal place for him because it was only four miles from the Elwood home in Newport Beach, and that proximity had seemed important the first year given the likelihood that he would have difficulties with social adjustment at college. They'd agreed that he should live in the dorm to experience being at least partway "out of the nest," while still being close enough to come home if he felt homesick or needed to talk to his parents.

Now, after a year, Steve wondered if he shouldn't have chosen a different campus—or even another university altogether. UCI was new and ugly. The community around it and all of central Orange County was new and ugly, with its blocks of identical, faux-Spanish tract houses and apartment buildings only recently sprouted from orange groves. He didn't need to be so close to his parents anymore; if anything, he needed more distance. But he was afraid it would hurt their feelings if he told them that.

The party was in a large apartment, and the living room was packed, with no place to sit except the floor. With cigarette smoke filling the air and an early Beatles album playing on the stereo, the party's locus was the big metal keg in the middle of the room. Steve grabbed a paper cup, and as he pumped it full of tepid beer, he saw a cute girl across the room, seated on the floor, looking like she wasn't with anybody. He maneuvered his way over and sat next to her. After introducing himself, he learned that her name was Melody.

"Crowded party," he said.

"Yes," she said. "Do you know anybody here?"

"No. A guy in my calculus class told me about the party . . . so I thought I'd come and see how it was." He had a sudden rush of self-consciousness and was glad the lights were too dim for her to see him blushing. He took a swig of beer. "Do *you* know anybody here?"

"Just my friend Janine over there." She pointed across the room, but Steve couldn't see where she was pointing.

They sat for a minute or so without talking. Steve quickly finished his beer and stood up. "I'm going to go get some more beer," he said. "Can I get you some?"

"No, thanks. In fact, I've already had a little too much."

"Okay. I'll be right back."

The room had gotten more crowded and he had to elbow his

way to the keg. By the time he refilled his cup and made his way back to where he'd been sitting, another boy had taken his place and was chatting animatedly with Melody.

That's okay. Really. What was I doing trying to talk to a girl? What right do I have? What do I have to say that would matter to any girl, anyway? Come to think of it . . . what the hell am I doing at a party?

He found a more isolated spot on the other side of the room and sat down alone. He sank deep into himself, once again thinking about how much he hated Irvine, fantasizing about transferring to someplace old and vibrant and liberal. Berkeley, perhaps. He imagined himself going to protests and love-ins, attending classes in century-old buildings.

A sudden roar of excitement jolted Steve from his reverie as all attention turned toward the center of the room. With raucous encouragement from his friends, a gymnast who'd apparently had a few too many beers was acting on a dare and trying to do a handstand on top of the beer keg. He failed, and his friends caught both him and the keg as they toppled. Undaunted, he prepared to try again, and again the crowd roared.

More convinced than ever that he had stepped into a place where he didn't belong, Steve started toward the door, but the keg-stander's audience blocked his way. He found a hallway and went down it, hoping there might be another door through which he could escape and go home. He tried the door at the end of the hall, but even before he touched the knob, it hit him: a smell that was sharply distinct from the pervasive cigarettes-and-beer odor. Though he'd smelled it only once before, he knew what it was.

The door opened into a bedroom where four guys and a girl were seated on the floor, passing a marijuana joint.

"'Scuse us," someone said. "Please get out and close the door."

"Unless you wanna join us," someone else said.

Steve had never smoked pot. He'd never wanted to. Now he did. If beer couldn't relax him enough to socialize like a normal human being, perhaps this stuff could.

"Either come in or get out," the first person said.

"Wanna join us?"

Steve hesitated for the briefest moment and then said, "Yes."

"Then get in here fast, man, and close the damn door."

Steve stepped inside and closed the door quickly, almost slamming it.

"Glad you've come to join us, my friend—except that we don't know you. Can you reassure us you're not a narc?"

"What's a narc?"

"If you don't know what a narc is, you probably aren't one. Siddown."

A girl handed him the joint. He took a quick puff and blew out the smoke without inhaling it.

"I can see you've never done this before," the girl said.

"No. I haven't."

"Give it here. Lemme show you."

The girl sucked the smoke in and held it in for several seconds before exhaling and handing the joint back to Steve. He imitated her, pulling the hot smoke deep into his lungs and holding it for as long as he could before coughing it out.

"Way to go."

"That's the way, man."

With only five other people sharing it, the joint came back to Steve quickly. He took a second hit, then a third and a fourth.

All he felt was lightheadedness, but he was suddenly afraid.

They were deep in the heart of Orange County, the most conservative county in California, and possession of marijuana was a felony.

"I gotta go now," he said nervously as he got up from the floor. "Thanks for letting me smoke."

"Any time, brother."

He let himself out of the bedroom and carefully closed the door behind him. He started down the hall, back to the party, thinking again that it was time for him to leave. The pot hadn't had any significant effect—it certainly wasn't going to enhance his social skills—and he started to elbow his way toward the front door.

Then, suddenly, the room began to drop like an elevator.

Caught unprepared for the delayed reaction, Steve leaned back against the wall. The falling accelerated, and he slid to the floor. But that didn't help either.

For several difficult minutes, he thought he was going to have to crawl back to the bedroom and humiliate himself by asking the veteran smokers for help with a bad trip. But then, as quickly as it had started, the falling stopped, and all at once the burst of confidence he'd hoped for happened. He looked around the room and saw people who were no longer intimidating, who were now his equals.

He stood up and looked around for Melody. He saw her, now sitting on a couch, with the boy who had taken his place. He scanned the room until he saw another girl sitting by herself.

"Hi," he said with a boldness that felt natural, as he sat down. "I'm Steve."

"I'm Vicki. Nice to meet you."

"Nice to meet you. Do you know anybody here?"

"Yes," she said, "I know Brent. This is his apartment. He's right over . . . no, he's not. He was there a minute ago. Anyway . . . he and my boyfriend are best friends. We all went to high school together."

He was relieved that she had a boyfriend. That took the pressure off. He didn't have to worry about what his chances might be; he could simply use her to practice his conversational skills.

"Is your boyfriend here?"

"No, he lives up in L.A. He goes to USC."

"Do you see him often?"

"About every other weekend."

"Is it hard being separated?"

"Yes."

He didn't feel like talking any more about her boyfriend, and when the train of conversation ended, there was no awkwardness. He just slid effortlessly onto a new track.

"What year are you?" he said.

"Freshman," she said. "And you?"

"Sophomore."

"Where are you from?"

"Right near here. Newport. And you?"

"North Hollywood."

"We lived in Studio City when I was a kid."

"Really! Did you go to North Hollywood High?"

"No, I went to Hollywood High for the tenth grade. Then we moved down here and I went to Corona del Mar. Did you go to North Hollywood?"

"Yes."

"I knew a lot of kids who went there. Did you go to Walter Reed Junior High?"

"No, I went to Sun Valley."

"Where'd you meet your boyfriend?"

"Junior high. But we didn't start dating till high school."

Suddenly, he felt self-conscious again. The conversation was starting to feel stagy and unnatural, and it reminded him that he was in an unnatural state. He feared that Vicki could tell he was high on pot; he wondered if she could smell it on his breath.

Who am I to be talking to this girl?

"Excuse me," he said. "I'm going to go get some more beer." Instead, he left the party and went out to his car. He wondered for a moment whether he was safe to drive, but then remembered someone saying that driving stoned wasn't as dangerous as driving drunk, and he hadn't had enough beer to be drunk.

He drove the entire three miles back to campus at fifteen miles per hour.

A few weeks later, Steve got a letter from his old high school friend Ron Cobin, who was at another of the new UC campuses—Santa Cruz. In the letter Ron invited him to come up and visit on a weekend when his roommate would be gone. Steve wrote back and accepted the invitation. From Ron's description, Santa Cruz sounded like a fun place for a short vacation.

He left on a Friday morning, skipping the day's classes, and headed north on Highway 101 with the top down on his Mustang. As he passed through the gentle green hills of San Luis Obispo County and the farmlands of the Salinas Valley, picking up Highway One at Castroville ("The Artichoke Center of the World"), he marveled at how different a world northern California was. After crossing the Pajaro River—an actual river, not a Los

Angeles-style concrete storm drain—into Santa Cruz County, he passed alternating thick forest and deep-green meadowland, scenery never seen in the state's brown, brushy southlands.

He got into Santa Cruz around five in the afternoon. Heading up High Street, following the directions Ron had mailed him, he felt the old houses that lined every street affect him in a way he couldn't fully comprehend. It was déjà vu, as if he'd lived in an old house, in a town full of old houses, in a previous lifetime.

After entering the UCSC campus and driving past some old farm buildings, Steve found himself at the bottom of a long sloping cow pasture with actual cows grazing in the distance; the university buildings were so far up the hill he had to squint to see them in the twilight as he started up the two-lane road. It was nearly two miles up to the central campus, and when he got there the beauty of what he saw stunned him. Stands of massive redwoods surrounded buildings that were as new as Irvine's but opposite in style and scale: small, complex and intimate, not monolithic and impersonal.

He found Ron Cobin in his second-floor dorm room at Stevenson College. Steve hadn't seen Ron since their graduation from Corona del Mar High nearly two years earlier, and he hardly recognized the hippie with the shoulder-length hair and full beard who greeted him at the door. The Ron he remembered had a surfer haircut.

"Let's go get some dinner," Ron said.

They went through the food line in the Stevenson dining hall and sat at a crowded table where Ron introduced Steve to more people than he could possibly remember. The dress and hair styles of the people at the table—and, it seemed, everyone else in the dining hall—were so overwhelmingly hip that Steve felt embarrassed by his straight appearance.

As they ate, one of the students announced that there was a party that night at someone's off-campus house.

"Wanna go?" Ron said.

"Sure," Steve said.

"Ever smoke grass?" Ron asked Steve on the way to the party. They'd never discussed the subject before.

"Just once," Steve said.

"Like it?"

"Well . . . I don't know. It was pretty weird."

"I'm sure there'll be dope at the party. Just wanted to make sure you're okay with that."

Steve had assumed—hoped, in fact—that there would be dope at the party. Not that he necessarily wanted to smoke; he was just curious to see what a full-blown pot party in a place like Santa Cruz—not an Irvine beer-keg party with a few people furtively sharing a joint behind a closed bedroom door—would be like.

"That's fine with me," he said.

"Far out."

The party was in an old bungalow-style house on the hillside just below campus. The scent was detectable on the street.

The living room was packed, but there was an ambience of mellowness. Everybody seemed to know everybody else. Steve immediately picked up on a sense of connection among the partygoers, a degree of comfort with one another, that had been absent at the Irvine party. A Grateful Dead album was playing on the stereo, but the music could hardly be heard above the low roar of easy conversation. The fragrance of burning incense mingled with the aroma of pot; joints were being shared openly, with no apparent concern for the danger of a police raid.

Ron pulled Steve around the room, introducing him. "This is Zach . . . George . . . Norman . . . Linda . . . Peter . . . another Linda . . . Adam . . . Patti. All of you, this is Steve, my old buddy from down south."

Steve sensed a certain reaction from the others when they learned he was from "down south" and quickly discovered that there was, among the Santa Cruz collegians, a stigma attached to anything or anyone from southern California. He also sensed that a transplanted and re-acculturated southern Californian could be quickly forgiven his origin, as was obviously the case with Ron.

Someone handed Steve a joint. He hesitated before taking a deep puff, then worried that he shouldn't have. He was in a strange place among strange people, and there was no predicting the pot's effect on him in that setting. But after the joint had come around to him the third or fourth time, he suddenly felt as if his hair had grown to his shoulders and he no longer stood out. There were none of the disturbing sensations he'd experienced that night in Irvine, just a euphoric glow of everything being all right.

He sat on a couch to get his bearings and found himself next to a girl who looked a little less hip than the rest. Her hair wasn't as long, and she wore jeans and a sweatshirt instead of the flowing floor-length dresses the hippie girls seemed to favor.

"Hi," he said. "I'm Steve."

"Hi," the girl said sweetly. "I'm Sharon."

After establishing that he was from "down south" and was visiting a friend, he wondered if he was talking too much.

"Wow . . . I'm really stoned," he said. "I hope I don't sound too weird."

"You seem totally normal. *I'm* really stoned."

"You seem pretty normal, too." Steve paused. "Have you been smoking pot a long time?"

"Just since last summer. My boyfriend turned me on to it."

This time Steve was disappointed that the girl was spoken for, but elated that he was doing so well at conversation and feeling so totally comfortable.

"Does your boyfriend go to school here?"

"Yes."

"So why isn't he here with you?"

"He went home to Walnut Creek for the weekend."

"And he doesn't mind your going to parties alone?"

"No. He doesn't take away my freedom."

After talking to her a while longer, he excused himself to circulate around the room, enjoying his pot-induced social confidence. He smoked a lot more dope and introduced himself to several other girls before the party began to wind down and Ron beckoned him away.

The following day Ron took Steve on a grand tour of Santa Cruz. They hiked up and down Pacific Avenue, the decaying downtown drag, with its beguiling nineteenth-century storefronts. They cruised endless streets in town, passing so many Victorian manses, turn-of-the-century farm houses and Craftsman bungalows that Steve was dizzy with the desire to inhabit one of them.

One day, he vowed, he would.

CHAPTER 12

Sophie and Craig

On Tuesday, August 20, 1968, Sophie woke around nine thirty in an upbeat mood, believing she was going to have a good day. It was her day off from her summer job as a seasonal assistant at the Santa Cruz post office. Craig and their temporary house-mate, Barry, were still asleep.

She went to the kitchen to scrounge up some breakfast. She craved an omelet, but she knew they were out of eggs. There was just enough milk left to pour over a bit of Kellogg's Raisin Bran. She didn't feel guilty about taking the last of the milk, because she hadn't been able to get either Craig or Barry to go to the store (she'd told them she was sick of always ending up having to do it herself) and neither of them ever ate breakfast anyway. She made herself a cup of instant coffee with hot water from the tap, eschewing the fancy drip-cone decanter Craig always made his coffee in.

Sophie had been living with Craig Murkovsky for seven months in the clapboard beach cottage off Seabright Avenue. Her parents had advised her against moving in with a boy she'd known only a few months; cohabitation, they had warned her, was little different from marriage, and a split-up could be every bit as messy and traumatic as a divorce. Craig's parents had given him a similar admonition. But they'd been spending so much of their time together that maintaining separate dwellings had no longer seemed to make sense. It was, after all, 1968. Living together wasn't a big deal anymore.

Now, after slightly over half a year, Sophie knew her parents had been right.

Larry and Ruth had come up to visit shortly after she and Craig had moved in together, and they'd liked him. He was nice—soft-spoken and gentle. But he was also lazy, self-centered, immature, insecure and possessive. In a way that Sophie could never quite understand, those faults seemed able to co-exist in Craig with "nice."

At first he had been responsible about sharing the housework, but he'd done such a poor job at the daily tasks—he was cursory at cleaning and inept at cooking—that Sophie had ended up doing them herself. He refused to make shopping lists, insisting he could rely on his memory, but invariably came back from the store two or three items short. And he was a slob. He left his clothes lying around and his half of the bathroom shelves a mess. When it got to the point where she couldn't stand it anymore, she grudgingly cleaned up after him.

Perhaps most maddeningly, Craig was paranoid about losing Sophie. He was jealous of her intellect and fearful that someone mentally superior might win her away from him. He constantly asked her if she was attracted to this or that person, demanding repeated assurances that he was the center of her universe. It didn't seem to register with him that his behavior was, in fact, driving her away. Scarcely a day went by that she didn't entertain the thought of leaving him.

Another big drag on Sophie's morale was Barry Fell, a friend of Craig's who had dropped out of UCSC five months earlier and been living rent-free in their tiny spare bedroom for three of those five months. She and Craig had taken pity on the soft, unassertive boy who, in leaving school, had lost both his dorm room and his parental allowance. He couldn't get his act together to find a job, couldn't afford a place of his own and couldn't stomach the thought of moving back in with his parents in Modesto. Before Sophie and Craig took him in, he'd been sleeping in his car.

Dropping out of school had also cost Barry his draft deferment. His reclassification to I-A status had alarmed him, but not enough to spur him to action; he called himself a pacifist, and had declared he'd sooner die than be sent to fight in Vietnam, but had abandoned his application for conscientious-objector status when he found the process "too big of a hassle." An attempt to get himself declared mentally unfit had failed, and now he had orders to report for induction the following Monday and still had no idea what he was going to do. Sophie was furious at him for running away from reality, disgusted with his whiny self-pity, and beside herself with worry over what was going to happen to him.

Barry's induction notice sat in the middle of the kitchen table as Sophie slowly sipped her coffee and ate her cereal, knowing he'd left it there to garner sympathy. She looked around at the filthy kitchen; a week's worth of dirty dishes lay stacked in the sink. Life was fucked. By what right could she have a good day?

Craig came into the kitchen just before eleven-thirty, while Sophie was washing the dishes, and lazily made his drip-decanter coffee. He stretched out on the living room couch, sluggish with summer indolence. At eleven-forty, Barry shuffled silently out of his room.

"Whaddya say, Barry?" Sophie heard Craig say.

"Huh?"

"C'mon. You can say more than that."

Barry grunted something unintelligible, then shuffled into the kitchen.

"Good morning, Barry," Sophie said.

"Mm." He poured himself a cup of the coffee Craig had left in the drip decanter for him. Then he darted back into his room, taking the cup of coffee with him and shutting the door.

"Hey, Soph?" Craig called to her from his spot on the couch.

"Yes?"

"Has he decided yet what he's gonna do?"

"No, but don't bug him about it, Craig."

"Why should I bug him? What good would it do? He's hopeless. You realize that, don't you? Six fucking days he's got!"

"Craig, will you cut it out? I'm sick of hearing you talk about how hopeless he is."

"You better help him make up his mind. You're the only one left he'll listen to."

"Would you leave him alone! I mean it, Craig—you don't *have* to be such a bastard with him."

"What the hell are you talking about?" Craig spoke softly even when he was angry or defensive. "How am I a bastard with him?"

"You know what I mean. It's the way you've always been with him."

"Now you're *really* fulla shit. I was the first real friend he had here."

Just then David Solinger popped his head in the door. David

was a friend Sophie and Craig had had in common before they met, a UCSC grad student in philosophy and a hard-core Marxist.

"Anybody home?"

"C'mon in, David," Craig said.

"What's happening?"

"Sophie and I were just having a little discussion about Barry."

"I noticed his car out front. He's still living with you guys?"

"Yep."

David started toward the kitchen. "What's happening with his draft thing?"

"He's getting inducted next Monday."

"No shit. So he's just gonna go?"

"I don't know what the hell he's gonna do. But you better not bug him about it or my woman in there'll get pissed."

David went into the kitchen, where Sophie was nearly finished with the dishes and the dish drainer stood full. "Sophie?"

"Hi, David."

He gave her an affectionate fondle on the rear as he edged past her, and she pulled away. She hated it when he did that and had asked him not to, but he still did it.

"Aha, washing dishes! Every time I see you you're doing something anal."

"Shut up." She flicked some water at him with the sponge. He laughed as he ducked.

"So where's our boy?"

"What boy?"

"The one who's about to be conscripted into the imperialist army."

"He's in his room. Leave him alone, please."

"Whaddya mean leave him alone? Someone's gotta help him."

"Not you."

"Who says not me?"

"I do. I'm protecting him."

"From what? From reality?"

"From you. From Craig. From everybody." She finished washing and started drying.

David picked up a towel and helped her. "Why are you protecting him?"

"Because I'm sick and tired of everyone bugging him. It's just messing up his head."

"How could anyone mess up his head any more than it's already messed up?"

"Just leave him alone, David. Okay? Please?"

"Your maternal instincts are touching. Wasn't he gonna get a shrink to write him a letter?"

"The shrink he saw refused to do it. I guess Barry couldn't act crazy enough."

"Of course he couldn't act crazy. All he knows how to act is pathetic. And that won't keep you out of the Army."

They finished the drying and joined Craig in the living room. Sophie picked up her guitar and played a soft, slow blues tune.

"So," Craig said, "what're you up to, David?"

"I'll give you one guess."

"Uh . . . ah! I know. You're trying to find some dope."

"What else?"

"Wish we could help you, man, but we're desperate, too."

"This is ridiculous. Why's this town suddenly so dry?"

"I dunno," Craig said. "Maybe 'cause they burned those pot

fields in Mexico." After a long pause, he said, "I know a cat up in Felton who might have some mescaline."

"Yeah, and I know where I could score some acid," David said. "But I don't want that. All I want is some good old-fashioned *weed*."

Craig shook his head. "Nobody I know's been able to score any grass."

"Jesus, we were *floating* in the stuff a few months ago! Why couldn't we have just saved a few lids and put 'em aside?"

"No, it never works that way. When you have it, you smoke it."

As Craig and David stretched out their debate on dope husbandry, Sophie started to drift downward. She fought it as she strummed on the guitar, determined that at the very least she wasn't going to show it to anyone. Not even Craig.

The day dragged on. It got hot. They left the front door open, letting in flies. In the late afternoon, Sophie went to the Albertson's supermarket near the center of town for the list that had grown far longer than she usually let it get. She thought getting something done might make her feel better. It did, but only temporarily.

When she got back home, Rodney Marr and Sylvia Rawlins, another living-together couple she and Craig saw often, were there. Everyone helped unload the groceries, and the mood grew festive for no particular reason. The group jumped on the gallon jug of Red Mountain wine Sophie had bought (a favorite of Craig's, not hers) and passed it from mouth to mouth. Craig put a Butterfield Blues Band album on the turntable of the portable stereo and the song "Walkin' Blues" came on.

"You wouldn't believe the political dream I had last night," Rodney said.

"I thought I was the only one who had political dreams," David said.

"Tom North is going to the Democratic convention in Chicago," Sylvia said. "He's gonna leave tomorrow and hitch all the way there."

"That's good," David said. "He'll get the shit kicked out of him there."

"Why is that good?" Sylvia said.

"The best way for chickenshit liberals like Tom North to get radicalized is to get the shit kicked out of them by the pigs."

"You're *terrible*," Sophie said.

"So what was your political dream?" David said.

"It was a dumb dream," Rodney said. "About Humphrey and Nixon. Let's change the subject. I thought we were gonna get some dope."

"We are," Craig said, "if Bob ever gets here."

"Bob?" Sophie said.

Craig informed Sophie that Bob Kelsey had phoned while she was out shopping. He'd just returned from a trip to the Bay Area and was coming over with a "surprise." Sophie knew that Craig wasn't comfortable around Bob; Craig knew that Bob and Sophie had a close friendship dating back to their freshman year, and had slept together once (which she now wished she hadn't told him). But because Bob had good dope connections, she knew that Craig had to stay friends with him.

"Hope he doesn't get busted on the way over," Sylvia said.

Fourteen minutes later, Bob strode confidently through the open doorway.

"Robert!" David said.

"Dope? Dope?" Rodney said eagerly. "Dost thou come bearing dope?"

"Sure do," Bob said, digging deep into the front right pocket of his jeans.

"Hallelujah!" David said.

"I don't believe it!" Craig said.

"*Cannabis sativa*?" Rodney said.

Bob pulled out a little foil-wrapped bundle and laid it on the coffee table. "Hope you guys have a pipe."

"Hash!" David said.

"Oh, my God!" Rodney said.

"Oh, wow," Sylvia said. "Hash!"

"A miracle has befallen us," Craig said. "Soph, where's our hash pipe?"

"I don't know. I'll have to look for it."

"I haven't had hash in *so* long," Rodney said.

"I think it's in the desk drawer," Craig said.

David picked up the chunk of hashish. He unwrapped it and examined it while Sophie rummaged through the desk drawer for the pipe. "This looks like some really fine shit," he said. "Where'd you get it?"

"An old friend," Bob said.

"Where?"

"Berkeley."

"Does he have any more?"

"No. He had this stashed away for a long time, and he wanted to get rid of it."

"I don't think it's here, Craig," Sophie said.

"Uh . . . try the middle drawer in the kitchen."

"We should invite Barry to join us," David said.

"Where *is* Barry?" Sylvia said. "Is he still living here?"

"Sure is," Craig said, "and he's getting drafted next Monday."

"Next *Monday*?"

"That's right."

"So what's he gonna do?" Rodney said. "Go to Canada?"

"Nah," David said. "He'll never get his shit together to do that."

"So he's just gonna go in the Army," Rodney said. "And be an agent of American imperialism. Kill people. Drop napalm. Then probably get killed himself."

"Don't talk like that!" Sylvia said. "I can't imagine Barry doing any of those things. And I don't want him getting killed. I care about him."

"I'm sorry," Rodney said. "That wasn't very nice. I care about Barry, too. I think we all do. But I think we all just wish he'd care more about himself."

Amid the conversation, Bob bent close to David and said something in a hushed tone.

"Hallelujah!" David said, and all eyes turned toward him.

"What's this?" Rodney said.

"Bob just told me some far-out news!" David said. "Tell 'em, Bob."

"What?" Sylvia said. "What is it?"

Bob cleared his throat. "While I was driving down here, I heard on the radio that the Soviet Union just invaded Czechoslovakia. Everybody's freaking out about it."

"No shit?" Rodney said. "That's great!"

"Why is that great?" Sylvia said.

"Because Czechoslovakia's been slipping away from communism a long time now," Rodney said. "A bunch of bourgeois revisionists have taken over. I read about that a few months ago, and it really bummed me out. Now . . . wow! I'm ecstatic!"

David picked up the jug of wine. "Let's drink to the revolution!" He raised the jug high and brought it to his lips to take a hearty swig.

"*¡Viva la revolución!*" Rodney tried to shout, but he didn't know Spanish pronunciation and *revolución* came out "revva-loo-shone."

"May there be one here soon," Bob said.

David handed the bottle to Sylvia. She took a few gulps and passed it on.

"I'm not sure that's such a good thing," Craig said.

"You're not sure what's such a good thing?" David said.

"The Soviets invading Czechoslovakia."

"Why not?"

"I don't think it's a cool move for them to make right now, with all that's happening here."

"Bullshit. It's a beautiful move *because* of what's going down here. They couldn't have timed it better. Just a few months before our election."

"What the hell do you mean? It's gonna help all the right-wing, John-Bircher types drum up support and sway the election. It's gonna get Nixon elected."

"That's exactly what we want. We *want* Nixon to win so things'll get really fucked up and the whole country'll get radicalized. Then will come the *revolución*." He pronounced it slightly better than Rodney.

"I don't quite agree with your reasoning," Craig said. "What if Nixon wins and things get fucked up, but not quite fucked up enough to start a revolution? Then we'll *really* be fucked."

"You need to have your consciousness raised," David said. "You need to smoke some hash."

Sophie came back from the kitchen waving the little brass hash pipe triumphantly. "You'll never guess where it was," she said, handing it to Bob.

"Matches?" Bob said as he broke off a chunk of the hash and crammed it into the pipe's tiny bowl.

Craig found a matchbook amid the clutter on the coffee table and tossed it to Bob. As Bob lit the pipe, Sophie went to the front door and made sure it was locked.

"Hey, Sophie," Sylvia said, "did you hear the news?"

"What news?"

"The Soviet Union just invaded Yugoslavia."

"*Czechoslovakia*," Rodney corrected her.

"They oughta do Yugoslavia, too," David said. "There's another bunch of bourgeois revisionists."

"Where'd you all hear about this?" Sophie said.

"Bob heard it on the radio," Rodney said.

"That's not good."

"What?" David said. "Don't tell me *you've* gone revisionist! Of all people! The only one amongst us raised by radical parents!"

"My parents were pacifists. They joined the C.P. because they were pacifists. They quit because of Hungary. And the Stalin revelations."

Bob took his turn on the pipe and passed it on to David. Sophie went to the window and fiddled with the curtains, trying to get them closed all the way.

"What are you doing, honey?" Craig said.

"Being paranoid."

"Don't do that," Rodney said. "It ruins half the fun."

"You're right," Bob said. "It *is* half the fun! If dope's ever legalized, I'll probably stop smoking it."

Sophie got the curtains closed and sat down next to Craig.

"This is incredible stuff," David said.

"I'll second that," Rodney said. "Just one hit and I'm completely smashed!"

"Thank you, Bob," Craig said. "Thank you, thank you, thank you."

"You're welcome," Bob said.

Barry emerged from his room. He walked timidly toward the group.

"Hi, Barry," Sylvia said warmly.

"Good to see you, man," Rodney said as he reached out to hand Barry the pipe. Barry took a deep draw without saying a word and handed the pipe to Sylvia.

"Barry," David said, "did you hear the Russians invaded Czechoslovakia?"

"No," Barry said flatly.

"You know," Craig said, "maybe that *was* a smart move for them to make."

"Right on, Craig," David said. "I knew you'd come around once you were stoned."

Barry went back to his room.

"You know what?" Bob said. "I've got proof it was a good move. I've seen two Roman Polanski films. The first was *Knife in the Water*, which he made back when he was still in Poland. Excellent film. Then I saw *Rosemary's Baby*, which he made after he came to

Hollywood, and it was a typical Hollywood piece of shit. He sold out once he came here."

"So what's the point?" Sophie said.

"The point is that westernization is bad. Americanization is bad. The revisionist pigs in Czechoslovakia were trying to turn back the socialist revolution and make Czechoslovakia more American. Which means more capitalist. And if they'd succeeded, the other Eastern Bloc countries would've followed right along."

"Right on, Bob," David said.

"Right on," Rodney said.

"Sounds like the domino theory," Sophie said. "In reverse."

"You're damn right," Bob said. "I believe in the domino theory."

"What happened to the Butterfield Blues Band?" Rodney said. "I wanna hear the other side of that album."

"I don't know if anyone has the strength to get up," Craig said.

Bob finally got up and went over to the stereo. He flipped the LP, restarted the turntable and turned the volume way up, distorting the sound coming out of the cheap speakers as the first side-two song, "Mary, Mary," began to play.

As the hash pipe circulated, the smokers slipped one by one into their private cocoons of euphoria. Sophie lay snuggled against Craig on the couch, but far from feeling comforted, she sank ever deeper into that dark void that was hers and hers alone.

Nothing was right. The loud, distorted music blaring from her crappy old stereo, and the spectacle of her stoned-out friends lying all over her living room, reminded her that the world was getting more fucked up by the day. Martin Luther King and Bobby Kennedy were dead. Soviet tanks were rumbling into Czechoslovakia to suppress a popular movement; they'd done the same thing in Hungary in '56 and her parents had quit the

Communist Party in protest. Innocent people were going to be killed, and her closest friends thought that was a good thing because Roman Polanski had made a bad movie. Richard Nixon was probably going to be elected president. She was stuck with Craig and his lazy oppressiveness. Barry was going into the Army, there wasn't a damn thing she could do about it and it would probably kill him long before he got to Vietnam.

"What's the matter, honey?" Craig asked her later, after the guests had left. "Depressed?"

She nodded.

"Same old thing? No particular reason?"

She nodded again.

He put his arms around her and pulled her to him. "It's okay, baby. It's okay. Everything's gonna be all right."

"Is it?"

"Yes. I promise. I'll *make* everything all right."

But she knew he wouldn't, and she knew that *nothing* would be all right until she left him. So why didn't she? Was it because routines were hard to break? Because change was scary? She couldn't quite figure it out. But she knew that someday soon, perhaps in one of her manic moods, she would make that jump.

The following Sunday morning, the day before Barry was to report, Sophie gently awakened him. She made scrambled eggs for the three of them while Craig made coffee in his decanter. After breakfast, they helped Barry pack up as many of his belongings as would fit into the one small suitcase he owned. Then they drove him the seventy-five miles to the Trans-Bay Terminal in San Francisco, stuffed a hundred and fifty dollars into his pocket—the amount they expected to make by selling his portable stereo, record collection and rattletrap of a '58 Oldsmobile—and put him on a Greyhound bound for Vancouver.

On the way back, about as far as South San Francisco, they talked about Barry. The rest of the way Craig grilled her relentlessly, demanding to know whether she wasn't just a little bit attracted to David or might not someday want to sleep with Bob again.

CHAPTER 13

The Kids

1969

The summer after Sophie's graduation from UCSC found her languishing in Santa Cruz with no clear or focused career goals. She had changed her major so many times—four by now—that she'd almost missed graduating with her class. She was a good writer but had no desire to do it for a living. She had musical gifts that brought her pleasure, but wasn't good enough on any one instrument to be a performer and didn't think she'd make a good music teacher. She had entertained vague thoughts of teaching history at the college level, but she would have had to go on to a PhD, and she was horribly burned out on school.

She was living alone now in a tiny studio apartment on East Cliff Drive, having managed at last to rid herself of Craig. Her UCSC classmates had scattered to the four winds after graduation; the off-campus radical crowd was still around, but she had begun to pull away from them. Besides the fact that Craig was still part of that group, she had grown weary of their ego trips, reckless rhetoric and foolish fantasies of imminent revolution.

Mood swings continued to plague her. One day she would be brimming with confidence, the world full of promise and possibility, and she would sit at her desk making lists of bold, ambitious career paths; the next day her universe would be gray, heavy and hostile, and she'd lie in bed feeling dispirited, hopeless and overwhelmed by that all-too-familiar nameless dread.

"I want to get out and do things," she told her parents on the phone during an up mood, "not spend two or three or four more years studying about doing things."

"But you don't seem to have any idea *what* you want to get out and do," her father said.

"I know."

"Any career likely to interest you is going to take at least a master's."

"I know."

Though the blacklist was now history, her parents were still struggling financially in its long wake. Larry (or rather Hank) had a modest name now as a TV sitcom writer, but the assignments were sporadic, and for long stretches in between there were only unemployment insurance and Ruth's teaching income. Their daughter's undergraduate education had put a big strain on them, and they'd looked forward to being relieved of that obligation when she got either a fellowship or a job after graduation; when neither happened, they had reluctantly agreed to continue sending her thirty-five dollars a week—slightly less than what they'd allotted her when she was living off campus as a student—while she explored options and did volunteer work in fields that attracted her. Their attempts to persuade her to come home were unsuccessful, as she now considered Santa Cruz her home and had developed the typical Northern Californian's aversion to the mere thought of living in L.A. Though she hated still being a burden on her parents, she could, on the small allowance they had agreed upon, go on living at the subsistence level to which she was now well-accustomed, rationalizing that it was only temporary and that sooner or later she'd find gainful employment.

She assisted first at a legal aid center that provided pro bono services, mostly to poor Mexicans with tenant-landlord or immigration issues. Her role was to interview the clients and take down preliminary information before referring them to one of the volunteer attorneys. Shortly afterward she began donating additional time to a free medical clinic that also served Santa Cruz's underclass, again performing triage duty. Then she fell into a third volunteering gig, helping out at a free-breakfast-for-kids program run by a black church.

The last would permanently alter the trajectory of her life.

Sophie had never worked with kids, she'd never been particularly fond of kids, and the notion of working with kids as a vocation had never entered her mind. She volunteered for the breakfast program as an afterthought and as a political gesture; she believed not enough was being done to help Santa Cruz's small black community. It caught her completely off guard, as she spooned hot oatmeal into the children's bowls, when one child after another wanted to talk to her, to form a relationship with her, to compete with the others for her attention.

As she sponged food remnants off the table in the church's small activity room after each breakfast, the kids gathered around her and inundated her with personal questions: How old was she? Where did she live? Was she married? Did she have a boyfriend? Then they began to share details of their own lives with her, telling stories of absent parents, divorce, parental fights, corporal punishments, mean teachers, mistreatment by white kids. Nothing had prepared her for the love that would burst inside her when those children befriended her. Especially Jimmy Moreland.

Jimmy was seven years old, and like most of the other kids in the breakfast program, he lived in a neighborhood of deteriorating 'fifties tract homes on the west side of Santa Cruz. He resided with his father and four-year-old sister in a tiny guest house behind the home of the better-off black family that owned the property. His parents had been separated for three years and he rarely saw his mother.

Jimmy adored Sophie. He followed her around and constantly wanted to talk to her. He was a highly intelligent child with a precocious awareness of the worlds inside and outside the circle of his own life; while he wasn't the only child in the breakfast program who had experienced poverty and racism at their ugliest, none of the others could step back and analyze those experiences the way Jimmy could.

On July 21, 1969, the day after Neil Armstrong became the first human to set foot on the moon, Jimmy stayed behind after the other kids had gone. "My daddy say they shouldn't be sending no people to the moon," he said as he helped Sophie clean up.

"Why is that?"

"He say it cost too much money. They should take that money to help poor people."

"I agree with your daddy."

They worked silently for a while.

"My daddy say Nixon and Reagan don't care about poor people. Who Nixon and Reagan?"

"Richard Nixon is the president of the United States. Ronald Reagan is the governor of California."

"How come they don't care about poor people?"

"I don't know. Maybe they just don't understand what it's like to be poor."

"But if he's the president, he should help people."

"I agree."

Again they were silent.

"I love you more than I love my mother," Jimmy said.

Sophie stopped working and looked at him. "I love you, too, Jimmy. But you shouldn't say that. I'm sure your mother loves you very much."

"No she don't. How come she never come to see me?"

"I don't know. She might have problems you're too young to understand."

"I ain't too young to understand nothin'."

"Maybe not," Sophie said as she hugged him and sent him on his way. "You be especially nice to your daddy today. He has a hard life. Hug him and tell him you love him. And be nice to your little sister."

"I will," Jimmy said, smiling sweetly over his shoulder as he walked slowly toward the door.

CHAPTER 14

The House

1969-1970

Sophie's epiphanic involvement with the children in the free breakfast program turned her career search in a new direction. She toyed with the idea of going back to UCSC and getting a teaching credential, but she couldn't stomach the thought of teaching in a public school. Based on what she'd heard from her mother and the kids and parents in the breakfast program, she was convinced that the American public school system existed for the purpose of inculcating kids with the established order of race and class distinctions. Then, in the fall of 1969, she heard that a group of local parents had established a "free school," a tiny private elementary school—of whose ilk many were springing up, she'd heard—with a loose structure, anti-establishment values and a minimal budget. It was called the Santa Cruz Open School, or SCOS.

Sophie took a volunteer position at the school a few weeks after it opened, working alongside the two paid teachers so diligently that the directors quickly recognized her as indispensable. When

several new students enrolled and a third full-time instructor was
needed, she was the obvious choice. She officially became a teacher
and began drawing a salary of $160 a month, slightly more than
what her parents had been providing her, allowing them to discon-
tinue their weekly dole.

She had by now moved out of her lonely apartment and into an
upstairs bedroom of an old house on Soquel Avenue, within walking distance of Santa Cruz's historical core. She shared the house
with a cohabiting couple, Karen DeWare and John Hudlinger,
neither of whom had any connection to the university high on
the hill above town. Karen was a junior-college dropout with a
rough childhood behind her, John a high-school-football-player-
turned-hippie who had never attended college. The pair had been
living together in rocky but survivable poverty since meeting in
San Francisco two years earlier, ultimately finding their way to the
mellow of Santa Cruz. They'd met Sophie at the free clinic where
she'd been volunteering (Karen had feared she was pregnant—false
alarm), and a strong bond had quickly developed. The three of
them ended up living communally in the four-bedroom house
with a series of transitory co-tenants.

"Victorian mansion" was the genre that defined many of Santa
Cruz's older homes. The dilapidated house where Sophie, John
and Karen lived fell just short of that designation. It had been
built sometime around 1910, and while it had some Victorian-
like details in its trim, it was actually an indefinable amalgam of
styles. A large house but not quite large enough to qualify as a
mansion, it was the only single home still standing on a block
given over to stores, office buildings and apartment houses. A
succession of students and hippie types had lived in the house,
with some unusual results: the downstairs rooms were all painted

yellow with white trim, the upstairs dark blue with light-blue trim. The exterior hadn't been painted in decades, and its white paint was peeling sadly off.

In mid-May of 1970, a reclusive man Sophie had suspected of being a hard-drug dealer abruptly vacated the large downstairs bedroom. Shortly afterward, the UCSC senior math major in the small upstairs room said he would be leaving immediately after graduation to take a job in the San Jose area, working on those mysterious, monstrous entities called computers. John and Karen were ready to advertise the two rooms, but events during the weeks that followed would create a different destiny for the old house.

First, Ray Sparman, one of Sophie's three fellow teachers at the Santa Cruz Open School, gave notice that he wouldn't be returning in the fall. He had decided that SCOS was too loosey-goosey for him and been offered a job at a more traditional and better-paying private school. Then Rob and Deirdre Buck, the charmingly flaky couple who had founded the school, announced that they would soon be moving with their two young children to a remote piece of property Deirdre had inherited in Trinity County, in California's far north. "We're going to live off the land," Deirdre announced proudly, "and grow our own food. Since we're vegetarians, we won't need meat, just the vegetables we can grow and the berries we can gather in the woods. And we'll have a goat, so we can have milk, and we'll make our own cheese and yogurt."

Thus did Sophie find herself the sole remaining faculty member and, by default, director of the Santa Cruz Open School.

The Bucks had operated the school in the garage and living room of their rented home, which the owner was planning to reoccupy as soon as they moved out. To keep the school running, Sophie needed two new teachers as well as a new location. She'd met a woman named Nora Weston—a middle-aged credentialed teacher disenchanted with the public school system after eleven years of teaching in it—whose presence would enhance the school's legitimacy. Nora had even offered to put up some money, a few hundred dollars at least, to help set up the school in a new venue. But neither she nor any of the school parents knew of a suitable site, and a tentative deal the Bucks had made to rent an old church building had fallen through.

Then, one day while she was thinking about the two rooms in the house that needed to be rented, Sophie came up with the solution. The newly vacant downstairs bedroom, a tacky fifties add-on intended as a family room, was large enough to serve as a multi-grade classroom. It had a door to the outside (which the suspected pusher had used for his secretive comings and goings), and the big dirt yard around the house would more than suffice for outdoor activities.

When Sophie proposed the idea to Karen and John, they were hesitant at first, but they liked children and ultimately relented. She didn't bother to ask permission of the absentee landlord, a phantom of a man they'd never met and about whom they knew nothing save that his name was Ernest Strohm and that he lived somewhere in the Bay Area. They made their rent checks out to him but mailed them to a Mr. Carlton, Mr. Strohm's property manager, who had been by the house only once since they'd moved in.

The Santa Cruz Open School had found its new home.

In the summer of 1969, two passions had taken hold in Sophie's heart. One was kids, the other feminism.

The feminist bug had bitten her in childhood, when she first came to perceive the depth of the societal expectations that seemed to have no rational basis. Why did only boys get electric trains for Christmas? Why could only boys play baseball and take shop classes at school? Why couldn't she play trombone or drums in the school band instead of flute? Her mother had offered a sympathetic ear on the subject and suggested that women's rights might one day prove to be her life's mission. So when the Women's Liberation movement erupted in 1969, it struck a deep chord with Sophie.

It inspired her to finally jettison Craig after being shackled for two years by his soft possessiveness. It had made her recoil in disgust from the cocky sexism of David Solinger and the other men in his little revolutionary circle, playing a part in her decision to break with that group—including, sadly, her longtime friend Bob Kelsey. It had imbued her with a fierce new sense of who she was, of how her story fit with that of womankind, and given her a shock to realize how imprisoned her mother had been—her own feminism notwithstanding—in the role of buttressing her husband through the blacklist. It had electrified her with an angry resolve to get her shit together and do important things; SCOS was important, but she needed to do something for female consciousness-raising. So early in 1970, she gathered together a small but diverse collection of women and began a weekly discussion group in the living room of her communal home.

With the school occupying the big downstairs room, a paying tenant would still have to be found for the little room with which Sophie shared the upstairs floor and its one bathroom. She resolved that the room should be occupied by a woman, preferably one with a strong feminist consciousness who related to kids and could help out at the school. That would leave the house all female except for John—for all his brash masculinity, a surprisingly non-chauvinistic man unthreatened by strong women. *How wonderful,* Sophie thought, *to have a school, run by two women, within a feminist commune!* Karen, whose women's-lib awareness was taking hold thanks to Sophie's weekly group, agreed in principle that the new housemate should be female. But one day in mid-June while Sophie was working at the legal aid center, Karen—having forgotten their conversation on the subject—offered the room to a man.

He'd come by while Karen was sitting on the front porch soaking in the early-summer sun. "Uh, excuse me," he called out to her, leaning out the window of his newish Volkswagen minibus. "You know of any places to rent around here?"

He was a big hulk of a fellow, intense- and moody-looking, but at the same time shy and appealing, with frizzy black hair and a full beard. He wore the round, gold-rimmed "granny" glasses that were wildly popular among the young and hip of both genders at the time.

"We have a room," Karen said. "It's small."

"Can I see it?"

When she showed him the room, he said he liked it.

"It's a communal house," she said. "We pool our money for food, and most nights we eat dinner together. We take turns cooking and cleaning."

"I like that," he said. "I like the idea of living in a commune."

"What's your name?"

"Steve. I'm a filmmaker. I'm from the L.A. area . . . I hope you won't hold that against me."

"I'm Karen. And no, I won't hold it against you. My friend

Sophie who lives here—she's from L.A., too. You'll meet her. She's really nice."

Steve looked around the living room. "This is a nice house. How many people live here?"

"Just Sophie and me and John, my ol' man. You'll meet him, too. And with you, that'll be four. Oh—and there's one other thing you should know. There's going to be a school operating in that back room. They'll be using the yard and maybe other parts of the house. If you don't like the idea of having kids all over the place, you'd probably be happier somewhere else."

"What kind of school is it?"

"A free school. My friend Sophie who I just mentioned, she's going to be running it with another lady."

"How many students?"

"I'm not sure. About fifteen, I think."

"What age?"

"Little kids. Elementary. It's been in operation for a year now. But they had to move their location, so now they're going to be here, and Sophie's going to be the director."

"How much is the room?"

"Thirty a month."

"I'll take it." Steve reached for his wallet and pulled out a twenty and two fives.

"You don't have to pay a whole month now. Just give me ten bucks for a deposit and the room's yours."

"No, I insist. Let me give you a month's rent, just to make sure I'm in. I really want to live here. I like the house . . . I like the vibes."

*

"I can't believe you did this without asking me," Sophie said as they sat in the living room waiting for the new housemate to arrive. "I *told* you I wanted this to be a women's house."

"I forgot," Karen said. "I'm sorry."

"I wanted a female environment here. I wanted a place where women could feel totally comfortable. You and me and another woman living here, Nora and me running the school here, no men except for John. I don't want some guy I don't even know living here. Living on *my* floor and sharing *my* bathroom, no less."

"Why would it be any different with some *woman* you didn't know? We gotta rent that room to someone."

"Obviously, Karen, our heads are in different places."

"Hey, come on, Soph, don't lay that on me. I'm for women's lib. I come to your meetings. But the idea of having another guy here doesn't bother me that much."

"Of course it doesn't bother you. You're not the one who's going to have to be in close quarters with him. Damn it, Karen! I wasn't going to have to share that bathroom with a man anymore! I wasn't gonna have to tolerate the toilet seat being left up."

"Look, I'm sorry I blew it, okay?"

"When he comes back, tell him you made a mistake, the room's not available."

"I can't do that. He gave me a whole month's rent to make sure he was in."

"Give it back to him. Tell him you're sorry, you made a mistake. The room's already been rented. Or you can just tell him the truth, that I want a woman in that room."

"I just can't do that," Karen said, looking down at the floor. "He was such a sweet, shy guy, and he wanted to live here so badly."

Sophie sat quietly for a few moments, giving her anger a chance to subside.

"Okay, Karen," she finally said. "We'll give him a chance. We'll let him move in. But he'd better be a guy who cleans up after himself. And if he's not—or if he has even a hint of male chauvinism—I'll personally throw him out on his ass."

"He's not a male chauvinist, Soph. He's a sweet guy. You'll see when you meet him. You'll like him."

"Everybody liked Craig. Everybody thought *he* was sweet."

"He's not like Craig."

A car pulled into the dirt driveway.

"That's probably him," Karen said.

Sophie went to the window.

"He said he was a filmmaker," Karen said. "He's from L.A."

"Just what we need. Another guy who thinks he's gonna be the next Truffaut."

"Sophie, he's nice. You'll see when you talk to him."

"He's probably a spoiled rich kid. Look at that. A brand-new VW bus."

"So what? Just because he has a new VW bus, that doesn't make him a bad person. By the way, what's happening with *your* VW? Isn't some guy supposed to be fixing it?"

Sophie continued to stare out the window. "You mean Warren? He can't do it. He knows how to fix VWs, but you gotta have metric tools, whatever those are, and he can't afford to buy them, so he just borrows someone else's whenever he needs to fix a VW. Except this time he hasn't found anyone to borrow from." She watched the new tenant unload his gear. "Look at that. What's all that crap he's taking out?"

"His filmmaking stuff, probably."

They watched in amazement as lighting stands, sound equipment, empty film reels, and boxes and trunks of every size and
shape came out the back of the minibus.

"Jesus Christ!" Sophie said. "*Look* at all that stuff! He's loaded
Hollywood into his bus and hauled it up here."

Steve came in through the front door carrying a large suitcase
in each hand. He had on worn jeans and a blue work shirt—a
classic uniform of the Santa Cruz hippie—which, along with his
chaotically frizzy hair and granny glasses, could almost conceal
his Southern California provenance. Sophie immediately noticed
the tentative, hesitant way he walked and held himself, which,
together with the strange timidity in his face, made him look
as if he were about to apologize for being somewhere he had no
business being.

"Hi, Steve," Karen said.

"Hi . . . uh . . . Karen. Right?"

"Yes."

"Steve, this is Sophie."

"Hi, Sophie." He set his things down and held out his hand. She
shook it politely. "I'm Steve Elwood. Pleasure to meet you."

During the silence that followed, Sophie saw why Karen had
been so unconcerned. He truly was shy, harmless and utterly lacking in the cocksureness she associated with young men who called
themselves filmmakers.

"So," she said, "Karen tells me you're from L.A."

"Yeah," he said, again sounding like he was apologizing.
"Actually I'm from Orange County, but I'm embarrassed to admit
that. So I just say 'L.A. area.'"

"So what brings you up here?"

It took him several seconds to formulate an answer. "I wanted to start making films. I got into filmmaking while I was at UC Irvine. I wanted to go someplace . . . someplace beautiful. You know, to work on my art. I came up here once to visit a friend . . . and afterwards . . . I just couldn't stop thinking about it. About Santa Cruz."

"That's good," Sophie said.

"Uh . . . okay if I start bringing my things in?" he said, still sounding unsure.

"You'd better," Sophie said. "Looks like you got a lotta things."

"Yeah . . . filmmaking equipment."

"Need any help?"

"Thanks. I think I can manage it."

"Let us help you," Karen said. "We're strong women. Right, Soph?"

"Yep," Sophie said. "Unless you're afraid of us breaking your equipment."

"Oh . . . no. Not at all. And I guess . . . yeah. I *could* use some help."

The two women followed Steve to his bus, where he handed Karen a box of microphones and Sophie an esoteric piece of lighting equipment.

"What kind of films do you make?" Sophie said.

"Nothing really, so far . . . just dumb experimental films. But . . . I'm into cinéma vérité. Films about the lives of real people."

"You're not going to make a film about *us*, are you?"

"No . . . well, uh . . . not if you don't want me to."

Steve grabbed two suitcases so big and heavy he could barely lift them, and the three of them trekked up the stairs to his room.

On their way down they heard John come in the front door. He brought in a big cardboard box. "Wel-l-l-l-fare food! Wel-l-l-l-fare food!" he shouted like Santa Claus, his craggy, half-hippie, half-mountain-man figure darting across the living room to the kitchen. He carried the heavy box with little effort, passing so quickly he didn't notice Steve at first. Karen and Sophie followed him into the kitchen with Steve trailing behind.

"Honey," Karen said, "this is Steve. He just joined our household."

"Glad to have you, brother." John held out his hand to Steve, who started to shake his hand the traditional way but adjusted quickly—albeit clumsily—when John thrust his fist upward for the "radical" handshake.

Steve looked on while Sophie and Karen removed and put away items from the box John had brought. A can of meat stew, a box of Velveeta-like cheese, bottles of corn syrup, a box of non-instant powdered milk, all with simple labels identifying their contents without any brand names.

"This is welfare food," Sophie said.

"Government surplus," John said. "Santa Cruz County doesn't have food stamps, so we poor folks have to make do with this shit. They give us a box of it every month."

"It's not that bad if you buy other stuff to go with it," Karen said.

"Where you from, Steve?" John said.

"Down south. Orange County."

"Whoa! Good thing you're coming *from* there instead of going *to* there."

"Yeah," Steve said. "Really."

"What were you doing down there?"

"Making films. Or trying to."

"A filmmaker. Far out."

John started to help Steve carry his things upstairs.

"Man," he said, "you got a lotta shit! How you gonna fit it all in that tiny room?"

"Uh . . . I can do it."

"You're not gonna have any room left for *you*."

"Yeah . . . I will."

"Okay!" John said. "Let's do it!"

It took the four of them almost half an hour to relay all of Steve's belongings to the upstairs landing, and it took Steve an hour and a half more of working alone to get it all crammed into the little bedroom. He didn't try to do it with any semblance of order; he was in too big a hurry to get everything out of the hallway and into the room, worried that his new housemates might already be thinking ill of him for having so much stuff and annoyed at having to help him carry it all up. He just stacked it all in one big pile against the wall opposite the bed.

When he finished, he was exhausted and hungry. It was near dinnertime, and though he remembered Karen's mention of communal dinners, he felt shy about eating with the group when it was only his first night there. So he slipped out unnoticed and drove around until he found a coffee shop. When he got back, he went to bed almost immediately without doing any unpacking save for his sheets and toiletries.

In the morning, even though Sophie had told him he'd be sharing the second-floor bathroom with her, he went downstairs in his pajamas and robe to the one off the kitchen. He met her on the stairs on the way back to his room.

"Where were you last night?" Sophie said. "We called you for dinner, but we couldn't find you."

"I went out to eat."

"Why? Didn't Karen tell you we all eat dinner together?"

"I . . . didn't want to impose."

"Impose? That's ridiculous! You're part of the household now."

"Yeah, but . . . I haven't made any contribution yet. I haven't put in any money for food. I haven't done any housework."

"Don't be silly. You'll be pitching in soon enough. Go find yourself some breakfast. There's cereal, eggs, milk, orange juice, instant coffee—help yourself. Don't be shy about eating. We each put in twenty bucks a month for food, and we divvy up the utility bills. Later on we'll figure out how much you owe for what's left of this month."

"Okay. Thanks."

"Also, that bathroom up there is yours, too. You don't have to go downstairs."

Steve spent the day trying to arrange the room to give himself access to all his film equipment—his editing table, projector, stereo, tape deck and precious sixteen-millimeter Bolex movie camera—and still have space left for the bed, desk and dresser that came with the room. At five in the afternoon, still a long way from finished, he took a nap.

About an hour later he drifted awake to the sound of an acoustic guitar and a lovely female voice singing a haunting ballad in Spanish. As he lay half awake, it occurred to him that the voice might be Sophie's.

By the time the song ended, Steve was fully awake and the guitarist was improvising sweet, interesting chords and snippets of melodies. He rose and went downstairs to see that the performer was indeed Sophie. She was sitting in the living room with Karen, John, and a woman who sat breast-feeding a month-old infant with no embarrassment at the presence of men. Steve averted his eyes.

"Was that you singing?" he asked Sophie.

"That was I," she said, randomly strumming and picking as she talked.

"You have . . . you have a very nice voice."

"Thank you."

"We all groove on Sophie's music," John said. "It's very cool having it here. Brings good karma."

"Yeah," Steve said. "I'm sure it does."

"So you're the new one here?" the woman with the child said.

"Yeah . . . I'm Steve," he said, still trying not to look at the woman's bare breast as she suckled the child. He saw that John didn't seem at all embarrassed, neither looking nor trying not to look.

"I'm Kathleen, and this is Jason." She nodded at the baby as she continued nursing him.

"Nice to meet you," Steve said.

"I hear you're a filmmaker."

"Yes."

"So . . . you have a movie camera?"

"Yes."

"Will you shoot some film of my baby?"

"Sure."

"Oh, that would be wonderful. I have a regular camera to take pictures of him, but I would love to have a little movie of him, too, even though I don't have a projector to watch it on."

"I'd be happy to do that." He quickly turned to Sophie, "How long have you been singing and playing the guitar?"

"I've been singing since I was a little girl. I started guitar in high school."

"She plays other instruments, too," Karen said.

"What others?"

"Just piano and flute," Sophie said. "And I'm a little out of practice on those."

"So, you really are a musical person," Steve said.

"Thanks to my mother."

"Is she a musician?"

"She was an acclaimed pianist when she was young. She could have had a concert career, but she became an elementary-school music teacher instead."

"Does she regret that?"

"Sometimes."

"Does she enjoy teaching?"

"Yes and no. She loves doing music with the kids, but she doesn't like the school system. She's had run-ins with principals . . . some of them were real assholes."

"I can imagine."

"The L.A. teachers went on strike last spring. My mom was a picket captain."

"Really? That's good."

"Things got pretty ugly. There's still a lot of bitterness toward the teachers who scabbed."

"That would be . . . I think . . . a very dirty thing to do—you know, to scab in a strike."

"You bet. Oh, by the way . . . sorry to change the subject, but there's something I forgot to tell you. You do know about the school, don't you?"

"Yes . . . Karen told me about it."

"Well, in addition to that, we have a little women's group that's meeting here tonight. We meet every Wednesday night at seven."

"Women's lib?"

"Yes."

"And you're the leader?"

"I don't like to say *leader*. I prefer *facilitator*."

"We all kind of run the group together," Kathleen said. "Sophie keeps the conversation flowing in a positive direction. I would never have learned to open up without her."

"That's great," Steve said. "I'm all for that."

"Anyway," Sophie said, "there can't be any men around while we're meeting in here. And we have a potluck dinner at the meeting, so there's no communal dinner Wednesday night."

"I usually go out for a burger and a beer," John said. "You're welcome to join me if you want."

"There's more potluck food than we need," Sophie said. "Karen and I went on a cooking binge today. You guys can have some if you want. Then you won't have to spend the money to go out."

"I still have a lot of unpacking to do," Steve said. "Is it okay if I stay up there in my room while you're having your meeting?"

"As long as you stay away from the living room, which means you won't be able to go downstairs at all. You'll be trapped up there."

"That's okay."

"Shall we start setting up?" Karen said.

"Yes," Sophie said. "John, Steve, the food's on the kitchen table if you want it. Just don't take too much, and you have to eat fast— it's only about half an hour till the women start arriving and you guys have to split."

*

After eating, Steve went back up to his room and looked at the mess he still had to deal with. It would take hours just to get his editing table in order; he wasn't even sure where all the components were. But he did have his big Sony tape deck set up on the dresser, its imposing reels ready to spin and record on command. The boxes with all his microphones and cords sat on the floor.

On his way to the bathroom, he heard Sophie's voice in the living room, and he could make out a little of what she was saying. When he came back to his room, he stood outside the door and listened in on the conversation.

"How many you think'll come tonight?" he heard Karen say.

"I dunno," he heard Sophie say. "How many did we have last week? Seven or eight?"

"Let's see, besides you and me and Kathleen, there was Grace, Emma, Nancy . . . and that new one, the real shy girl who wouldn't talk. What was her name again?"

"Oh, what *was* her name? . . . Maureen? Marlene? Something like that. But don't say 'girl,' Karen. There are no girls in our group. We're all over eighteen."

"Sorry, I wasn't thinking. Old habits die hard, I guess."

"We have to watch things like that. All those little ways we put ourselves down."

Steve heard Sophie and Karen greet the women as they arrived. As he eavesdropped, unable to pull himself away, a notion crossed his mind. He went back into his room and took out his best microphone, a Sennheiser that had cost more than the tape deck itself, and plugged it into the deck with a twenty-five-foot cord. Uncoiling the cord, he tiptoed back to the spot in the hallway where he could hear the conversation and set the mike next to the railing above the stairwell. He put a fresh reel of tape on the deck and started recording.

While in the back of his mind he knew it was wrong to record the women, his thought process went: *I support women's lib. I'm interested in it. I want to be informed about it. I'll never be able to go to one of their meetings, but if I tape this meeting I'll be able to listen and learn.* On one level he knew it was a bad rationale, but once he'd developed the excuse, he was on a one-way track.

As the tape reels rotated at three and three-quarter inches per second, Steve continued to putter about the room, rearranging objects and boxes, feeling alternately guilty and determined about making the recording. At one point he plugged his stereo headphones into the jack on tape deck and listened to a few minutes of the meeting at which his presence was forbidden.

"My ex-ol'-man wasn't exactly the *macho* type, like Nancy's," Sophie said. "He was more of a passive-aggressive type. Everybody but me thought he was the nicest guy in the world."

"What does that word mean, *macho*?" someone asked.

"It's a Spanish word that's used a lot in Mexico," Sophie said. "It literally means the male of a species of animal, but it's also used to describe a super-masculine man . . . I'm sorry, I thought I'd already talked about that word. I use it a lot in feminist discussions because it's a trait you find in a lot of chauvinistic men—the desire to be as masculine as possible in every way, and that includes treating women as—"

Steve set the headphones down. He shouldn't have been listening. He shouldn't have been recording. But he left the tape deck running as he continued rearranging his room. He knew the meeting was over when he heard Sophie playing the guitar.

He stopped the recorder and removed the microphone from its hidden spot, coiling the cord and replacing the mike in the box with the others. As he rewound the tape, he felt guilty once again.

He thought he should erase it, but he couldn't bring himself to do it after going to all that trouble. When the tape finished rewinding, he shut the machine off and stared at the reel, wondering what he was going to do with it.

The following day, Sophie knocked on his door.

He'd been listening with headphones to his tape of the women's meeting. When he heard the knock, he quickly stopped the machine. "Come in."

Sophie noticed the headphones. "What are you listening to?"

Steve had a thing about lying. He just couldn't do it. As a child, he had never told a lie to his parents, not even one of omission. Once when he was eight, while they were living in Studio City, he had admitted to his mother that he'd ridden his bike on the wrong side of Laurel Canyon Boulevard for a block on the way home from school, knowing the admission was going to cost him his bike privileges for a week. If he hadn't told her, she never would have known. But not telling would have been the same as lying.

So he told Sophie the truth. In a nervously joking manner, he told her he'd taped the meeting because he was a supporter of women's lib and was interested in knowing what sorts of things were discussed at a women's lib meeting.

Sophie hesitated for a long moment. Then she asked him in a soft but angry tone: "Who are you?"

"Who am I?"

"Yes. Who are you?"

"What do you mean, who am I? I'm Steven Elwood."

"Are you a pig?"

"*What?*"

"Are you a pig? Are you some kind of undercover agent? Police? FBI? Come in here pretending to be a filmmaker?"

"Of course not!"

"Then who sent you to record what goes on here?" Sophie spoke rapidly and angrily. "Did someone send you in here to spy on *me*? Because I lead a women's group? Because some sexist-pig police agency is threatened by a little group of women asserting themselves? Yeah, well, you can go tell whoever sent you to fuck off and you can get out. *Now*. Go pack up all your expensive toys, whomever they belong to, and get the hell out of this house. And don't *ever* bring your slimy ass around here again."

"But I—"

"*Go*! Do it now or we'll start throwing your toys out the window and smash every window in that pigmobile of yours."

"I'm not a pig," Steve said, choking back tears. "I'm so . . . so sorry. I did a very stupid thing. I'll go right now . . . and erase the tape. You can watch me to make sure I do it. And don't worry—I'll leave. Right away. I won't stay in a place where anyone suspects I'm a pig."

"Well, surely you can understand why I—"

"The last thing I could ever do is be is an informer, believe me. I support your cause . . . but that doesn't change anything. I blew it. I did a stupid thing . . . and now you'll always suspect that I'm a pig. So I'll split. I'll erase that tape . . . or even better, I'll just *give* you the damn thing . . . and then . . . I'll pack up and go back down south. This whole Santa Cruz thing . . . it was a stupid idea, anyway. It's obvious I'll never fit in here. Jesus Christ. Me, a pig. An informer. My father was blacklisted for refusing to be an informer. My God, that you could even suspect me of—"

"Your father was blacklisted?"

"Yeah, he was."

"What was he blacklisted from?"

"From writing. He's a screenwriter."

"My father was blacklisted, too, and he's a screenwriter. What's your father's name?"

"Arthur Elwood. What's *your* father's name?"

"Lawrence Hearn. Arthur Elwood? I've never heard that name. Strange, I thought I knew just about all the blacklisted people in Hollywood, or at least knew of them from hearing my parents talk about them."

"Hearn doesn't ring any bells, either. Wait—God! Back when I was *really* little . . . maybe three or four years old . . . there were these two girls I used to play with. And I think . . . yes! One of them, I'm pretty sure, was named Sophie."

"And I'm remembering now that I used to play with a little boy named Stevie. My friend Laura and I used to play dolls with him. Does that ring any bells? Could that have been you?"

"Yes. Sophie and Laura."

"It had to have been you. Do you really remember Laura? Laura Gelman?"

"Yeah . . . I remember Laura. I don't remember her last name, though. Or yours. I was really little . . . I probably wasn't even aware of last names yet."

"This is incredible."

"Yes. It is."

"Steve, I'm *so* sorry I let paranoia get the better of me. I feel just awful. Our dads were both blacklisted, we played together as kids, and I thought you were a pig!"

"It was my fault. It was very uncool of me to make that recording. I'll give you the tape and you can destroy it."

"That isn't necessary. Just erase it, and please, don't ever do that again. Those women trust each other and feel safe in that room. It's their place, where they can be vulnerable with no fear of being put down. It took months for some of them to open up. They would absolutely freak if they knew a man was listening in on them, let alone recording them."

"You have my word, I will never do it again. In fact, I will never tape or film *anything* in this house."

"That's okay, just don't do it secretly. And not on a Wednesday night. And I want you to tell me more about your dad being blacklisted."

"I really don't know anything. He never talks about it."

"That's sure the opposite of *my* dad." She didn't press him further.

From then on, Steve trod softly with his camera and recording equipment, never using them in the house without permission. He was diligent with his household chores, taking on more than his share of the cleaning and meal preparation and going out of his way to interact with his housemates in a friendly and respectful manner. He picked up after himself, kept his half of the bathroom shelves immaculately clean and, once Sophie had warned him about it, never, ever left the seat up.

CHAPTER 15

SCOS

Once past their initial misunderstanding, having recognized their common background and recalled their childhood friendship, Steve and Sophie became friends again. Steve also developed a warm rapport with Karen, who, it seemed, found his quiet ways endearing. With John he never felt entirely comfortable; the overbearing jolliness of his sole male housemate irritated him, and it often seemed that John wanted to "cure" him of his shyness (he'd always hated it when people tried to do that). John was also an aficionado of astrology, in which Steve disbelieved—he insisted on doing Steve's chart, declaring that his housemate's status as a Gemini with a Pisces moon and Capricorn rising thoroughly explained his personality—and spoke often of the various gurus he admired, which Steve also found off-putting. Yet a mutual if standoffish respect slowly grew between the two men of such disparate personalities.

For a week or so after his arrival, out of sympathy for her lack of a car, Steve ferried Sophie around in his bus to the places she had to go to round up equipment and supplies for the school: private and parochial schools for castoff desks and chairs; stationery and office-supply stores for batches of slightly defective pencils, crayons and writing paper; someone's basement where the Bucks had stored some of the furniture they'd used to run the school at their home. On each run, they would load up the bus with as much stuff as it could hold and bring it to the house, where they would stash the new items alongside the things they'd already collected.

One day Steve asked Sophie nervously, as if he'd had to work up sufficient courage, "Would you mind very much if . . . if I filmed you while you're doing some of these things?"

"Why do you want to film me?"

"It's exciting, this whole thing of getting ready for the school . . . and all the other things you're involved in. It's . . . it's drama."

"Well . . . I don't know . . . I guess I don't mind."

So he began shooting, quickly using up most of his stash of raw film stock capturing Sophie's peregrinations through the lens of his Bolex. He couldn't seem to stop filming her, and when he wasn't filming her he couldn't seem to let her out of his sight.

He caught himself noticing little things about her: the distinct timbres of her speaking and singing voices; the scent of her lavender soap; the words she used frequently; the statements she made about her beliefs and values, all of which reflected his own. In the bathroom he shared with her, he knew from memory the exact locations of her personal care items: her glass and toothbrush, her hairbrush, the soap and shampoo she left on the rim of the tub, even the box of tampons she unabashedly kept on the toilet tank. One day while she was gone, he dared to enter her room—guiltily—and inspect the posters on her wall (Che Guevara and Jefferson Airplane), her photos, her guitar case, and the books in her improvised bookcase of gray cinder blocks and unfinished pine planks, Malcolm X's autobiography and Eldridge Cleaver's *Soul on Ice* prominent on the top shelf.

He took it all in, mentally recording everything that was there.

During his first month in the house, Steve had the opportunity to become the savior of Sophie's independence.

"Did you say you had a VW you were getting fixed?" he asked her one day.

"Yeah, but there's a hang-up with the guy who's working on it."

"What kind of hang-up?"

"He needs metric tools. I have no idea what metric tools are. All I know is he doesn't have them and he can't work on a VW without them."

"I have metric tools," Steve said.

"You *do*?"

"Yeah . . . I have a set of wrenches. I keep them in the back of my bus. I bought them . . . well . . . I bought them thinking I was going to, you know, learn how to do my own car maintenance. Which I'm ashamed to say . . . I never did."

"Is that what metric tools are? Just wrenches?"

"Yeah. They're wrenches sized in millimeters. You need them to work on any foreign car—not just VWs—because almost every other country except us uses the metric system."

"Would you be willing to lend your wrenches to the guy who's fixing my car?"

"Sure."

With Steve's tools in hand, it took Warren only a few days to get Sophie's VW up and running. Now she no longer had to bum rides to get to the places she needed to go. It was only for the hauling of loads for the school that she still depended on Steve and his bus.

Steve began to participate actively in Sophie's various pursuits instead of just filming them. He went with her to the free breakfast program on the two or three days a week she still went. Jimmy Moreland had moved away, and though his absence had taken a lot of the joy out of her work there, she kept up a minimal involvement out of a sense of duty. For Steve, however, it provided the same revelation it had for Sophie a year earlier. It was his first experience being around children, and they took to him right away, just as they had to Sophie. They pursued him, bombarding him with the same kinds of personal questions they had once asked Sophie: Where did he live? How old was he? Was he married? Did he have a girlfriend? Was Sophie his girlfriend? He didn't mind answering the questions; his shyness seemed to dissolve when he was with kids.

Sophie also continued to work a few hours a week at the legal aid center. Steve accompanied her there one day, too, and watched in fascination as she used her fluent Spanish to pre-interview the non-English-speaking clients and serve as interpreter when they met with the lawyer.

"How did you learn to speak Spanish so well?" he asked on the way home. "Did you study it in school?"

"We lived in Mexico City for two years when I was a kid."

"What were you doing in Mexico City?"

"Trying to escape the blacklist. Word got out that there were jobs in the Mexican film industry, so some of the blacklisted people went down there. Most of them didn't make it. My dad didn't."

"You were there two years?"

"Yes, and it was a disaster. We ended up worse off than before.

We'd rented out our house, and when we got back it had been trashed."

"What a bummer."

"What was it like for *your* family?"

"How do you mean?"

"How did your family survive? During the blacklist?"

"Well . . . I dunno. I don't remember ever being poor. I guess my dad still managed to make a living."

"How?"

"As far as I know, he just kept on writing. He's always been a writer. I don't think he ever did anything else."

"Did he use a pseudonym?"

"A what?"

"A phony name. That's what my dad did."

"I dunno. I don't think he did that, but . . . I just don't know. He never talks about it."

"You said that before. Why doesn't he talk about it?"

"He said it was too painful."

"It was painful for my dad, too, but he *loves* to talk about it."

"I guess my dad was more sensitive."

"I guess."

Steve called his parents that night, and afterward he recounted the conversation for Sophie.

"It was strange. There was this long silence after I said your parents' names . . . Then, finally, my mom said, 'Yes, we used to know them, but it was a very long time ago.' Then there was another long silence, and she said, 'We haven't had any contact with them in many years.' Then my dad changed the subject and asked me if my bus was running okay."

Sophie looked at him suspiciously for a fleeting moment and then looked away.

The next time she spoke with her parents, she didn't mention Steve.

One day while he was taking her in his bus to pick up some discarded bulletin boards at a church, Sophie recounted to Steve all about her relationship with Craig, how it had begun and how it had gone sour. Steve told her about a brief relationship he'd had with a woman in his class at UC Irvine. Then he suddenly blurted out to Sophie, his face turning a deep shade of burgundy, that he'd been in love with her since his first day in the house.

This bold and abrupt declaration caught Sophie so off guard that she had no idea how to respond. She struggled to form words that would be both kind and honest.

"I'm flattered," she finally said. Then, after a long, pensive pause: "I have a really strong aversion to romantic relationships right now. It's been over a year now since I ended my relationship with Craig, and I'm still reveling in the autonomy it gave me." She paused again. "Most sexual relationships are inherently oppressive to the woman, anyway."

"You really think so?" Steve said, still red in the face.

"Yes, I do. It's been an ongoing topic in my Wednesday-night group. Three of the women are in relationships the rest of us are trying to encourage them to break free of. It's heart-rending to see how trapped they are, just like I was with Craig."

"What about John and Karen?"

"I wish I could say they're an exception, but they're not. John's a nice guy, he's relatively non-sexist and they have, relatively speaking, a good relationship. But even so, Karen feels trapped in a lot of ways."

"Really?"

"Yes. But I strongly believe that non-oppressive relationships between women and men are possible, as long as they remain platonic—as long as sex doesn't intrude. You and I are a good example of that."

"I see," Steve said, somberly but acceptingly, his face back to its normal color.

"I talked about you with the group last week. I said lots of nice things about you. How non-chauvinistic you are, the way you treat me as an equal, what a great friendship we have."

"Thanks."

As the summer days passed, Sophie spent more time planning for the opening of the school and less on her other activities. By the middle of July, she had dropped her volunteer work at the legal aid center, the free clinic and the free breakfast program entirely. She did, however, keep the women's group going. That was the one thing she couldn't give up.

"I want to be part of your school," Steve told her one day.

"You do?"

"Yes. I would really enjoy working with the students. I could teach filmmaking."

"That would be great. We wouldn't be able to pay you, though. It would just be a volunteer thing."

"That's okay."

"You don't need money, anyway. You've got that huge allowance from your parents."

It was twice the amount Sophie's parents had given her before she started working at the school. "It's not *that* huge, but you're right. I don't mind being a volunteer." He paused. "Yeah, my parents give me a pretty generous allowance. They wanted to give me more, but I refused. I wanna live a simple life up here, not a spoiled-rich-kid life."

Sophie called Nora Weston, the experienced teacher she had been counting on, and left a message with her daughter. Nora didn't call back, though, and Sophie left two more messages. When she still didn't call back, Sophie began to get nervous, but she continued with her planning and preparation, which included making a call to Joanne Vaughn.

Joanne was a poor but proud thirty-four-year-old Vietnam War widow and the mother of three SCOS kids. She'd been an energetic volunteer at the school the previous year when the Bucks were in charge.

"I really don't want to be heavily involved next year," she'd said to Sophie in the spring. "It's taken up way too much of my time. It's hard enough with three kids. I need some time for *me*."

"What if I offered you a full-time paid position?"

"As a teacher?"

"Yes."

"Are you serious?"

"Absolutely."

"But I didn't even finish college."

"Doesn't matter. You're self-educated. You know more than a lot of teachers do."

"I'm flattered . . . but—"

"No buts. You're hired."

"No. I can't, Sophie . . . I just can't do it. I'm sorry."

At first Sophie had accepted Joanne's refusal and advertised at the university for a third teacher, but no one had responded. So now, as she waited for Nora to call, she beseeched Joanne to reconsider. She finally brought her around by offering a salary larger than her own and greatly reduced tuition at SCOS for her children: forty dollars a month, the usual per-child fee, for all three.

Soon after they reached their agreement, Joanne had Sophie and Steve to dinner to discuss plans.

"You really think we can pull this off?" Joanne said over a feast of Spanish rice she'd prepared with rice from her welfare-food box and vegetables from the local food co-op.

"Sure we can," Sophie said. "You and me and Nora. We've got what it takes."

"And what's Steve going to do?"

"I'm going to teach filmmaking," he said shyly. Intimidated by Joanne's strong personality, he hadn't said much during dinner.

"You may end up teaching more than that," Joanne said.

"Are we gonna get a horse this year?" Joanne's nine-year-old daughter Michelle said.

"That's right," eleven-year-old Susan said. "Rob and Deirdre said we might get a horse."

"I don't think so," Joanne said. "Rob and Deirdre are gone, and I have no idea how they thought they were going to get a horse, or where they planned to keep a horse. Rob and Deirdre talked about a lot of things that were exciting and totally impractical."

"I wanna have a horse," Michelle said.

Michelle was bright, vivacious and mischievous—the opposite of her serious older sister, from whom she tried to steal the show throughout the evening. Six-year-old Geoffrey made car and train noises all through dinner, ignoring his food.

"Stop making those noises and eat your dinner," Susan said, playing mother.

"I don't like this food," Geoffrey said.

The two girls were immediately drawn to Steve and he to them. After dinner they physically pulled him into their shared bedroom and made him sit while they told him everything they believed he ought to know about SCOS.

"You and Mom and Sophie should be more strict this year," Susan said. "Rob and Deirdre weren't strict enough. The kids were always running around and screaming, and nobody learned anything."

"But don't be *too* strict," Michelle said. "Or it'll be like public school. I *hated* public school."

"I didn't hate public school that much," Susan said. "I liked my fourth-grade teacher. But I wouldn't want to go to junior high in public school. The teachers are mean and the boys are always fighting. That's what my friend down the street says."

"Sophie wants to add a grade each year," Michelle said. "I hope we don't. I don't want any teenagers at SCOS. They'll ruin everything."

Steve was industrious and inventive in helping plan the school. He helped Sophie forage for materials and supplies, finding yet more ways to get them cheap or free. But they still needed money. Sophie was counting on the stake Nora had promised, but Nora still hadn't returned any of her calls.

Finally, one morning in late July, Nora did call. She told Sophie she was sorry, but she couldn't be part of the school. Personal reasons.

This was it. Without Nora as a teacher—and without Nora's money—they simply didn't have the human or financial resources to open in the fall, even with Joanne aboard.

Crushed, Sophie retreated to her room. This was the end. The Santa Cruz Open School, the joy of her life, was gone. All that planning, all that collecting of materials, had been for naught. She was out of a job and would once again have to turn to her parents, while the kids she had loved and nurtured and taught to handle freedom would be forced back into the regimented environment of public school. She lay on her bed, lost in darkness. *Who was I kidding? Who was I to think I could run a school? Who was I to think I could do* anything *significant?*

But the next day, when her mood lifted slightly, she realized there was no way she could give it up.

She called some of the school parents and asked if they would give her an advance on their first month's tuition payment. There were only a few she felt comfortable asking, and from them she raised $120.

Then she thought of her own parents. To go to them for yet more money felt brazen—they had given her a substantial handout to tide her through the income-less summer—but $120 wasn't nearly enough. So she called them.

"It's a desperate situation," she said to her mother. "Much as I hate to ask you, the Santa Cruz Open School will cease to exist if I don't get some funds together real quick."

"We're not very flush at the moment," Ruth said. "You know it's been almost a year since your father's had an assignment. And we just gave you a big chunk of money."

"I know. But any little amount you can spare . . . You know that if the school disappears, so does my income. And my present mission in life."

Ruth agreed to contribute fifty dollars and Steve threw in a hundred from his allowance, bringing the total to $270. With that they could do something.

Sophie put up fresh notices on bulletin boards around town and on kiosks at the university seeking an experienced teacher or even a newly-trained one, but she knew what a long shot it was that anyone with the desired qualifications would respond on such short notice.

The inevitable reality began to descend on her. It scared her. Several times a day it threatened to drive her back into the darkness and the despairing belief that continuing the school was a lost cause.

That reality was that Steve, with neither training nor experience, was destined to be the third full-time teacher at SCOS.

CHAPTER 16

Day One

On a mid-August evening, twenty-three adults packed the living room for the first parents' meeting of the school year. The parents had known since June that the Bucks were leaving and had voiced near-unanimous confidence in Sophie's ability to carry on for them, and they knew and trusted Joanne as well. But Sophie had assured them that the third teacher and co-director would be a mature person with teaching experience, and when she announced that Steve Elwood—twenty-two, untested and unknown to them—would be that third person, their skepticism was as justifiable as it was discomfiting.

Several parents threw questions at Steve about his educational philosophy and teaching approach. Sophie had prepped him for this, and though his discomfort before the crowd was visible, he did a passable job of articulating a middle-of-the-road stance: freedom but not too much of it, adequate attention to the "three R's" but with plenty of room for creative expression. Then Leanne

Mason, an intimidatingly distinguished-looking mother in her forties, spoke up. "You say you've never taught. Have you had any experience at all working with children?"

"Well . . . I worked in the free breakfast program," Steve said, looking down to avoid Leanne's withering gaze. "With Sophie."

"And what did you do before that?"

"Uh . . . I studied filmmaking."

After the meeting, Leanne approached Sophie. "Are you really confident that this man can help you and Joanne run the school? Do you even know that he can teach?"

"I have total confidence in him," Sophie said. "He's wonderful with kids."

Sophie went over to Steve, touched his arm reassuringly and led him around the room, personally introducing him to parents. Some were friendly and open, most likely seeing his intelligence and perhaps charmed by his self-effacing modesty; others were less warm. She overheard a few grumbling and talking about sending their children elsewhere. She got a sick feeling that maybe the three of them really were in over their heads. But there was no turning back now.

During the week that followed, two sets of parents gave notice that their children would no longer be attending SCOS. One wrote an effusive apology and enclosed a check for forty dollars, a month's tuition, as a guilt-assuaging donation. Happily, though, some new parents who had attended the meeting signed their children up.

The final three weeks before school started were frantic and crazy, but much got done. More than half the parents had now paid the first month's tuition—twenty to forty dollars a month, on a sliding scale according to ability to pay—generating almost three hundred dollars more for the materials that still needed to be bought. With only twelve days to spare, Sophie, Steve and Joanne succeeded in turning the downstairs bedroom into something that actually looked like a schoolroom, complete with chalkboards, tables, desks, old but usable books, discarded office-cubicle dividers for separating the grades, a couple of barely-functional typewriters and a globe so old it lumped Vietnam, Cambodia and Laos together as "Indochina."

They also considered the idea of clearing out the abandoned garage in the back so it could be used as an activity area, though Sophie had her doubts about whether it was possible. Besides a hulk of an early-fifties Plymouth, the ramshackle structure was cluttered with old car parts and other useless stuff, and the concrete floor was unspeakably filthy. But Joanne persuaded Sophie to call on school dad Cal Wright, a forty-year-old Tennessean with a drawl that belied his politics and a vintage four-wheel-drive pickup that he and his wife used to transport furniture for their antique-refinishing business.

"I think I can do it," Cal said. "My truck's almost as old as that wreck in there, but I believe it can do the job." He then proceeded to drag the wheel-less old Plymouth out of the garage to a spot in the backyard where the children could play in it once it was cleaned up.

While Cal hauled the remaining junk from the garage to the municipal dump, Karen and John pitched in to help Sophie, Steve and Joanne clean the floor and walls of the garage. The five of them scrubbed for hours with an industrial-strength solvent provided by Cal, and when it was clean they set down a scrounged piece of carpet remnant almost big enough to cover the floor. For the final touch, they moved in a homemade knee-height art table someone had donated. With the garage doors open for light and ventilation, they now had an open-air art studio.

"I can't believe we did this," Steve said.

As they stood looking over their accomplishment, Sophie suddenly threw her arms around Steve, feeling both proud of and protective of him. He was a big teddy bear—the kids were going to love him. Surely, with a little coaching and encouragement, he would be a great teacher.

The first parent to arrive on the morning of the first day of school was Cal's wife, Toni Wright. A peppy woman in her mid-thirties with prematurely graying hair tied back in a ponytail, she arrived in Cal's old pickup with their two children, six-year old Sheila and four-year-old Kenny, who was just along for the ride and crying loudly because he wanted to go to SCOS like his sister but wouldn't be old enough for another year. Toni led the two kids up the front walk as Sophie and Steve stood in the doorway to greet them. Kenny continued crying, ignoring his mother's repeated glares. Sheila leaned back shyly against her mother's waist in the presence of a large, unfamiliar male.

"It's okay, sweetie," Toni said to her daughter. "That's Steve. He's going to be one of your teachers."

"Come," Sophie said, taking Sheila by the hand, gently coaxing her from her mother and leading her into the house. "Let me show you our new school."

The next to arrive was Estelle Baumgarten, a new parent, with her six-year-old son Paul. Steve showed the shy boy around, but he showed no interest in anything until Steve led him to the old Plymouth. Paul immediately climbed up into the driver's seat and began turning the steering wheel back and forth in excited, silent motions.

After getting Sheila settled with a dollhouse in the main room, Sophie returned to her post at the front door. After a few minutes another new student arrived, Joey McComb, a short, gawky twelve-year-old with a close haircut and glasses.

"Why don't you just go on in and meet the other kids," Sophie said to Joey. "You're old enough that you don't need a grown-up to show you around. I'd like to stay here and rap with your mother a bit."

Anne McComb was an overweight woman in her late thirties with stringy blond hair and a few too many wrinkles for her age, her persona an odd combination of feisty and pitiable. She'd told Sophie she was living on a paltry child-support settlement from an ex-husband who could easily have afforded to pay more. Sophie had agreed to accept Joey for fifteen dollars a month even though the bottom of the sliding scale had been set at twenty. Anne was a zealous political activist; at the first parents meeting she'd tried to solicit volunteers for prison reform, welfare rights, the Salinas Valley lettuce pickers' strike and opposition to the Vietnam War. Sophie had heard several parents say yes, they supported those causes, but no, they didn't have the time. Today Anne was fixated on Angela Davis, the radical black professor who had been fired from UCLA and was now a fugitive, accused of complicity in a courthouse shootout in which four men, including a judge, had been killed.

"I'm really worried about Angela," Anne said. "I'm afraid they're gonna kill her when they catch her. They don't wanna let her go to trial, 'cause they know she's innocent."

"I hope that isn't true," Sophie said, trying to edge away tactfully so she could circulate and supervise. "That they're going to kill her, that is."

"I hope not, too. By the way, you may have to help Joey integrate socially. He's got a near-genius IQ—not that I take IQ's that seriously—but he doesn't relate well. He's off in his own little world."

By the time Steve returned to his station at the front door, Sophie had managed to break free of Anne McComb, and Joanne and her three children were just arriving.

The Vaughn kids needed no tour of the school. They'd spent many long days there while their mother worked with Steve and Sophie to get things ready. Little Geoffrey headed straight for the old Plymouth, where he and Paul Baumgarten quickly established a friendship around the car and took turns "driving," Paul silent and Geoffrey providing the sound effects. Susan and Michelle, who had both been passionate about helping to organize the school and making sure everything was just right, went to check out the art studio they'd helped set up in the former garage. Susan knelt at the big low table in the middle of the room and began sorting through the chaotic array of crayons, colored pencils and Pentel pens that had all been donated together in a box, categorizing the items and culling out the felt-tip pens that had dried from being left uncapped. Michelle grabbed a broom from the corner and swept the dust from the bare concrete along the uncarpeted edges of the floor.

A girl appeared at the entrance. She was blonde like both of the Vaughn girls and between them in age.

"Come on in," Susan said.

The new girl walked in slowly, as if testing the water.

"What's your name?" Michelle said.

"Melissa. I'm new here."

"I'm Michelle, and this is Susan."

"Are you sisters?"

"Yes."

"I can tell."

"How old are you?"

"Ten."

"I'm nine and she's eleven. You're right in between us. What's your last name?"

"Zweickert."

"Ours is Vaughn. Our mom's Joanne. She's one of the teachers."

"Oh, yeah, I met her. She's nice. Are you the only ones here?"

"Our little brother's here. That's all I know."

"No," Susan said, "I saw two other kids, a boy and a girl. They're little, though. One of them's playing with my brother in that old car out there." They could hear Geoffrey's *Brroommmmmm! Brroommmmmm! Brroommmmmmm!* from where they were.

"My little brother's here, too," Melissa said. "Do you know what we're supposed to do?"

"Whatever we want," Michelle said. "Until everyone gets here. Then we'll have a big meeting."

"How many kids are in this school?" Melissa said.

"About fifteen, sixteen," Susan said.

"Any others our age?"

"Yes."

"How many?"

"I'm not sure. Some of the kids who went here last year aren't going to be here anymore, and there are going to be some new

ones. Like you. I don't know . . . I think maybe about five or six."
Susan paused. "Where did you get that dress?"

"My mom got it for me in San Francisco."

"It's really nice."

"Thanks."

"It's old-fashioned. I like old-fashioned things."

"Me, too."

"We find a lot of old-fashioned things at thrift shops," Susan
said. "We buy all our clothes at thrift shops."

"We have to," Michelle said, "'cause we're poor."

"We're kind of rich," Melissa said matter-of-factly. "My mom
gets child support from both my dad and my ex-stepdad. She got
divorced from both of them."

"Our dad was killed in Vietnam," Susan said.

"Really?"

"He stepped on a land mine and got blown to pieces," Michelle
said.

"That's horrible," Melissa said. "How old were you when it
happened?"

"I was seven," Susan said. "Michelle was five."

"That must've been really hard for you."

"It wasn't that bad. He and my mom had been separated for
a long time. I hardly even remembered him . . . Michelle doesn't
remember him at all."

"Are there any *boys* our age at this school?" Melissa said.

"There are a few," Susan said.

"I hope they're not icky and obnoxious, like some of the ones in
my last school."

"They're not too bad."

"There was this one boy in my class—he had a crush on me and he followed me around all the time like a little puppy dog," Melissa said. "It was so embarrassing! Everybody teased me about it instead of teasing him like they should have."

"What a bummer," Michelle said.

"When I was in fourth grade, in public school, there was a boy who liked me," Susan said. "It was really embarrassing. I didn't like him, but I felt sorry for him. Nobody liked him."

Joey McComb was suddenly at the entrance to the garage, a silent apparition. He said nothing but stared, grinning, at nobody in particular. The girls exchanged dismayed frowns.

"What does *he* want?" Melissa said.

"What do you want?" Michelle asked him.

Joey said nothing. He just continued to stare.

"Do you know him?" Melissa said.

"No," Michelle said. "He's new."

"Speaking of what we were just talking about . . ."

"Could you please leave us alone?" Susan said politely. "We're having a private conversation."

No response except the stare and the silly grin.

"What's the matter?" Melissa said. "Don't you know how to talk?"

"Look," Michelle said, "would you *please* leave us alone? Pretty please?"

Joey responded by sauntering into the garage, walking around and pretending to inspect the art supplies.

"Let's just ignore him," Michelle said.

"I don't want to talk in front of him," Melissa said.

"Let's go somewhere else. He can have this room all to himself . . . We can finish organizing that stuff later."

The girls filed out of the garage and headed toward the house. They went through the door into the main schoolroom.

Joey followed them.

"He's following us," Melissa said.

"God," Michelle said, "what's his *problem*?"

While the girls looked for a place to sit and talk, Joey stood near the doorway with his hands in his pockets, staring at them.

"What's your problem?" Michelle said in the most sarcastic tone she could muster. "Are you mentally retarded or something?"

Joey remained silent.

"Please leave us alone!" Susan said. Her pleading tone of voice betrayed some compassion for the boy, perhaps a desire to spare him the scathing mockery of the two younger girls.

"I don't think I wanna go to this school if *he's* gonna be in it," Melissa said.

"Let's go tell Mom," Michelle said. "Maybe she'll kick him out for bugging us."

The girls found Joanne and complained while Joey continued to stare, a few feet away, with his forced silly grin.

"Come here, Joey," Joanne said. He didn't budge but didn't try to evade her when she moved close to him. "Do you really think that's a good way to relate to people? Following them around and staring at them?"

Before Joey had a chance to answer, little Sheila Wright appeared with a bleeding finger. "Can I have a Band-Aid?" she said demurely.

Susan stayed with Sheila while Joanne went to get a bandage.

"Susan," Joanne said when she got back, "could you do this for me? I have to supervise."

After bandaging Sheila's finger, Susan looked around for

Michelle and Melissa. They had vanished, apparently successful at last in shaking off Joey—who was off at the far end of the yard, having what looked like a serious conversation with Steve.

Kids big and little, veteran and newcomer, continued to straggle in for more than an hour as the three adults dealt with one calamity after another: a skinned knee, an overflowing toilet, Michelle and Melissa (Susan had managed to escape) complaining nonstop about Joey, who intermittently continued following and annoying them. Some of the parents who came to drop off their children wanted to "rap" with the staff, seeming not to notice how busy they were, while others inundated them with questions.

An all-school first-day meeting had been scheduled for ten o'clock, but at ten-thirty things were still chaotic. With considerable effort, the three teachers finally managed to shepherd everyone into the living room.

The kids sat on the floor and on the couches, and though they were squirrelly at first, they settled down quickly. Some of the older children, especially Susan, were helpful at calming the little ones.

Sophie and Joanne did nearly all the talking while Steve sat next to them, silently surveying the room. Sophie welcomed the students and introduced herself and her partners. She and Joanne laid out the school's central philosophy along with the vague motto the Bucks had come up with the previous year: "Grow, be free, learn how to handle freedom." Joanne went over the list of rules the three of them had concocted (there had been none the previous year):

1. No put-downs.
2. Treat everybody the way you would like to be treated.

3. Take responsibility and clean up after yourself.
4. Do your best at everything.
5. Do your thing and let others do theirs.
6. Be free, but don't take away anyone else's freedom. (Sophie realized as Joanne read them that Rules 5 and 6 were redundant.)
7. Hands to yourself.
8. No running or screaming unless it's part of a game.

After the rules had been discussed and general announcements made, Sophie picked up her guitar and conducted a sing-along, gradually seducing the reluctant group into participation, while Joanne and Steve sat at the kitchen table making last-minute adjustments to the schedule of classes and activities for the day.

By the time the meeting was over and the day's timetable mapped out, it was lunch time. The kids were supposed to have brought their own lunches, but several hadn't, and at least two complained that theirs had been stolen. Sophie and Joanne had anticipated this and bought peanut butter, grape jelly and a loaf of whole-wheat bread.

"I only eat white bread," one of the middle-grade boys said.

"Whole wheat's better for you," Sophie said, "and it tastes better once you get used to it."

Unmoved, the boy opted to go without lunch rather than eat the healthier bread. Two other lunchless ones also claimed they ate only white bread, but were hungry enough that they gave in. The lunch hour and the subsequent cleanup spilled over into what was to have been the first twenty minutes or so of the afternoon program, necessitating a further rejiggering of the schedule. An additional delay resulted from a near-fight between two ten-year-old

boys, another skinned knee and some arguing and pouting by children who didn't like the activities to which they'd been assigned.

When the activities were organized and under way, a semblance
of organization began to take shape. For the first hour, Joanne
played games in the backyard with the six youngest kids, the five-
to-seven-year-olds, and did art in the garage during the second
time slot. Meanwhile, Sophie and Steve took the eight- to twelve-
year-olds into the garage and had them do free writing—anything
they wanted to write about themselves—sitting on cushions on
the floor around the low art table; for the final hour, they brought
them into the house and split them into two groups, Sophie with
the middle-graders in the living room and Steve with the pre-teens
around the kitchen table, to discuss expectations for the school
year. Sophie's discussion with the middle group revolved mostly
around "Do we get to do this?" and "Do we have to do that?" while
the older ones, Steve reported, were mostly concerned about the
quality of interpersonal relations. Steve expressed special concern
about Joey—identifying, Sophie figured, with the boy's combination of high intellect and poor social skills—and the difficulties he
was likely to have with the other kids in his age group.

By the time the school day ended, Sophie was exhausted to the
point of desperation. It hadn't really gone that badly for a first day,
once they'd gotten a handle on things, but she couldn't shake the
vague, unfocused feeling that they should have done something
differently. She ended the day discouraged, demoralized and worried about whether Steve was really going to cut it as a teacher.

And so it went, that day and the next day and the rest of the
week and the week after that.

CHAPTER 17

Tami

The well-scrubbed fourth-graders of the public school stood at attention reciting the Pledge of Allegiance. Tami Hagar, who wasn't as well-scrubbed as the others, didn't. She held her hand over her heart like the others and her mouth approximated the words, but she just couldn't stand still. She didn't know why she couldn't hold herself rigid like the other children; she just couldn't. When she tried, she got nervous because she knew that she wasn't standing still enough, that she stood out, and that Mrs. Colombe (pronounced co-LUM-bee, she'd instructed the class) was going to scold her. The harder Tami tried to keep all the muscles of her body stiff, the more nervous she became and the less control she had over her twitching and fidgeting. She'd spent most of the summer dreading the start of school, knowing it was going to be like this.

"One nation under God . . . indivisible . . . with liberty and justice for all."

"Tami," Mrs. Colombe said softly, approaching Tami's desk after the children had sat down, "do you need to use the restroom?"

Tami shook her head vigorously.

"Are you feeling ill?"

Again, she shook her head.

"It's distracting when you fidget like that during the flag salute." As Mrs. Colombe paused, all eyes were on Tami. "It's disrespectful, too."

Tami stared down at her desk. She was a pretty girl with light skin and long brown hair, but her hair was unbrushed, her clothing unclean and unkempt.

"Are you sure you're feeling all right, Tami?"

All was silent for several seconds. Then, suddenly, Tami burst into tears. She covered her face, dropped her head to her desk and sobbed loudly. Mrs. Colombe tried to put a comforting hand on Tami's shoulder, but it was shrugged off.

The teacher strode to her desk and quickly wrote out a referral slip. "Emily," she said to a tall girl with curly red hair, "would you please escort Tami to the nurse?"

As she followed Emily to the door, Tami saw, out the corner of her eye, a boy displaying a note he'd written in large block letters: "HER MOTHER IS A HIPY."

Tami sat outside the office while the nurse finished dealing with a second-grade boy who had thrown up in class. By the time she was called in, she'd calmed down and hastily dried her tears.

"What's the matter now, Tamara?"

"Don't call me Tamara. Call me Tami."

"Okay. What's the matter, Tami?"

"And it's T-A-M-I, not T-A-M-M-Y."

"Okay, Tami. Now tell me what's wrong."

"Same old thing."

"What same old thing?"

"I get nervous."

"What makes you nervous?"

"School."

"That's what you said the last time. What's making you nervous at school today? The day's hardly started!"

"Everything."

"Are you having trouble doing your work?"

"No."

"Are you having problems with the other children?"

"No."

"I don't think there's anything wrong with you, Tamara," the nurse said, making a notation at the bottom of the referral slip. "You go on back to class now."

Tami did not go back to class.

After dropping the referral slip in a hallway wastebasket, she walked unnoticed out the elementary school's unlocked main gate, down the driveway, up two blocks and onto Highway Nine.

State Highway Nine wound north and south through the Santa Cruz Mountains. To the north lay the rustic San Lorenzo Valley, where Tami and her mother lived. At its southern terminus was the city of Santa Cruz, where the San Lorenzo River rolled lazily under the railroad trestle by the boardwalk into Monterey Bay. Tami walked on the narrow shoulder of the curving two-lane road, facing the oncoming southbound traffic, until she reached a spot where she could see each approaching vehicle a hundred yards or so away and be sure it wasn't a California Highway Patrol car before she held out her thumb.

After several cars had passed her by, an old Chevy van driven by a long-haired young man pulled over.

"Where you wanna go?"

"Santa Cruz."

"Hop in."

"Can you take me to the Catalyst?"

"Sure."

After they'd driven a short distance, the man said to Tami, "Shouldn't you be in school?"

"No school today. They're having teachers' meetings."

"You're pretty young to be hitchhiking. Your parents know you're doing it?"

"My mom knows. I do it all the time."

Fifteen minutes later they were in Santa Cruz, where Highway Nine straightened out and became River Street, which passed directly by the Catalyst.

The Catalyst was a restaurant and bar on the bottom floor of the old St. George Hotel, a hip hangout frequented by a broad spectrum of Santa Cruz denizens. The lawyers on their lunch hour, who walked over the bridge from the ugly concrete monolith of the county courthouse, were the only ones who could afford the pricey entrees and sandwiches. To the students and hipsters who came, it was a place to hang out and have a beer, meet friends or check out the postings on the bulletin board:

Couple w/baby & dog desperately need house. Can pay up to $100/month. Call Jim or Kathy, 426-7278

Free Yoga class. Tuesday nights 7:30-10:30.
Santa Cruz YWCA

Mellow Capricorn male, 24, desperate for bread. Will do
anything legal. Call Michael 423-9136

Tami knew her mother would be there.

Alice Hagar was in her early thirties. She had lank, dark hair and a
disturbingly wasted-out face.

"What are you doing here?" she said to her daughter.

"I freaked out at school. I just couldn't hack it."

"How did you get here?"

Tami stuck out her thumb.

"Damn it, I told you I don't want you hitchhiking. It's dangerous. You're just a kid."

"How else was I supposed to get here?"

"You *weren't* supposed to get here. You were supposed to stay at
school. What made you freak out?"

"The other kids. And the teacher."

"How do you mean?"

"All those kids are so straight. I just can't relate to them. And
that Mrs. Colombe . . . she's so uptight. They all hate me."

"What makes you think they all hate you?"

"They stare at me all the time and they whisper to each other."

"You're probably just imagining it. I've told you over and over
again that you're too sensitive."

"I'm *not* imagining it. And I'm *not* too sensitive. Wanna know
what happened this morning? Mrs. Colombe sent me to the nurse

just 'cause I couldn't stand still during the flag salute, and this boy named Richie wrote 'Her mother is a hippie' on a piece of paper, and he showed it to all the other kids while I was walking out."

"That's *his* trip."

"He didn't even know how to spell 'hippie.'"

"He's probably just afraid of anybody that's different. Some people are like that."

"I know. That's why they all hate me. 'Cause I'm different."

"You just have to ignore them. It's *their* bad karma. Don't let them put it on you."

"Mrs. Colombe hates me, too."

"How do you know that?"

"The way she looks at me. The way she talks to me. She scolds me just 'cause I can't sit still all the time."

"Well, now, that's wrong. Maybe I should go have a talk with her."

"No. I don't want you to. She'll treat you like she treats me."

"Then I'll go to the principal."

"He'll treat you bad, too. They'll all treat you bad, especially now that I ditched. They'll say you're a bad mother."

"Well," Alice said, putting her arm around Tami, "we'll work it out some way or another. Actually, I'm kind of glad you're here. I'm lonely."

"Why do you hang out here? It just bums you out."

"It does not. I like it here."

"You just wanna meet a guy."

"That's bullshit. I have lots of friends that hang out here. It's just early. They're not here yet."

Tami glanced at her mother's half-full mug. "Can I have some of your beer?"

"No."

"Why not?"

"'Cause it's not cool for kids to drink. I could get busted. And you could get taken away from me and put in a foster home, 'cause they'd say I was an unfit mother."

A stocky man with a beard, leather jacket and biker boots appeared at their table and eyed Alice up and down. "Uh . . . excuse me," he said.

"Huh?" Alice said, startled.

"I know you from somewhere."

"I don't recognize you."

"Did you use to live in Oakland?"

"No."

"The Haight?"

"No."

"Did you ever live on a big commune just off of Highway One? Near Big Sur?"

"No."

"Well . . . all the same, I'm just positive I know you from somewhere." He paused. "Mind if I sit down?"

"Yes," Tami said loudly. "We mind."

"*Tamara*," Alice said. "Don't be rude. Of course you can sit down."

The man seated himself between Tami and her mother.

"I don't want the rest of my beer," Alice said. "You can finish it off if you want."

He downed the half-mug in one big gulp. "Thanks," he said. "By the way . . . I'm Arnie."

Tami sat and sulked. She could tell the man was a loser. She could also tell he was destined to become part of her family.

"I'm Alice, and this is Tami. Don't mind her rudeness. She was having such a bad day at school she left and came here."

"Well, now, I'm sorry to hear that, little lady. What happened at school? Kids pick on you? Flunk a spelling test?"

Tami looked away.

On their way out of the Catalyst that day, Alice and Tami stopped and looked at the bulletin board. Among the ads was a poster seeking students for the Santa Cruz Open School, fees on a sliding scale.

Alice enrolled Tami the next day.

CHAPTER 18

Challenges

Sophie didn't want the Santa Cruz Open School to be all white. She wanted at least some of her students to be educationally neglected children of color whom she could liberate from the racist public school system. She had tried to recruit the children from the free breakfast program, but none of their parents had shown any interest. During the summer she had plastered ads in English and Spanish all over Santa Cruz's predominantly minority neighborhoods announcing the school's emphasis on cultural pride, but not a single black or Mexican parent had responded. So despite Sophie's commitment to pluralism, SCOS remained as homogeneously Caucasian as a segregated school in 1950s Alabama.

A fair number of white middle-class families in 1970 Santa Cruz were raising their children in accordance with the "do-your-own-thing" ethic that permeated California's hip coastal towns at the time. Many of these parents enrolled their children in, and in some cases helped found, "free schools" like SCOS. Santa Cruz and its environs also had a growing population of white, formerly middle-class single moms who, cheated out of fair divorce settlements or otherwise deprived of the means they'd been accustomed to, had found themselves and their children tumbled from the comfortable bourgeoisie into the sad, demeaning culture of the welfare check—a dejected group of women who lived in run-down housing, drank cheap wine, smoked pot and brightened their lives only slightly with an unfocused mix of the laid-back lifestyle of the hippies and the tattooed, swaggering cult of the men with motorcycles who hovered at the periphery of that milieu. Free schools, with their atmosphere of tolerance, attracted these alienated mothers as well.

The longhaired kids of these two overlapping spheres were amazingly similar and surprisingly likable, startling though their language and attitudes could be. Without boundaries of age or gender, they cursed, discussed sex and bodily functions in the same crude language as their elders and aped the latter's anti-establishment styles in outlook and ornamentation. Even after just a year of teaching them, Sophie knew what these children were all about. She knew how they lived and understood the nuances of their emotional lives. Joanne, she knew, had an even deeper comprehension of these hip kids, being herself the mother of three of them—one of many reasons why her presence in the school was needed. Sophie knew the mind games sophisticated children could play on adults and most of the time knew how to avoid being sucked into them. She also knew that Steve, lacking such savvy, was vulnerable.

At first the children reacted guardedly to Steve.

"He's weird," Sophie overheard some of them saying.

Then Tami Hagar, the streetwise nine-year-old newly plucked from a hostile public-school environment, began following Steve around and talking to him. One by one, the other girls turned to him, intrigued to be in the presence of a big, imposing man who was kind and sweet, not rough or intimidating. Within a short time, he had bevy of young female admirers.

As she watched Steve, beguiled by the interest and affection of those lovely creatures, respond in kind, Sophie initially thought it charming. But as she observed him day after day walking and talking with the girls, from six-year-old Sheila Wright to eleven-year-old Susan Vaughn, sometimes giving shoulder rides to the littler ones, she began to worry. Not that she saw anything inappropriate in a sexually-tinged way—her concern was with Steve's naïveté and susceptibility.

"He's gonna get hurt," Sophie said to Joanne, who nodded in agreement.

The question of academic instruction at SCOS was a difficult one. The Bucks had been neglectful in this area—something Sophie was determined to change—and when it was first announced that academics would be mandatory and that the better part of each day would be devoted to lessons, there were protests.

"This is supposed to be a free school!" Lauren McNeely, one of the younger girls in the eight- to ten-year-old group, said.

It took some one-on-one intervention to convince the protesters—most of whom were in the middle group—that "free school" did not mean a school without lessons, and of how embarrassing it would be to fall behind their public-school peers in reading, math and the other basics. But what finally clinched it was a lively, ingenious speech by, of all people, Steve.

"Let's show everybody that free-schoolers are just as smart as public-school kids," he yelled to the assembled school. "Let's study and work like crazy. Let's make sure *everybody* is reading and writing and doing math at the grade they should be at. Let's make sure *everybody* knows the science and social studies for their grade. Let's memorize our times tables. Let's learn to spell twenty new words each week. Let's have the world's most beautiful handwriting. We're a small school, and you have three good teachers who can take all the time they need to help anybody who needs help. We can go on field trips . . . and play games . . . and do activities to make learning more fun. Let's do it, and let's have fun doing it! *That's a challenge!*"

To Sophie's and Joanne's amazement, the pep talk drew cheers. Steve himself was amazed at how his enthusiasm had—at least for that moment—trumped his shyness. He was even more amazed at how that enthusiasm had infected the kids. And thereafter, the three teachers never forgot that *challenge* was a magic word.

Little by little the three SCOS teachers began to find their footing with each other, to learn how to work together, to complement each other's talents while respecting one another's sensibilities. Sophie learned not to resent Joanne's take-charge attitude, while Joanne kept reminding herself that despite now being a full-fledged teacher, she hadn't intended to take on a leadership role. Both women learned how to avoid hurting Steve's feelings, using gentle tact when they had to remind him of his duties. Steve had turned out to be a passionate and dedicated teacher and was slowly learning to be more assertive with the kids, but he was absentminded. When working with individual students or on a special project, he often lost track of time—there being no bells at SCOS to mark the end of instructional periods—and forgot when it was time to move on to the next class.

Things continued to improve. There were fewer chaotic days and a growing sense that a mission of purpose was being carried out. Some days were downright wonderful, with teachers and students pulling together as a cohesive, focused unit happily on task. Karen and John, who hadn't really thought of themselves as part of the school, got involved; she frequently helped out with supervision, especially at lunchtime, and he became the official athletic coach.

There were still, of course, some days that dragged with malaise and crackled with testiness. Each such day brought a new lesson to the adults.

Steve had meant to teach only filmmaking at SCOS, and though it turned out he was needed for academics as well, he didn't neglect his main interest.

He wanted to make a film about the school that had come to be the center of his life, but film was expensive, processing even more so. Even if he used only his Bolex, shooting silent black-and-white and adding voice-over, the one-hour film he envisioned would strain his budget; were he to shoot in color and rent a full professional synch-sound outfit, even a twenty-minute short could easily top a thousand dollars. He hated the thought of asking his parents for more money, generous as they'd been in providing him with an allowance as well as equipment, film and a VW bus in which to haul it all around. Perhaps at some point, he thought, he might ask a few of the better-heeled school parents like Dan and Leanne Mason to kick in a hundred or so apiece and then importune his own parents to match those contributions. But for now, he contented himself with letting some of the older kids play around with his Kodak Super-8 Instamatic camera, paying for film and processing out of his allowance.

Joey McComb, who had developed an interest in filmmaking and a strong bond with Steve, took his teacher's instructions to heart and shot carefully planned footage of SCOS's students and teachers at work; the results showed talent and promise. The other three boys in the film class were less cooperative. "Hold the camera still!" Steve continually shouted at them. "Leave that zoom lens alone!" But despite his constant admonition to plan out their scenes and use slow, deliberate camera work, they wasted roll after roll on wild panning and zooming shots of one another's zany, uncontrolled clowning antics.

The boys also made Joey—with his social ineptitude, quirky intellect and seriousness about filmmaking—the butt of constant teasing. When Steve defended Joey and took the boys to task for their behavior, they began to tease him as well. Exasperated, he disbanded the group and continued to work alone with the awkward protégé who hung on his every word.

Filmmaking was no longer Steve's sole interest. He was enjoying his other teaching as well, especially science and math. And, of course, there were the girls, who continued to brighten his days with their fond attention.

One day the younger and middle age groups went on a field trip to Harvey West Park, a patch of green at the bottom of a hill beneath the site of the old Santa Cruz Mission. Adjacent to the park was an old cemetery, where they went first for a discussion of death and dying as well as an arithmetic lesson. Steve was officially in charge; Sophie had stayed at school with the older kids and Joanne was home sick with the flu. Mark Brandsteader—the boyfriend of Martha Miller, mother of the two Zweickert children—had offered to come along and help supervise. Mark was twenty-eight, nine years Martha's junior, an easygoing guitar player who was good with kids.

"Okay," Mark said at one grave site, "Mr. Hilliard was born in 1867 and died in 1941. How old was he when he died?"

Steve felt slightly resentful. As teacher, he'd intended to be the one to carry out the lesson. Mark, an impromptu volunteer, was taking over.

They continued to examine the old epitaphs, calculating the ages at death, the number of years since burial and how old the deceased would be today. All enjoyed the lesson, but several of the girls were jittery to be in the presence of the dead and made their fear known. Steve was prepared for the girls to gather around him and cling to him for protection from the spirits—indeed, he was looking forward to it. But to his dismay, they clustered around Mark instead.

After the cemetery excursion, there was a birthday party in the park for Kevin Zweickert, Melissa's younger brother, who was turning seven. Martha showed up with her son's cake and Mark's guitar. After "Happy Birthday" had been sung, Mark played a few tunes while his newfound female devotees hung on him. When he began giving shoulder rides to the younger kids, Steve asked some of the little girls who'd been regular riders on *his* shoulders if they wanted a ride. "No, thank you," they all said.

Unable to accept the alienation of his girls, Steve continued to hang around them, hoping they would at least divide their attentions between him and their new man friend. They didn't, and he realized with intense hurt that they were tired of him. Like him, Mark was softly masculine, but *unlike* him, Mark was new and interesting.

In the days that followed, the girls who had been fondest of Steve—especially Michelle Vaughn, Lauren McNeely and Melissa Zweickert—continued to snub him. Only Susan Vaughn and Tami Hagar remained loyal.

He was desolate. He hadn't realized how emotionally dependent he'd become on those girls. It humiliated him to have to admit he had needed them more than they needed him, to know he'd lost their respect by being just another child among them. For the next two weeks, he wandered about in a daze, feeling pathetic. He taught his classes halfheartedly. He hardly spoke to Sophie or Joanne and avoided contact with Karen and John.

It was Sophie who brought him out of it.

"Stop being an idiot," she said to him one day. "Just let those girls be and they'll come around again. Quit sulking and pay attention to the other kids. Pay attention to the boys."

Steve took her advice. He forced himself to teach his academic lessons with renewed vigor. He worked on his rapport with the older boys and, under John's tutelage, even played some touch football with them, though he'd always been terrible at sports. And he began once again to work seriously with Joey, this time focusing more on social skills than on filmmaking.

Finally, one day, he said to Sophie: "I'm back. I'm over it."

She hugged him. The big teddy bear. She knew what had made those little girls love him, and she knew they would love him again. She also knew that her own friendly affection for Steve was turning into something stronger, which scared her.

*

Sophie's resistance to the seeming inevitability of romance with Steve boiled down to two specific concerns.

Her first qualm was that changing the nature of their relationship could alter the delicate balance of the separate lives they'd been leading under the same roof and the working partnership they had fostered with such care in the school. If they became lovers and it didn't work out, things would get even more complicated and, potentially, ugly. And in the meantime, whatever occurred between them—good or bad—would be food for gossip among students and parents alike.

Her other worry was the weekly women's meeting. She continued to feel a commitment to the group and had managed to keep it going despite the much stronger demands of the school. In her zeal to help the women break free of the oppressive relationships many of them were in, she'd created the perception that she was altogether opposed to romantic and sexual liaisons—which, in fact, she had been for a long time after terminating her relationship with Craig. But during a meeting in late October, she shared her changed feelings about Steve with the group, bracing herself to be called a hypocrite.

To her surprise, the members not only showed no disapproval but urged her on. After nearly a year of Sophie's being their trusted and beloved mentor, the women of the group now mentored her.

They all knew and liked Steve.

"He's such a nice, gentle guy," one of them said.

"He's one of the only men I've ever seen who's truly not a male chauvinist," said another. "He's strong. He knows who he is. But he's not—what's that Spanish word again?"

"*Macho*," Sophie said.

"That's it. He's not macho. That's such a great word, I'm going to start using it."

In spite of all her reservations, Sophie found herself sitting very close to Steve around the campfire during a whole-school camping trip a few weeks later. The three directors of SCOS had felt good enough about how things were going and how everyone was getting on to propose the trip: all three teachers, several parent volunteers and the students sleeping out in the open for two nights at a creek outlet on the Big Sur coast. And so here they were, the grown-ups enjoying the quiet of their first night in the outdoors after the kids had gone to sleep. Sophie and Mark sang and played their guitars, the others singing along softly to a string of old traditional folk ballads from Sophie's extensive repertoire.

When it was bedtime for the adults, Sophie and Steve placed their sleeping bags side by side. She said some sweet things to him about how wonderful he was with the kids, and then suddenly they were kissing with a wholly unexpected passion. Conscious of the proximity of the sleeping children, Sophie cut the romantic moment short and didn't allow a repeat of it the following night.

Monday morning, the kids who had been on the trip were keyed up and excited. It took most of a lesson period to get them calmed down, but "Get your act together and work like you always do— that's a challenge" did the trick for most of them.

After lunch, the fourth- and fifth-graders did a math practice session, with Susan in charge. She had them do some long division, reviewed subtraction with borrowing and quizzed them on their multiplication tables. Susan was an extraordinary tutor; the middle-group kids respected her and, most of the time, behaved for her. When they didn't, she knew how to refocus them in a calm and mature way.

She was drilling the group with flash cards in one of the partitioned-off sections of the schoolroom when Joey suddenly popped his head out from behind the divider. The children grimaced and sighed. Susan tensed. Like the others, she knew that Joey took to annoying people any time he was bored and that the middle-groupers, especially the girls, reacted dramatically to his annoyances.

"*Get out!*" Melissa said.

"Go away, Joey," Lauren said. "You're not welcome here."

"Don't be rude," Susan said firmly. "Joey, why aren't you in class?"

"I have independent study."

"Then you should be studying."

Not about to take orders from a girl a year younger than he, Joey crossed his arms over his chest and stood silently, his body language saying, *Make me.*

"What kinda trip are you on now, McComb?" Robby Mason said. "Trying to act tough or something?"

"Get the hell out of here, Joey!" Tami, who had developed an aggressive streak along with her new-found self-confidence, said.

"*Tami*," Susan said.

"You're such a retard," Melissa said. "You spent the whole camping trip being obnoxious and bothering people . . . and when you weren't doing that, you were off collecting shells or looking at the stars. You're the weirdest boy I've ever known."

"Come on, Melissa," Susan said. "Stop it. You know the rule about put-downs."

"Guess what *I* saw!" Joey said.

"We don't give a shit what you saw," Tami said.

"*Tami*," Susan said.

"I saw Steve and Sophie kissing," Joey said.

Susan couldn't control the outburst that followed.

"Bullshit!" Robby said.

"Liar!" Lauren said.

"Liar!" Melissa said.

"You're such an *idiot*!" Lauren said. "Everyone knows Steve and Sophie aren't boyfriend and girlfriend. They're just good friends, and they work together in the school."

"Not anymore," Joey said, grinning.

"McComb, you're so fulla shit," Robby said.

"It's true," Michelle said softly, bringing the argument to a halt.

Susan couldn't hold her tongue any longer. "Shut up, Michelle! We weren't supposed to tell anyone."

Michelle and Susan had overheard their mother talking to Sophie on Sunday night after they got back from the trip. Joanne had cautioned them not to gossip about it.

The first night back in the house, Sophie and Steve were too tired to do anything but fall, exhausted, into their separate beds. But on the second night, she invited him into her room.

As they sat on the bed, he reached for her first. He gently touched her hair and ran his hand over her face, and she put her hand behind his neck and pulled him to her. They made love with an intensity that startled and frightened Sophie, who had been intimate with only three men before and had never known what she experienced that night. And the next night. And the night after that.

Sophie found herself on a manic high that lasted weeks. She typed out new plans for the school, proposing at a parents' meeting that they add a junior high and a high school the next year and seek out either a university grant or a well-moneyed benefactor to help them buy a piece of land and construct a beautiful new school building for SCOS—to include, of course, a fully equipped film production studio for Steve and his students.

"Aren't you getting a little ahead of yourself?" Dan Mason said. "We still haven't figured out how we're going to pay for the rest of *this* school year, in our present humble abode."

"I think we've got to think big and dream big," Sophie said. "Or we'll never get beyond where we're at now."

Though everyone knew it was her changed relationship with Steve that had escalated Sophie's ambitions, that change didn't seem to hinder her work in the school, or Steve's. If anything, it enhanced and energized it.

Life was good.

CHAPTER 19

Larry and Arthur

Sophie hadn't gone home for Thanksgiving for the past few years. With most of the extended family in the East, her parents had never made a big deal of the holiday. This year she stayed in Santa Cruz and shared a small turkey with John and Karen.

Steve's family took Thanksgiving very seriously, and his parents made the reservations for his flight home. Thursday night was the traditional Elwood Thanksgiving dinner, which Steve dreaded every year. Jovial Uncle Mike—his mother's brother—and garrulous Aunt Vivian, neither of whom Steve could stand, had driven down from Fresno as usual with their teenage sons, Randy and Marty, whom he disliked even more. He did the job on the bird with his mother's new electric carving knife.

"So . . . I hear tell that you're the principal of a school," Aunt Vivian said to Steve after they were all seated.

"That's absolutely not true," Steve said. "*You* didn't tell them that, did you, Dad?"

"I told them you were a vice principal," Arthur said. "That's true, isn't it?"

"No. We don't even *have* a principal or vice principal. I'm just one of three co-directors."

"Well, now, that's just a vice principal by a different name, isn't it?" Aunt Vivian said. "How many teachers work under you?"

"None. There's just us three."

"What kind of school is this?" Uncle Mike said.

"It's . . . well, it's an experimental school of sorts."

"Experimental in what way?"

"Well . . ." He talked briefly about SCOS, keeping the details as vague as possible. Unlike the hosts, the guests were all conservative (the subject of politics had to be carefully avoided) and would have disapproved of the whole "free school" concept. The moment Steve yielded the floor, his cousins began to gab excitedly about their high school football team's recent string of wins. He tuned out.

Friday night, the guests gone, the three Elwoods dined on leftovers.

"How's the boat?" Steve said.

"Haven't taken it out in a while." Arthur said. "Having some engine trouble . . . I keep procrastinating getting it fixed, but I gotta do it. I gotta get out in that boat. It relaxes me, lowers my blood pressure. How's the bus running?"

"Great."

"Are you driving carefully all the time, Steven?" Rosemary said.

"Yes, Mom."

"I worry about you. I know how you sometimes get lost in your thoughts and don't pay attention to your surroundings."

"I know, Mom. Don't worry, I'm always attentive when I'm driving."

"Promise me you'll be *extra* careful when you drive down here for Christmas."

"I promise."

"I especially worry about you on those long highway trips, Steven. All it takes is just one moment of inattention . . . "

"I know, Mom. I promise I'll be careful."

"Sure you don't want to fly again?"

"No, I want to have my car while I'm down here."

"You can drive one of our cars. You can drive the Caddy."

"No, I want my own car. I don't want to be the rich kid driving around in a Caddy. You know how I feel about that."

"Then you can drive the station wagon."

"Mom, I really want to have my own car. Don't worry, I'll be *very* careful."

Steve had made no mention of Sophie the entire weekend. He didn't like to discuss his love life with his parents, though the only time he'd ever mentioned a girlfriend—a short-lived relationship during his senior year at UC Irvine that had, despite its brevity, given him his first sexual experience—they'd been respectful and not pried too much. He also remembered how uncomfortable the mention of Sophie's surname on the phone had made them. But after they'd discussed Steve's driving and speculated briefly about who might run against Nixon in '72, Rosemary began asking her son about his living situation.

"What is it like, living in a commune?" she said.

"It's nice," Steve said. "I like it."

"Does everyone share the housework?"

"Yes."

"Who does the cooking?"

"We take turns."

Then his father asked him, with visible unease: "Is the Hearn girl still living in your house?"

"Yes, she is," Steve said, "and her name is Sophie, not 'the Hearn girl.'"

"And you and Sophie are still just friends, I take it?"

"Well . . . actually, no. We're more than that now."

Arthur turned pale. "You are?"

"Yes. Is that a problem?"

His father said nothing.

Rosemary broke the silence. "We were friends with Larry and Ruth Hearn at one time, many years ago . . . but we had a falling-out."

"What kind of falling-out? What happened?"

"I think your father would prefer we not discuss it. Let's just leave it at this: It would be uncomfortable for your father and me to have any contact with the Hearns."

"When did this falling-out happen?"

"A long time ago."

"Then shouldn't you have gotten over it by now and made up with them?"

"Did you not just hear your mother say we didn't want to discuss it?" Arthur said, his face turning from pale to angry red.

"Yes. But I don't agree. If it was something that terrible, I think you should tell me."

"Trust us," Rosemary said. "We can't stop you from dating Sophie Hearn, but you must not ask us to discuss what happened between her parents and us. Are you serious with her?"

"Depends on what you mean by 'serious.' We're not getting married tomorrow, if that's what you mean . . . but yes, we are doing a thing. "

"What the hell does that mean, 'doing a thing'?" Arthur said.

"It means we're involved," Steve said, suddenly feeling defiant. "Romantically, if you want to put it that way."

"Listen, both of you," Rosemary said. "We all need to cool down. Steven, you're a big boy now. It's your own business what girl you choose to date, or 'do a thing' with, or whatever other terms you kids are using these days. Yes, any encounter with the Hearns would be uncomfortable for us, but that's not your problem—or Sophie's. You go and live your life."

"Thanks, Mom," Steve said, picking at his cold turkey.

Arthur sat silently, not eating.

Sunday morning, after they'd dropped Steve off at Orange County Airport, Arthur turned to Rosemary. "I'm going to have to go and see Larry Hearn. It'll be awful, but I have no choice now. I've gotta go talk to him—if he'll talk to me."

"What for?" Rosemary said.

"What for? What the hell do you think for?"

"What are you going to say to him? That you don't want his daughter 'doing a thing' with your son?"

"Of course not. You think I'm a complete idiot?"

"Then what *are* you going to say?"

"I don't know. I haven't thought it through yet."

Arthur called Information in L.A. to make sure the Hearns' phone number was still the same as it was in his old address book: State 5-6461. It was, only now the operator gave it to him as "Area Code 213, 785-6461." He dialed the number.

"Hello?"

"Ruthie?"

"Yes, who is this?"

"This is Art Elwood." He took a deep breath and braced for her to hang up on him, but she didn't. There was just a long silence.

"Yes . . . Art," she finally said, coldly. "What can I do for you?"

"Is Larry around?"

There was another long silence. "Yes," she finally said, "he's here."

"May I speak with him, please?"

"Yes. Just a moment."

He heard Ruth set the phone down and, a few seconds later, an extension being picked up. Doubtless Larry was in his study. A twenty-year-old picture of the dark room with the venetian blinds flashed briefly in his memory.

"Hello?"

"Larry?"

"Yes?"

Arthur knew that Larry knew it was him. Ruth would have told him immediately. "Larry, this is Art Elwood."

"Yes, Art," Larry said icily. "What is it?"

"I need to talk to you."

"Go ahead."

"No, I mean in person. I'd like to meet you somewhere."

"Can you give me some idea of what this is about?"

"I'd rather we discussed it in person."

"Okay, then . . . when and where would you like to meet?"

He'd expected Larry to resist and had a speech prepared to persuade him. "Uh . . . I dunno. Anywhere . . . any time that's convenient for you. We live down here in Newp— . . . We live in Orange County now, but I'll come up there. Just pick someplace near you. A nice restaurant. I'll treat you to lunch."

"Well . . ."

"Do you remember that little place in Studio City that had terrific fish and chips? It was called Charles', if memory serves, but it was originally called The Keg . . . and the restaurant was actually shaped like a keg. Is it still there?"

"Yes," Larry said. "It's still there."

"So then, let's meet there," Arthur said.

"When would be a good day for you?"

"Any day you want."

"How about Tuesday?"

"Tuesday's fine."

"Tuesday it is then. See you there—noon?"

"That's fine."

"Very good. Charles', Tuesday at noon." Long pause. "Thanks, Larry."

"Good-bye, Art."

Arthur had wanted to be first to arrive. He thought he'd allowed plenty of extra time, but he ran into a bad tie-up on the Santa Ana Freeway just before the downtown L.A. interchange and it remained bumper-to-bumper all the way through Hollywood and on into Cahuenga Pass. He began to sweat when, at noon, he was only passing the Capitol Records tower; he feared Larry would give up and leave. But Larry was there, alone in a booth sipping a beer, when Arthur walked into the barrel-shaped eatery at 12:17.

They shook hands stiffly.

"Hello, Art."

"Hello, Larry."

"Have a seat."

Arthur had known the meeting was going to be difficult, but he felt even more awkward than he'd expected.

"Thanks for coming," Arthur said.

"That's okay."

"You look good."

"Thanks."

"Have you ordered yet?"

"No, I was waiting for you."

"I'm not very hungry. How about we split a fish and chips?"

"Fine by me."

The waitress came and took their order.

"How's Ruthie?" Arthur said when the waitress was gone.

"She's fine," Larry said, still coolly. "How's Rosie?"

"Keeping herself busy."

"You working?"

"Some sitcoms, a bad movie or two in the offing . . . worthless shit, but it pays the mortgage. How about yourself?"

"Getting by."

"Rotten racket. Worst fucking industry in the world. I'd dig ditches if I had it to do over."

The waitress returned and poured Arthur's beer into a tall glass.

"Thank you," he said.

"I'll have your fish and chips shortly."

Arthur took a sip of his beer. "I'll get right to the point."

"I'm listening," Larry said.

"Well . . . I guess you must be aware by now that my little boy and your little girl are . . ." He paused.

"Are what?"

"They're romantically involved. They're dating. You weren't aware of that?"

"No, I wasn't. I wasn't even aware that they'd met."

"Yes. Apparently they met up there, in Santa Cruz."

"I see."

"Back last summer, after he graduated UC Irvine, Stevie said he wanted to move up there. We thought it was a good idea for him to get away on his own, so we encouraged the move. He'd developed a strong interest in filmmaking while he was at Irvine . . . You know, once Stevie gets interested in something, he's very single-minded about it. He's been that way since he was a kid. So anyway, we buy him some equipment so he can pursue his interest up there in Santa Cruz. He lets his hair grow long, he goes on up there looking like a hippie and moves into one of those communes . . . and as it turns out, I guess, your Sophie was already staying there."

"Okay."

"At first they were just friends, but apparently now they're going together. 'Doing a thing,' as Stevie put it."

"I see."

Arthur sat silently for a long moment, staring into his glass to avoid making eye contact. He took a hearty swig of the beer. "Stevie means everything in the world to me," Arthur said, "*Everything*. Nothing else matters for shit."

Larry didn't respond.

"Larry . . . I've been so ashamed all these years of what I did. So very, very ashamed . . . I couldn't bear to tell him. I've kept it from him all these years."

Larry was still silent.

"Maybe that was as big a mistake as what I did. But I couldn't bear it otherwise. The shame, Larry . . . the shame and the guilt, knowing that what I'd done could never be undone." His voice broke. "Have you any idea what it's been like?"

"You wanted to make sure I wasn't going to tell him. Is that why you wanted to see me?"

"For *his* sake, Larry. Not mine." He saw disdain in Larry's face. "He doesn't deserve to suffer for what I did, Larry. He's a good kid . . . an honest kid . . . and *very* smart. And very moral. He's a much better person than I am, Larry. He would never have done what I did. *Never*. But he's sensitive. Very sensitive. He had a rough childhood . . . got teased a lot for his shyness and high intelligence. It would just destroy him if he ever found out."

"Don't worry, Art. I'd have no reason to tell him."

"What about Sophie?"

"I'd have no reason to tell her, either."

"Thank you, Larry, thank you. You are a true saint. Unlike me."

"It's all right, Art."

"I'm sure your girl has grown up to be a marvelous young lady."

"Yes, she has."

As they sipped their beers, neither tried to fill the silence.

The waiter arrived with their fish and chips and two extra plates. Larry divided the mound of thick fries and the big golden-battered pieces of fish.

"Just gimme one piece," Arthur said. "I'm not very hungry."

Neither spoke as they ate.

"This lunch is on me," Arthur said after Larry asked for the check.

"No, that's okay. We can split it."

"No, I insist."

"How about I leave the tip?"

"Okay. I'll let you do that."

They laid their cash on the table and got up to leave. "It was good to see you," Arthur said. "Give my love to Ruthie."

"I will. Give my best to Rosie."

"And thank you again, Larry. A million times thank you."

"It's okay, Art."

They parted without shaking hands.

"He's lied to his son all these years," Larry said.

"Cowardice compounded upon cowardice," Ruth said. "That doesn't surprise me in the least."

"He begged me not to tell his son. Or Sophie."

"What did you say?"

"I assured him I wouldn't."

"That's better than he deserves."

"He apologized."

"I should've hung up on him."

"He was pitiable."

"There are others more deserving of my pity."

When Steve told Sophie what his parents had said during the Thanksgiving visit, the troubling thought that had occurred to her earlier once again crossed her mind. Once again, she suppressed it.

She had still made no mention of Steve to her parents. His initial report of his parents' reaction back in July had made her wonder if there'd been some kind of trouble between her parents and the Elwoods, and she'd instinctively held off even though Steve had several times pressed her to tell her parents about him. Now, when he told her the latest, she was glad she hadn't. Unlike Steve's parents, hers would have told her exactly what had caused the rift. And she didn't want to know.

Steve did.

During the three weeks between Thanksgiving and the start of Christmas vacation, Steve became so obsessed with the mystery of the falling-out between the Elwoods and the Hearns that he could think of little else. Sophie, Joanne, Karen and John all tried to get him off it and into the holiday spirit.

"Don't let it get you down, man," John said. "It's your parents' trip, not yours."

While Steve continued to wonder and worry, life went on. A Christmas tree and a large cardboard menorah (a nod to Paul Baumgarten's heritage and half of Sophie's) went up in the schoolroom. Holiday songs were sung, cards and gifts exchanged. Finally, on the day before vacation, the adults bade the students a fond farewell.

CHAPTER 20

Ups and Downs

Nineteen seventy-one began well for the Santa Cruz Open School. Students and teachers greeted each other with hugs, and the kids were eager to get back to their routines, even to academics.

Steve reported to Sophie that the two weeks with his parents had been unbearable, with the prohibited subject an all-pervasive cloud in the air. He also told her, with abundant and eager affection, how thankful he was to be back with her again. He told her about some ideas for the school he'd dreamed up during the long drive back, among them that he teach a class in the history of audio-visual technology—film, radio, television and sound recording. Joey and some of the other kids had shown fascination when he'd told them that television had been a new thing when he was a child, that all television had once been black-and-white, that his family had been the first on the block to own a set—"My friends all used to come over to watch 'Howdy Doody'"—and that families had used to sit around and listen to radio dramas.

As the weeks passed, more pupils enrolled and more parents became active and volunteered. One artsy-craftsy mom donated a pottery wheel and an old kiln and offered to teach ceramics. A father volunteered to teach auto mechanics using the defunct Plymouth to practice on. Another parent had a friend who kept a mare and gelding on her place just outside town, and groups of kids—always including the Vaughn sisters, SCOS's resident horse experts—were allowed to come once a week and ride. The three co-directors saw the social environment in the school improving steadily and a strong sense of esprit de corps developing among the students, and so good was the feeling among the adults that parent-teacher meetings were almost festive. More and more, the teachers and volunteers found ways to develop critical thinking and social awareness by drawing links between the curriculum and the students' life experiences.

Steve continued to work one-on-one with Joey, and as he taught the boy to better his social skills, he found his own improving as well. He felt less intimidated at meetings and became gutsier about speaking up. Anne McComb couldn't stop talking about how much happier Joey was at school. Other parents had equally effusive praise.

"Paul's ahead of his older brother now in math," Estelle Baumgarten told Sophie. "I don't want to pull David out of public school in the middle of the year, but I'm going to enroll him for sure next year."

Word got out about the school's success. Teacher trainees from UCSC and San Jose State came to do field work, and people interested in starting their own free schools came from as far away as Berkeley and Sacramento to study SCOS.

Steve and Sophie were crazy in love. They spent as much time together as they could and slept nearly every night in Sophie's room; Steve's bed became a surface on which to stack film cans and tape reels. They did things away from the house whenever possible, attending plays on the UCSC campus and art films at the Nickelodeon Theatre, going hiking and camping in the Santa Cruz Mountains and—when in a playful mood—riding the roller coaster and eating cotton candy at the boardwalk. They began to talk, gingerly at first, about a possible future together.

One day in late February, Tami Hagar invited Steve, Sophie and Joanne, along with her two best friends, Michelle and Melissa, to dinner at her house.

Sophie and Joanne tactfully declined. They didn't much care for Tami's mother. Alice Hagar was the least responsible of the SCOS parents with regard to tuition; though they'd agreed to accept ten dollars a month from her plus a few days of volunteering at the school, she'd gone for two months now without paying or volunteering.

"I've been to her place," Joanne said to Steve, who had agreed to go and represent the faculty. "It's squalid and depressing. God only knows what she'll serve you for dinner. Probably some of that canned welfare meat we all eat every day. I was very reluctant to let Michelle go, but I don't want Tami to feel snubbed."

Tami and her mother lived in the densely-forested mountains above Santa Cruz, near the rustic village of Felton, where many poor white families lived with their children beneath the majestic and ancient trees in little rented cabins like Alice's; Sophie called it the "Redwood Ghetto." It was dark when Steve arrived with Michelle and Melissa (who were once again being nice to him), shifting into first gear as he coaxed the bus up the steep, muddy driveway and stopped alongside the two motorcycles that were parked there. The three of them tramped up the long path to the front door. It had rained that morning; the air was chilly and moist, and the dirt path, like the driveway, was a river of mud.

Michelle had been to Tami's house before. "Brace yourself," she said as they neared the door. "Her house is always dirty and her mom has a creepy boyfriend."

The aroma of roasting beef reached them. It wasn't welfare meat.

Tami and her mother stood in the doorway smiling. "Hi," Alice said. "I'm so glad you all could come."

Steve and the girls wiped the mud from their shoes as best they could on the worn welcome mat before stepping inside. The inviting smell of the roast mingled with the scent of burning firewood and the dreary odors of beer and cigarette smoke. The interior of the cabin was dirty and decrepit—funky, some would say—in a way that suggested apathy more than poverty, a state of languid disarray. An old wood-burning stove heated the living room.

A man whom Alice introduced as Arnie lounged blissfully in a tattered easy chair in a corner of the room, sipping a can of Coors and filling the room with smoke from his unfiltered Camel. On a bare mattress in the opposite corner, another burly man with biker tattoos on his arms, clad in a sleeveless T-shirt, leather jeans and motorcycle boots, lay fast asleep. Next to him, a thin woman with frizzy blond hair and the same wasted look as Alice sat breast-feeding a small baby. Taking in the scene, Steve forced a smile.

There was no place to sit in the living room, so Steve and the girls sat at the kitchen table, the only relatively clean place in the cabin. Tami put out the place settings—an old unmatched set of stainless-steel flatware, plastic plates, and rectangles of paper towel for napkins—while the guests made small talk with Alice. After about fifteen minutes, Alice took the roast from the oven and called out, "Dinner's ready, everybody." Arnie guzzled the last of his beer, crushed out his cigarette and slunk lazily to the table.

"Hey, Louise," Alice called to the woman with the baby, "you and Dale want some dinner?"

"I don't think we're gonna eat. I'm not hungry, and Dale's crashed out."

"*Good*," Tami said, "that means more for us."

"Now, that's no kind of an attitude to have," Alice said. "We share what we have."

"But you stole it for us, not for them."

"You *stole* that?" Steve said as he took his seat at the table.

"Alice is a master shoplifter," Arnie said.

"You think we can afford to *buy* stuff like this?" Tami said.

"How did you manage to shoplift a whole roast beef?" Steve said, trying to sound curious rather than judgmental.

"It's easy," Alice said. "I've got this big puffy ski jacket. I just slip it into the sleeve from in front. It doesn't even make a bulge, the jacket's so puffy."

"Aren't you afraid of getting busted?"

"My mom's magic," Tami said. "She can't get busted."

"It has to do with karma," Alice said. "Why doesn't everybody pass their plates up?"

Tami, Michelle and Arnie shoved their plates toward Alice. Steve handed his over with more reserve while Melissa sat quietly, her empty plate in front of her.

"Hey, one at a time!" Alice said. She took each plate and cut a smallish slice for each child, a larger one for Steve. "Don't you want any, Melissa?"

"No, thank you."

"She's a vegetarian," Michelle said.

"That's okay," Alice said. "I'll find you something in the refrigerator."

"Gimme a nice big rare piece," Arnie said. "I'll take her share."

Alice cut two huge slices, bigger than all the others put together, and set them on Arnie's plate.

"Hey!" Tami said. "How come *he* gets so much?"

"I got a bigger stomach than you," Arnie said.

"Well, Steve's bigger than you, and he got a lot less."

"Tami," Alice said, "what'd I tell you before about bitching and whining at the table?"

"Tami," Arnie said, "why don't you be a vegetarian like your friend? Then I'll eat your meat, too."

"*Shut up.*"

"Tamara," Alice said sternly, "don't talk to Arnie like that."

"Tell *him* not to talk to *me* like that."

"Will you stop being so sensitive? He was only teasing you. Come on, let's just enjoy our dinner, okay?"

Things continued to go well for the school through most of the winter. Then, in early March, things took a turn for the worse. The spirits of the students and the faculty alike began to droop. The wave of creativity that had carried the teachers along for months ebbed into static routine, academic lessons became rigid and uninspired, and the kids began complaining that it was "just like public school." The friendly spirit among the students deteriorated. Joey started to regress in his interpersonal development and was once again the target of teasing. Parent meetings, which for a time had been almost party-like, turned into scratchy, argumentative gripe sessions.

Steve and Joanne didn't know what to do, leaving Sophie to take it all on her shoulders even though she was feeling the same malaise as everyone else and fought every day to keep the demon depression at bay. The three of them talked and talked and finally agreed that the school needed something big and exciting to shake things up.

Then, in an up mood, Sophie hit on it.

A trip to Mexico.

Three years earlier, as a research project for an independent-study class at UCSC, she'd spent two weeks in a little farming village in the interior of Baja California called San Gregorio del Valle. It was far from any of the tourist areas and could be reached only by a dirt road from the old coastal highway between Tijuana and Ensenada. Sophie proposed that the whole school caravan down there during Easter break, with parent volunteers providing cars and drivers, and spend the week enjoying a unique intercultural experience.

The minute she first mentioned it at a parents' meeting, though, she realized it was totally unrealistic. It was a crazy idea, born of a manic high and fraught with peril.

The response was wild enthusiasm.

CHAPTER 21

San Gregorio

"It's nuts," Sophie said. "We can't possibly go through with this. I wish I'd never thought of it."

"No way to back out now," Joanne said. "Everybody's really into it."

Anxious but resigned, Sophie sent a telegram (there were no telephones in San Gregorio) to Juan and Margarita Hernández, the couple who had hosted her on her earlier visit. They wired back that they'd be delighted to receive Sophie and her students and that there would be more than enough families in the village willing to take in the children and their adult supervisors.

Planning began, and once again the school was alive with positive energy. Parents volunteered to be drivers and chaperones. They organized bake and rummage sales to help raise money for the kids who wanted to go but couldn't afford the twenty-five-dollar fee the three teachers had calculated would be needed to cover the expenses of the trip. Sophie drove up to San Francisco to pick up the tourist visas from the Mexican consulate, and went into high gear with the Spanish class she'd been teaching. As the trip's details began to take form, her anxiety subsided and she found herself swept up in the excitement. Steve was excited, too. It would be a wonderful filming opportunity, and it would be romantic, traveling to an exotic place with Sophie—though they wouldn't exactly be alone.

Early Saturday morning, the first day of spring break, a four-car caravan—Steve's minibus, the Wrights' pickup, Martha Miller's station wagon and Mark Brandsteader's van—headed south, carrying seven grown-ups and eleven kids. Driving in shifts for ten hours, barreling through Los Angeles and San Diego without stopping, taking only brief breaks for gas, restrooms and fast picnic meals in San Luis Obispo and Oceanside, they reached the Mexican border just before sunset.

When the small band of gringos finally bumped over the dirt road into San Gregorio del Valle around eight o'clock, the Hernándezes were waiting in front of the town hall to greet them. The families who had volunteered to put them up were there as well, crowded together inside the little building as they awaited the arrival of their American guests. The SCOS children and adults—save for the three men, who had decided to pass on the total-immersion experience—were quickly farmed out; one by one, they disappeared into the night with their host families, to be led through the village's unlighted streets to the homes where they would spend the week. After Joanne, Sophie, Toni and Martha also headed off with their designated hosts, to be lodged in the homes where the younger kids had been assigned, Steve, Cal and Mark laid their sleeping bags on the concrete floor in the back of the town hall.

For the young adventurers, the inevitable culture shock set in immediately. Some of the little ones cried at the strangeness of the smells, the cacophony of incomprehensible speech. It was after ten by the time the last of the young Americans settled in for the night, calmed by the kindness and warmth of their hosts.

"*¿Cómo te llamas?*" Reyna Tenorio asked Susan Vaughn.

"*Me llamo . . . Susana,*" Susan said, using the name Sophie had given her in Spanish class, where she had been the fastest learner. "*¿Cómo se llama usted?*"

"*Yo soy Reyna.*"

"Uh . . . *mucho gusto . . . Reyna,*" Susan said, groping for the words she had learned as she reached out to shake Reyna's hand. Though she spoke with a passable accent, she still couldn't quite manage the rolling of the *r*'s, and she remembered too late Sophie's instruction to use the polite *usted* with grown-ups and the familiar *tú* when conversing with a peer.

Reyna was thirteen, two years older than Susan. They were in the small bedroom they would be sharing that week in the tiny green stucco house without an indoor bathroom that was home to the Tenorio family.

"*¿Cuántos años tienes?*" Reyna said.

It took Susan a few moments to figure out that Reyna was asking her age. "*Tengo . . . once años,*" she said. "*¿Y tú?*"

"*Yo, trece,*" Reyna said. "*¿Cómo se llama tu escuela?*"

"*Mi escuela*"—Susan strained to remember what Sophie had taught her—"*se llama . . . Escuela . . . Abierta . . . de Santa Cruz.*"

"*¿Escuela Abierta?*"

"*Sí.*"

"*¿Qué significa 'escuela abierta'?*"

Susan shrugged apologetically; explaining free schools in Spanish was beyond her ability. She stood by silently while Reyna turned to make up the bed for her.

Joanne had planned on placing her two younger children in the home where she herself would be staying; but Michelle, Tami and Melissa insisted on being housed together, and one family, the Becerras, was happy to take in all three. Sophie took them aside and gave them a mini-lesson in cultural sensitivity, a quick review of rudimentary Spanish and some suggestions on how to deal non-verbally with the language barrier.

María Luisa de Becerra, the family matriarch, prepared the beds in the immaculately clean bedroom where the girls were to be housed. The three of them stood and watched while their hostess turned down the sheets, making occasional comments that they couldn't comprehend but that conveyed warmth and affection.

They were lying on the beds, trying them out, when the three young Becerra girls appeared in the doorway.

"Hello," the ten-year-old and the twelve-year-old said together.

"Hello," the six-year-old said.

The three American girls breathed a deep sigh of relief. "Oh, good!" Melissa said. "You speak English!"

The three sisters wagged their right index fingers back and forth in a motion that Sophie had taught her students was a perfectly polite way, in body-language Spanish, of saying "no."

Hello, *okay* and *bye-bye*, as it turned out, were the only words of English they knew. Still, they managed somehow to exchange names.

"Your dresses are very pretty," Melissa said. While the SCOS girls were clad in jeans and sweatshirts, the Becerra sisters had put on their best Sunday dresses to receive their guests.

The sisters gave each other a puzzled look.

"Very pretty," Melissa said as she walked toward them, pointing at their dresses. "Very pretty." She touched each of the three dresses. Suddenly, a word Sophie had used to describe a flower in one of their Spanish lessons came to her, and she carefully enunciated: "Bo-NEE-ta."

The sisters smiled.

"*Gracias*," Ofelia and Evangelina, the older ones, said.

"*Gracias*," Lilia, the six-year-old, said.

In the morning, the Americans awoke to a landscape of little stucco and cinder-block houses along a short unpaved main street with the small municipal building at one end, a plaza with a church at the other, plowed fields all around and scrubby brown mountains in the distance. In the town hall, volunteers from the community served up a communal breakfast of eggs, spicy chorizo and refried beans.

"Eeeew," some of the little ones said when they saw and smelled food that was nothing like the mild, inauthentic Mexican cuisine that Northern California kids were used to. Most, however, were willing to try it. For those who just couldn't cope, there was toasted *pan Bimbo*—white bread—and the mildly sweet, multi-shaped pastries known as *pan dulce*.

After breakfast, while the San Gregorio families were at

Sunday Mass, the teachers led the kids in a meeting to discuss
how everyone had handled their first night as guests in a foreign land. Though a few complained about crowded quarters and
primitive amenities, most were animatedly positive about what
they had experienced so far and immensely proud of whatever
little bit of Spanish they'd managed to muster thanks to Sophie's
last-minute lessons. When the villagers returned from church,
Sophie organized games in which the SCOS students and their
local counterparts could participate across the language gulf.
Soon the American and Mexican kids were laughing and having fun together, inventing nonverbal communications and conducting impromptu language lessons in both directions, stopping
only when it was time for afternoon *comida*, the main meal of the
day, served by the host families.

In the evening, the three unadventurous men sat in the empty
town hall sipping Dos Equis beer. Mark strummed softly on his
guitar, while Steve reloaded his Bolex with a fresh roll of Kodak
Tri-X black-and-white film, wishing he'd spent the extra for color
and wishing he could be alone with Sophie in this romantic place
instead of bunking with Mark Brandsteader and Cal Wright. He
wasn't comfortable around either of them; Cal especially made him
uptight. But he could never have coped with lodging in a village
home, trying to relate and interact across a linguistic and cultural
barrier, when he had a hard enough time relating and interacting
with people of his own language and culture.

"How long you been shootin' movies with that thing?" Cal said.

"A little over a year."

"Looks pretty intricate. Must take a lotta skill to operate it."

"It's pretty simple once you learn the basics."

"The only kinda camera I know how to use is my little Instamatic."

"They make Instamatic movie cameras, too," Steve said. "I have one. You're welcome to try it any time."

"So, you get sound and everything with that camera?"

"No, not sound. You need a much more expensive camera and a special synchronized tape recorder for that."

"So then how do you film people talking?"

"You don't. If you're a low-budget filmmaker like me, you just shoot scenes where people are doing things but not talking. Then, afterwards, you can record a narration or a music track. You can add that in later because it doesn't have to be precisely synchronized."

"So you're gonna do that with this film?"

"Yes."

Out of the monthly funding he got from his parents, Steve had bought enough film to last the week; he'd gone for the cheaper black-and-white option so that he could buy more film and make a longer movie without having to hit up his parents for more money. Filming turned out to be a touchy operation, however, as some of the villagers were sensitive about the gringo with the fancy camera filming houses they imagined were hovels to American eyes. But just as Steve had learned to go gently with the camera in his communal house, he learned quickly where he could and couldn't film in San Gregorio.

By Tuesday, some of the kids were edgy and had begun whining for the comforts and diversions of home. The grown-ups conferred and decided that Steve and Sophie would take the nine- to twelve-year-olds on an outing to Ensenada, an hour's drive away, in Steve's bus. There was little room to spare and they hadn't planned on including any of the host children, but Susan insisted on bringing Reyna. So they all bumped together, packed tightly into the bus, over the twenty-two-mile dirt road that connected San Gregorio to the coastal highway. An additional twenty minutes on the highway brought them into Ensenada, where they parked near the beach.

"Why is everything so dirty here?" Robby Mason asked Steve as they walked along a street of tourist shops near the waterfront.

"Because Mexico is a poor country," Steve said, lifting his camera to get a high-angle shot of the passing parade of American tourists. "They can't afford to keep things clean all the time."

"Is everybody in Mexico poor?"

"No, not everybody. There are rich Mexicans, and there are middle-class Mexicans, but most are poor. At least, by our standards."

"Why?"

"Because Mexico is a Third World country. It's still developing. Remember we talked about that in class?" Steve raised the camera again to film Melissa as she stopped to admire an abalone-shell pendant on a leather-string necklace hanging outside one of the stores.

"Do Mexicans hate us because we're rich and they're poor?" Melissa said into the lens of the unhearing camera.

"No, most of them like us," Steve said, lowering the camera. "They only dislike us when we're disrespectful to them, or when we flaunt our wealth."

"What does 'flaunt' mean?"

"It means showing off. Acting like we're better than they are because we have more money."

They resumed walking and then stopped again, this time to

watch a man in a little sidewalk shop tooling designs into leather belts and purses. Steve filmed the man, who smiled broadly, and then filmed the kids watching him.

"You were flaunting last night," Melissa suddenly said to Tami. "You were showing off your money to Ofelia."

Steve stopped filming.

"I was *not* showing off!" Tami said. "I was just showing her what American money looks like!"

"You were *too* showing off. You had a big proud grin on your face."

"A dime and a dollar bill—that's all I showed her. It's not like I had a whole bunch of money to show off. I'm not exactly rich, you know."

"You're rich compared to them. And you *were* showing off."

"*Shut up*, Melissa. *You're* the one who's always bragging about how rich you are. You talk about it all the time, how much money your mom gets—"

"You're fulla shit."

"That's enough, girls," Steve said. "This isn't the way we treat each other at SCOS."

"How come a peso's only worth eight cents?" Melissa said, abruptly changing the subject.

"Because that's the rate of exchange," Steve said. "A peso buys the same as eight cents buys. Ten pesos buys the same as eighty cents. Come on, let's walk faster. We're gonna get separated from the group."

The kids kept wanting to stop and look at the craft items, searching for things to spend their money on. When it was time for lunch, they crossed the street and headed back toward where Steve's bus was parked. Another side of the street, another row of shops with pretty, touristy things. They were almost back to the bus when they realized that Tami was missing.

Steve waited at the bus with the kids while Sophie backtracked on one side of the street, Reyna on the other, asking the shopkeepers if they'd seen a nine-year-old *gringuita*, with long brown hair and a light complexion, acting like she was lost. Steve feared that Tami had slipped away from the group on purpose, in a snit over Melissa's accusation of "flaunting."

"It's your fault," Michelle said. "You hurt her feelings when you said she was showing off her money."

"Shut up," Melissa said. "I was just kidding her."

"No you weren't. You were laying a guilt trip on her, for serious."

"You're a fucking liar! Tami's my friend, and she understands me. She knew I was just kidding her."

"Bull*shit*. She's *my* friend, too, and I understand her a lot better than you do. She's very sensitive. I could tell she was hurt, for real."

"Hey," Steve said, "Let's cut it out. There's nothing to be gained by this."

The girls glowered at each other.

A long forty minutes went by, the kids cranky with hunger and Steve worried sick. Finally, Sophie and Reyna appeared with Tami in tow, her face streaked with tears.

She'd not, it turned out, left the group on account of Melissa's teasing. She had only stopped to admire a beautiful doll in a shop window, wishing she could afford its two-hundred-peso price.

After lunch, as Steve and Sophie sat holding hands on the beach, Tami looked out at the ocean. "Is that the same ocean as the one back home?"

"Yes," Sophie said. "That's the Pacific Ocean."

"Could you get all the way back to Santa Cruz by walking on the beach?"

"You could, but it would take you a long time."

"How far is it?"

"I don't know . . . maybe five, six hundred miles."

"How long would it take?"

"Months, probably." Sophie looked northward along the beach and Tami followed her gaze. Steve picked up his camera and filmed both of them from behind.

All in all, the trip was a success. It was a happy group of kids and grown-ups that assembled in front of the town hall Friday morning to prepare for the long drive home, with lots of warm good-byes, hugs and exchanges of addresses. The adults spoke of how wonderful it had been—no major mishaps other than Tami's getting lost and, miraculously, only two cases of "Montezuma's revenge."

Though Tami had pretended to be eager to leave, she cried when it was time to go. Sophie knew why. She knew Tami had never been so warm and safe, so loved and protected, as during those five days in the Becerra home.

"Are we going to drive straight through like we did coming down?" Mark said as they prepared to pile into the cars.

"I don't know," Martha said. "We're all pretty tired. I vote for stopping somewhere for the night."

"Like where?"

"I don't know . . . I guess L.A. would be the halfway point."

"Where would we stay in L.A.?" Toni said.

"I don't know," Martha said. "A park?"

Everyone had brought a sleeping bag just in case there hadn't been enough beds in the San Gregorio homes.

"Most city parks won't let you camp overnight," Mark said.

"Hey," Sophie said, "maybe my parents would let us stay for the night."

"Would they have room for all of us?"

"Not in the house, but we could camp out in the backyard."

"That seems like a big imposition to make on your folks," Martha said. "But if you think they'd be cool with it, that'd be great."

As soon as they were back over the border in San Ysidro, California, Sophie called her parents collect from a pay phone and asked their permission to have the group descend on them. After a lengthy consultation, they said yes.

Three hours later, the SCOS convoy rolled into Van Nuys and pulled up in front of the modest ranch-style house that had been the Hearn family home for as long as Sophie had lived.

Sophie still hadn't told her parents about Steve, and during the drive up from the border she'd worried about how, given the bad blood between the two families, they would react when she presented him to them. She hoped they wouldn't connect the surname with his parents.

But they did. And if they were at all discomfited, they took great pains not to show it. They welcomed Steve warmly to their home, recalling how he and Sophie had played there together as children. Sophie saw him react with pleasant surprise and hoped that perhaps this would release him from his preoccupation with the two families' mysterious falling-out.

While Larry barbecued hamburgers on the backyard grill, the little kids played little-kid games with Joanne and the older ones played ping-pong or sat around singing with Sophie and Mark. Steve circulated and provided general supervision. When the hamburgers (and a grilled-cheese sandwich for Melissa) were ready, everyone talked about how glad they were to be back in the USA eating American food. Larry and Ruth were fascinated by the group's experience in Mexico. Mark, Martha and the Wrights, whom Sophie had told about her father and the black-list, were eager to talk to him about it, and Larry was more than happy to oblige.

"Were you one of the Hollywood Ten?" Cal said as they sat in the living room after dinner.

"No," Larry said. "I wasn't that important. But we knew most of them."

It was during this time, while the rest of the kids were playing games in the backyard and her father was holding court in the living room, that Sophie brought Tami, the two Vaughn girls and Melissa into her old bedroom, which they'd asked to see. The room remained much as it had been during her junior high and high school years.

"You had this whole room all to yourself?" Tami said, her voice and expression characteristically combining amazement with a touch of sadness.

"Yes."

It felt at once strange and pleasant for Sophie, to be standing there alongside those Santa Cruz girls—embodiments of her present-day life—as the room's primeval memories swirled about her.

"Can we sleep in here with you tonight?" Tami said.

"I'm not sleeping in here tonight," Sophie said. "I'm camping out with you guys in the backyard."

"Did you have a lot of toys when you were little?" Michelle said.

"I had a lot of dolls. I had dolls of every size, shape and nationality."

"Do you still have them?"

"Yes, but they're packed in boxes in the garage. I haven't seen them since I was nine years old."

"Can we see them?"

"I don't know if I can find them. They're up on a high shelf somewhere. But I'll go look and see."

"Can we come with you?" Tami said.

"It's very dirty and dusty in there," Sophie said.

"We don't mind."

"No, we don't care," Michelle said. "We're dirty anyway from the trip."

"Are there spiders?" Melissa said.

"Probably," Sophie said.

All four girls made gestures of aversion and ran back out to rejoin the group, so Sophie went to the garage alone to look for her old dolls. She remembered, in particular, a Mexican doll in traditional dress that probably looked like the one Tami had admired in Ensenada. If she could find it, she wanted to give it to Tami privately when they were back in Santa Cruz.

She entered the garage through the side door and smelled the familiar smell of dust and decomposing cardboard. She looked up and saw boxes everywhere: boxes on the low shelves, boxes on the high shelves, boxes on top of boards set over the rafters, only an occasional one labeled. Her parents had never been very good about labeling boxes of things. She knew that many of those boxes had been there since before the family's move to Mexico City in 1956 and remained in place, never unpacked, after fifteen years. Her dolls would be in one of those.

She set up the extension ladder and climbed up, peeking in all the unlabeled boxes she could reach on each shelf, moving the ladder sideways to reach more boxes, repeating the process again and again. She found no trace of the dolls. They could have been in one of the boxes on the rafters, but her parents' cars blocked her from placing the ladder there.

She decided to give up on the dolls, but an item she'd noticed on one of the uppermost shelves had piqued her curiosity. She climbed back up and looked at it again. It had appeared at first to be a small reddish-brown suitcase, but when she tugged on it, she was startled to find it so heavy that it could have been filled with bricks. She rotated it so its end was facing her and saw a speaker and a socket for a power cord. A small brass plate—she could barely make out the lettering in the garage's dim light—identified the weighty object as a Webster Chicago Wire Recorder. Nearby on the shelf she found a small cardboard box with the faintly penciled words "wire recordings" in her father's familiar block lettering.

She pulled the device off the shelf by its translucent-red plastic handle and its weight nearly pulled her off the ladder and sent her crashing to the garage floor. For a scary moment, the machine swung wildly back and forth, but she managed to regain her balance, descend the ladder, and lower the thing safely to the concrete.

Kneeling, she opened the clasps and lifted the dust-caked lid. She saw knobs and levers that triggered a long-ago memory of getting in trouble by touching them. At the top, toward the rear, was a thick spindle holding a spool of metal wire. She pulled out a little of the wire—it was like a guitar string, only much thinner. When she let go, it curled into a tangled mass. She grew excited at the thought of bringing this thing to Steve, fascinated as he was by vintage equipment, old machines, the long-obsolete technologies of yesteryear. Surely he'd want to show it to the students in his History of Audiovisual Technology class.

She climbed back up the ladder and brought down the "wire recordings" box. Leaving the recorder and the box on the floor of the garage, she went into the house to ask her father if she could borrow them. But when she saw him still regaling his guests with tales of the blacklist—he was telling the story of her schoolmate who had almost blown his pseudonym—she decided not to interrupt him. That thing had obviously been up on that high shelf for many, many years. He had most likely forgotten it was there and would never miss it. So she lugged the heavy machine out front and set it, along with the box of wire recordings, into the rear cargo space of Steve's bus.

When she got back, the kids and the grown-ups were rolling out their sleeping bags on the grass of the backyard. Steve had already laid Sophie's bag out next to his near the warmth of the barbecue pit.

"I have a surprise for you when we get home," she said.

CHAPTER 22

Crises

The Mexican adventure, wonderful though it had been for the participants, failed to fulfill its purpose of revitalizing the school and boosting morale. The kids who had been on the trip couldn't stop talking about it, but those who hadn't gone felt left out and resentful. As the excitement died down, routines were reestablished and spirit-breaking boredom once again set in.

Sophie and Joanne grew impatient with Steve. He was so obsessed with the editing of the film footage he'd shot in Mexico that he was neglecting his duties in both the school and the house. During the short breaks between instructional periods, he would dash up to his room to do "a little" work on the film and then become so engrossed that he'd forget when it was time for the next class to begin, forcing someone to go up and fetch him. He spent countless after-school hours at his editing viewer, often refusing to join the group dinner and conveniently "forgetting" his assigned household tasks.

His single-minded involvement with the Mexico film became a serious issue between him and Sophie.

"I feel like you've been ignoring me," she said to him one day after school.

"*Ignoring* you?"

"It's like I don't exist anymore."

"I haven't been ignoring you. I'm just busy with the film."

"I know you are. And I understand that the film is important to you. But you can't just shut out everything else."

"What am I shutting out?"

"Besides me, you're shutting out the school. And the kids. And the house."

"That's not true. You're exaggerating."

"You haven't even bothered to look at the old recording machine I almost killed myself carrying down the ladder in my parents' garage. I thought you'd be fascinated by it."

"I'm just too busy with this right now. I promise I'll look at it later."

After this frustrating, dead-end conversation, Sophie's mood dropped like a rock. Steve had always been able to pull her at least partway out of her depressions, but this time he made only a halfhearted effort, his head still deep in the film. He apologized and went back to his work, leaving her to swim alone through the relentless hours of darkness.

As Sophie struggled to deal with Steve's inattention, the interpersonal environment in the school continued steadily downhill. Melissa and Lauren became the center of a clique that was bullying and intimidating other girls. A newly-enrolled twelve-year-old boy named Chad developed an instant mutual enmity with Joey, who was also once again being teased and rejected by the other kids (his mother had kept him home from the Mexico trip, fearing it would place too much of a strain on his social skills). The conflict between Chad and Joey was an issue Steve was obliged to deal with, both of them being in his History of Technology class, and he wasn't dealing with it well. The two boys' altercations frequently disrupted the class and forced an early adjournment, which the others resented.

Steve knew he was causing all manner of trouble by letting the Mexico film consume him, but he couldn't seem to stop. Though he realized he was hurting Sophie and shirking his duties in the school, he was stuck in a groove he couldn't find his way out of. Feeling a need to escape, he took to smoking pot nearly every afternoon after the kids were gone, but the drug sent his mind into an even more distant place and made the already-bad situation worse.

After a few weeks of this, Sophie and Joanne decided that enough was enough. They confronted Steve one day after school at his editing table.

"You've got to stop running away," Joanne said. "What you're doing isn't fair to the school and isn't fair to Sophie. You've got to come back on board and focus on the kids, and on the woman you love—if you still love her."

"I know your Mexico movie is important to you," Sophie said, "and I know you need to work on it, but it's not your main job here. Your main job here is teaching and helping us run the school."

"The kids have been asking, 'Why is Steve ignoring us? Is he mad at us?'" Joanne said.

"And you've got to stop getting stoned every day," Sophie said. "You've stopped helping out around the house. You hardly ever eat dinner with us, and whenever we try to talk to you, you act spaced-out. It's really bugging Karen and John. It's like you're not really here anymore. And you need to show more leadership with Chad and Joey. Their fights are becoming a major source of negative energy in the school. Anne is really upset about it and she's threatening to pull Joey out."

"So let her pull him out," Steve said. "At least that'll solve that problem."

"How can you talk like that!" Sophie said, her eyes angrily piercing his. "What's happened to you? What's happened to all the love and caring you had for the kids? All the wonderful stuff you were doing with Joey, and now you're just going to abandon him? You've changed, Steve. And I don't like the change. It's hurting me. It's hurting us, and it's hurting the kids."

Throughout all of this, Steve had sat and glared defiantly, but now his angry expression turned to sadness. Later in the evening, when they were alone in Sophie's room, he managed to summon up a weak apology for his behavior and an unconvincing promise that he'd "try" to do better. Then he immediately became amorous.

She pushed him away. "I won't make love with you when you've been smoking dope."

"Why?"

"You're not a good lover when you're stoned. You're not sensitive and gentle like you used to be."

"You're imagining that."

"No, I'm not."

"I need to get high. It helps my creativity with the film."

"Then we'll just have to not sleep together while you're working on the film. And by the way, I think that's bullshit. I don't think getting stoned makes you more creative. It just makes you more self-absorbed."

Steve had no answer for this. He hung his head and left the room.

After Sophie's and Joanne's scoldings, Steve went into a depression. He wanted to ask Sophie to help him pull out of it, as he'd done for her so many times, but how could he now?

Suddenly the Mexico film, for which he had jeopardized everything that mattered to him, no longer felt important. The flickery black-and-white images of San Gregorio he saw when he cranked the film through the viewer made him think, *So what?* So he'd gone to Mexico and shot some film—who would watch it other than the people who'd been on the trip? For what reason had he spent all that money? To what end had he neglected everything he loved?

He knew he couldn't fix it by begging pardon and pledging to change his ways. He'd lost all confidence in his ability to control his own behavior. How could he make promises without knowing if he could keep them? How could he apologize when he knew he might go right back to doing the things he'd apologized for? His world was slowly collapsing and he had nothing to hold on to. He thought about professional counseling, but that would've required asking his parents for money; they would have wanted to know what it was for, and he didn't want to discuss it with them.

He ended up confiding in the one person besides Sophie whom he knew understood and appreciated him, the person who had brought him into the house and into the life he now knew: Karen.

"You're a beautiful person, Steve," she said as they sat at the kitchen table. "The way you've been isn't the real you. It's just a bad trip you're on. Just be yourself again."

"I don't know what myself is anymore."

"Yes, you do. Just look at the inner you. Shut out the Mexico movie and the dope and all that other garbage."

"But what do I *do*? How do I undo all the damage I've done?"

"Don't try to do it all at once. Just do it a little at a time."

So that was what he did. He took a small step, then another. He smoked less dope. He cut down on the time he was spending on the Mexico film and became more attentive to Sophie. He made sure he was doing his share of the housework. By increments, he reengaged with the children and once again began to work closely with Joey.

Then one evening he asked Sophie to come out to dinner with him.

"Of course," she said, clearly surprised and delighted.

He took her to a seafood restaurant on the Santa Cruz wharf, a romantic place they'd gone to once before. He had made up his mind to talk to her but wasn't sure what he was going to say or if he'd have the courage to say it. He had planned on waiting until they finished their dinner, but before the waiter had even come to take their orders, he looked into her eyes and a tear rolled down his cheek. He tried to say something and couldn't. She put a finger over her lips; he knew she knew what he'd wanted to say. She reached across the table and took his hand just as the waiter arrived to take their order.

"We're not quite ready yet," Sophie said and watched the waiter walk away. "Let's get out of here."

They left the restaurant and walked slowly toward the end of the wharf, arms around each other, listening to the barking of the sea lions. No words were needed.

The old Steve returned.

He got his priorities back in order. He flushed what was left of his dope down the toilet. He continued to work sporadically on the Mexico film but spent most of his time helping Joanne and Sophie figure out how to deal with the multiple problems that had developed in the school. Once back on board, he became a fount of ideas; in one all-day Saturday meeting, he helped author a new set of plans that entailed new rules, new activities, a more engaging curriculum, regular rap sessions with the students to address the social environment, and a new strategy for helping Joey.

The plans were a surprising success. The kids accepted and, for the most part, abided by the new standards. They participated constructively in the rap sessions, and while the cliquish behavior among the middle-grade girls didn't go away entirely, it diminished noticeably after the teachers took a hard line on put-downs and disrespect. Steve was once again working one-on-one with Joey, who was being treated slightly better—even by Chad.

Sophie and Steve got their relationship back on track, and Steve, determined never to let things go bad again, was more loving and attentive than ever before. Once again they were spending their time outside of school hours together, sharing experiences, making plans—albeit vague ones—for the future.

*

Mr. Carlton, the property owner's agent, knocked on a Saturday afternoon. Karen answered the door, Sophie close behind her.

"I'm afraid I've got some bad news for you all," Mr. Carlton said.

"What's that?" Karen said.

"This property's been sold. You have to vacate by May 20 at the latest."

"*What?*" Sophie said.

"Mr. Strohm's been trying to sell this place for some time now, and he'd hoped to sell it sooner. So you've all been living on borrowed time, so to speak."

According to Mr. Carlton, Mr. Strohm had found a buyer willing to meet his price, a developer who planned to demolish the old house and erect a large—and lucrative—apartment building on the lot.

"Ernie wants to close the deal as soon as possible," Mr. Carlton said. "He's not a wealthy man, you know. This piece of property was his only real asset. The buyer's anxious to get started on his project and Ernie's anxious to get his money, so they agreed on a short escrow. They're closing May 21."

"That's not enough time," Karen said.

"Thirty days' notice. It's in your rental contract."

"We're running a school here," Sophie said.

"A *school?*"

"Yes."

"What kind of school?"

"Kindergarten through seventh grade."

"Well, now, I'm not even sure that's legal. It certainly wasn't what Ernie had in mind when he rented you this place. He rented it as a residence."

"Can't we just have until the middle of June? When school ends?"

"You'd have to take that up with the new owner, and I can almost guarantee you he'll say no. From what I understand, he's planning to come in with the wrecking ball the day escrow closes."

They called an emergency meeting for parents, where they learned that none of them had room in their homes for the school and nobody knew of a suitable site. Not even worrying yet about where she and Steve and John and Karen were going to live, Sophie got on the phone and called everybody she knew who might know of a place—a church, a vacant house, anything—where the school could function for just a month. She got a few leads, but none panned out.

It was desperation time.

A few days into May, one of Sophie's former free-clinic colleagues told her of a community center in Watsonville, fifteen miles to the south, that might have a room available to rent. She called and made an appointment with the director.

It was a long shot. The head of the center hadn't sounded particularly enthusiastic when Sophie had described the school. And then, even if it worked out, there was the geography. Fifteen miles was a long way for the parents to drive twice a day five days a week. But she was in no position to rule out anything. It would just be for a month. The parents could carpool, and Steve could ferry some of the kids in his bus.

She headed out in her VW on a beautiful sunny morning, leaving Joanne and Steve in charge of the school. As she drove south on the Highway One freeway, she was in a surprisingly up mood.

She felt a surge of pride in Steve. How he'd changed; how far he'd come in such a short time. How he had grown in his ability to work with kids, and what a miracle worker he'd been with Joey. How beautiful their relationship was once again. She hoped the meeting with the community-center director, successful or not, would be quick so that she could get back to Steve and the kids before the end of the school day.

The morning dragged for Steve. He hated having to teach the middle- and upper-grade children together. He filled some of the time with joint lessons on history and science that were appropriate for both levels, but they still had to do their math, reading and writing assignments separately, and it was stressful to have to keep going back and forth between groups. At the same time, he had to keep a handle on the social dynamics, especially the negative interaction between Joey and the middle-grade girls, a few of whom still occasionally baited him with cruel "cooties" cracks, laughing at his angry responses.

But then came the History of Audiovisual Technology class, which was always fun and satisfying for Steve. He had a great rapport with the five pupils in the class, all boys from nine to thirteen (an attempt to get some girls in had failed) with a strong interest in the topic. With Chad and Joey in at least a temporary cease-fire, the class was running smoothly.

Joey was the most eager participant. When Steve showed the group how he was editing the Mexico movie, every step of the process had fascinated Joey, every piece of equipment, even the type of glue he was using to splice his edits. He'd listened intently when Steve spoke of a wonderful new medium called videotape that might one day replace movie film. On this particular day, however, Joey had something else on his mind.

Joey spent every other weekend at his father's mountain home in Los Gatos, off the freeway to San Jose. He'd described the house in detail to Steve: the redwood paneling, the huge picture windows, the outdoor hot tub with the spectacular view. Now he was breathlessly giving Steve the news about the new stereo system his dad was planning to buy.

"He's getting a Marantz receiver and an Ampex tape deck. It's the coolest deck you've ever seen." Joey then recited a long checklist of the tape recorder's features and specifications, delving into data that was beyond even Steve's comprehension. It always pleased him to see the lonely, alienated boy excited about something.

Soon class was over and it was lunchtime. An idea suddenly occurred to Steve.

"Joey," he said, "I have something to show you that I think you'll find interesting. It's part of the history of sound-recording technology, and I was planning to bring it to class sometime this week, but I'm going to show it to you first."

"Cool," Joey said.

"I'm going to go up now and get it ready. Go eat your lunch. By the time you're finished, I'll have it all set up. Then I'll come get you."

Sophie's conference with Rosa Barrios, director of the Centro de Comunidad de Watsonville, went better than she'd expected. It turned out she had been one of the first Chicanas to graduate from UCSC. She was amazed by Sophie's command of Spanish and fascinated by her story.

"So, your *papá* was on that Hollywood blacklist?"

"Yes."

"You know the movie *Salt of the Earth*? About the miners' strike?"

"Of course."

"Wasn't that made by blacklisted Hollywood people?"

"Yes, and they were all friends of my parents'."

"Really! I'm impressed. You must have had a very interesting childhood."

"Maybe a little too interesting."

They talked about the workings of a free school and the makeup of the student body.

"Unfortunately, it's all white," Sophie said. "I tried my best to get at least some minority kids, but I couldn't find any black or Chicano parents who were interested."

"That's because schools that are loosely structured are a turn-off to minority parents. They want their kids in regular schools so they'll learn to survive in white society."

"I understand that. I wish I knew what to do about it."

"If you moved your school here, I might be able to find you a few Chicano kids. I know a lot of parents who are very unhappy with the schools here in Watsonville."

"Would you have room for us here?"

"How many rooms would you need?"

"Two small ones or one medium-sized. We have partitions we use to divide the rooms. And remember, it's just for one month."

"We have a medium-sized room you could use for a month."

Sophie had but a moment to enjoy the elation of a huge problem solved before reality hit and she realized that it couldn't possibly work.

The distance was too great. The parents would balk at driving that far, and organizing carpools would be a nightmare. Anne McComb would never make that trip in the old wreck of a car she drove—she'd just pull Joey out for the last month. Some of the families lived in the hills and would have even farther to drive. Alice Hagar's car had broken down some time ago and she couldn't afford to get it fixed, so she'd been depending on a neighbor to bring Tami into town each day and would certainly have no way of getting her to Watsonville. Steve could accommodate six or seven kids in his minibus, but driving all over the mountains to pick up the more isolated kids in the morning and bring them back in the afternoon would hardly be feasible. In her desperation, she'd failed to think it through adequately.

"You know," she said sadly, "now that I think about it, it wouldn't work. It's too far for the parents to drive."

"That's a shame," Rosa said. "But you know what? I have an uncle here in town who owns a small warehouse in Santa Cruz. Could you have your school in a warehouse?"

"We could have it anywhere that has a roof over it."

"I don't know if he's using it for anything right now. If he's not, he might rent it to you for a reasonable price if it's just for a month."

"That would be perfect."

"Let me call him and see if he's home."

Rosa dialed her uncle's number, but there was no answer. She said her uncle, a retired factory supervisor and a heavy drinker, sometimes went out to buy liquor but was rarely gone for long. Eager to jump on this possible salvation, Sophie decided to stick around while Rosa made repeated attempts to contact him. As midday approached, Rosa invited her for a free lunch at a home-style Mexican restaurant owned by another, non-drinking uncle.

When they returned, Rosa tried again and finally reached the uncle with the warehouse. Luckily, he was sober. He said no, the warehouse was not being used, and he'd be happy to meet with Sophie at his house in an hour.

Knowing she wouldn't make it home until late afternoon, Sophie decided to call Steve and tell him to cancel the emergency-update parents' meeting they'd scheduled for after school. She used the community center's phone and called collect, since Santa Cruz was a long-distance call from Watsonville, and heard John answer and accept the charges in an uncharacteristically somber voice that startled her.

"Sophie," he said before she had a chance to say anything, "you gotta come home right away."

"Why? What's wrong?"

"Steve."

"What's the matter?"

"He's acting strange. *Very* strange."

John recounted how he'd been sitting in the living room reading when Steve had gone up to his room at lunchtime.

"He was holed up in there the whole lunch hour," John said, "and for a while I could hear, like, faint voices from a radio or something. Then after a while the voices stopped, but he was still in his room with the door closed. Then lunch was over and it was time for him to go teach his students, but he still didn't come out of his room. So then Joanne called through the back door and told me to go up and remind him to come down and teach his class, 'cause the kids were waiting. So I go up and knock on his door. He doesn't answer, so I knock again. I said, 'Hey, Steve, they want you down there, your students are waiting for you,' and he yells back at me, 'Go away! Leave me alone!' in this real angry tone I'd never heard from him before. It kind of freaked me out. So I said, 'Hey, Steve, what is it?' a coupla times, no answer. I try the door—it's locked."

"Jesus Christ," Sophie said softly. "What the hell's going on?"

"I have no idea," John said. "So anyway, I told Karen to go up and see if he'd talk to her, 'cause I know he really digs Karen, so she went up and knocked, tried to talk to him through the door, like, 'Hey Steve, the kids are waiting for you, what's wrong, what's the matter?' and all that, but he *still* doesn't answer. So I guess Joanne took over and worked with all the kids together. Anyway, that's the way things stand right now. School's over, the parents are starting to come for the meeting, and Steve still won't talk to anybody or come out of his room. Something's eatin' him real bad."

"Go knock on his door again and tell him I want to talk to him."

"Right on. I'll have Karen do it."

Sophie waited, oblivious to the cost of the phone call.

Karen finally got on the phone, deep trouble in her voice. "Soph," she said, "I don't know what's going on. I told him you were on the phone and wanted to talk to him. I could hear sounds coming from inside the room—it sounded almost like he was packing or something—but he wouldn't answer."

"I'll be there in twenty minutes," Sophie said. "Tell the parents the meeting's called off."

She made a vague and hasty explanation to Rosa, asked her to call her uncle and cancel their appointment, jumped into her car and sped off.

As she pulled into the driveway, the first thing Sophie noticed was the absence of Steve's bus. The children were gone except for Joanne's three and a few others who hadn't been picked up yet.

Karen reported the following: Shortly after she and Sophie had finished talking on the phone, Steve had suddenly burst out of his room carrying two suitcases. He had descended the stairs rapidly and tramped through the living room, tears streaming down his face. After dropping a note on the kitchen table, he'd gone out the back door, avoiding the kids, and driven away in his bus.

"He was freaked out, man," John said. "*Really* freaked out. Never seen him like that before."

"Soph," Karen said, "here's the note he dropped on the kitchen table, and another one he left upstairs taped to your door. I've only read the one from the table." She handed Sophie the two notes, both written on lined yellow paper from a legal pad. One was folded over several times and had Scotch tape stuck to it.

The unfolded note was addressed to nobody:

I'm leaving and not coming back. This is for good. I've left all my stuff here. Don't want it. Sell it or give it away. I know this is sudden, but I have to go. Sophie can explain why. Sorry to all the kids and everyone else I'm leaving behind, especially Joey. Love you all. Steve

The folded note said:

Sophie, I can't stay here. Can't be here. Can't be with you. Not your fault. Play the recording on your dad's old machine and you'll understand. Goodbye. Sorry. I love you and will always love you. Steve

*

In the days and weeks that followed Steve's departure, Sophie would curse her impulsive decision to take the wire recorder from the garage of her childhood home. On the day Steve left, after reading his note, she went to his room and found the ancient thing in the middle of the floor, still powered on and humming, the open box of wire spools sitting next to it. The spool he had left on the recorder had a faded label with several names in her father's printing, one of them "Elwood."

When she turned the playback lever—as she'd once done naughtily as a child—she heard the sounds of a noisy room gradually quieting down. Then she heard someone call Arthur Elwood's name.

She instantly knew what the recording was, and she knew she would soon know what she hadn't wanted to know.

Poor though the sound quality was, Sophie could clearly hear Arthur respond as he was asked to repeat and spell his name and to recount his personal history, his education, his experience as a screenwriter in Hollywood. She listened to Arthur's lengthy recitation of his employments and assignments with studios, his memberships in trade organizations. Then she heard one of his questioners refer to a Communist Party registration card of which they had a photostat (another old technology) and ask Arthur if the card was his.

He said yes, it was.

On the staticky, tinny recording, Sophie listened to Arthur Elwood as he remorsefully confessed to having joined the Communist Party in the early 1940s, calling it a mistake born of naïve idealism. She heard him chronicle, in long-winded detail, the various liberal causes he and his wife had championed—unionism, anti-fascism, world peace, racial equality—and how they had "foolishly" embraced Communism as a means to those ends.

Then she heard Arthur Elwood name names.

Many names.

She felt sick and dizzy as she heard the father of the man she loved give the questioning congressmen names of people who had been in the Party with him, people who had served on committees with him or been at meetings with him. One after another she heard him spell out the names for the clerk to stenograph into the record, painstakingly betraying to the inquisitors the names that would be on the next round of subpoenas.

Hearn. H-E-A-R-N.

Yes, among the names he offered up—regretfully, he said for the record—was that of his "dear friend" Larry Hearn, who he claimed had recruited him into the Party.

Now it all added up.

The "falling-out" between the two families. Steve's saying his father had continued writing under his own name during the blacklist period—making enough money to live the good life in Newport Beach, with a boat and a Cadillac, enough to buy his son thousands of dollars' worth of filmmaking equipment and a brand-new VW minibus—but had said the blacklist was "too painful" to talk about.

Steve had lived proudly in the belief that his father, like Sophie's, refused to cooperate with the House Un-American Activities Committee. But Larry Hearn had recorded the truth from the radio, never imagining that his old toy, forgotten and left on a high garage shelf for two decades, would one day reach out from the past to haunt another father's lie.

CHAPTER 23

Set on Edge

The day after Steve left, Sophie called Newport Beach Information and got his parents' phone number. She dialed the number and Rosemary Elwood answered. Sophie nervously identified herself.

"Hello, dear," Rosemary said, sounding normal at first. "I remember you when you were just a tiny little thing."

"Have you seen Steve?"

Rosemary burst into sobs. "He came here last night, while I was up in the bedroom reading and Artie was working late in his study," she said, struggling to compose herself. "He went into his father's study . . . and said the most horrible things to him . . . and then he left before I even knew he'd been here."

"Oh, no."

"He'd found out something we'd kept from him, something his father wasn't proud of . . . we'd kept it from him because we knew how much it would hurt him . . . it was the reason your parents never spoke to us again. I went into Artie's study and found him sitting there crying. It took me at least ten minutes to calm him down enough to tell me what had happened. We don't know how Stevie found out. I'm sure you must have known about it from your folks."

"No. They never told me. He found out by listening to a recording."

"A recording?"

Sophie told her about the wire recorder. Rosemary made no response at first, as if she didn't quite grasp it. Finally she said, "Your father made that recording?"

"Yes," Sophie said.

"And Artie was on it?"

"Yes."

"His . . . his testimony? All of it?"

"Yes."

"And Stevie heard it?"

"Yes."

"Oh, my God," she said. Then, after a long pause: "You have no idea how ashamed Artie was of what he did." She paused again. "When Stevie was a teenager, he somehow got the notion that his father had done what your father did. Artie couldn't bear to tell him the truth, knowing how it would diminish him in Stevie's eyes, so he let him go on thinking that. You have no idea what lengths Artie went to to keep him from finding out. We moved down here to Newport to minimize the chance that he'd come into contact with Hollywood people. People who would know."

"I'm so sorry. It was my fault."

"No, of course it wasn't your fault, dear. Like you said . . . there was no way you could've known what was on that recording."

"Do you know where he is now?"

"No, and I'm worried sick." Rosemary choked up again. "If you hear from him, please tell him to call his mother right away."

After Steve was gone, Sophie found out just how loved she was.

When the SCOS parents learned what had happened, they went into action. They contacted Rosa Barrios' uncle in Watsonville and arranged to rent his Santa Cruz warehouse for four weeks, then pitched in to move the school there. They helped Sophie, John and Karen move out of their beloved old house, clearing out the last of their belongings just before demolition day, and helped figure out what to do with Steve's stuff—they donated his camera and moviemaking equipment to UCSC's nascent film program, the rest to Goodwill. They came to the school's new location to help out with everything, including teaching; some days it seemed there were as many adults there as children. Sophie was there as often as she could manage, and when she was, everyone was overjoyed to see her. When she couldn't cope, she stayed away and everyone understood. When she needed to be alone, she was left alone, but when she needed company there was always a parent ready to invite her to dinner.

The kids missed Steve terribly, and those who had been closest to him made it known how hurt and abandoned they felt. Joey simply refused to go to school for the last four weeks.

Joanne did a wonderful job of explaining to the students of each age level as much as they were able to grasp about why Steve had left. The younger ones were told that he and Sophie had had a parting of the ways and he'd needed to go off and be by himself, but the eleven- to thirteen-year-olds got the full story, and they understood.

They got a crash course on the Hollywood blacklist and the many issues connected with it. There were discussions about betrayals, deceptions and tangled webs, whether parents should ever lie to their children and whether children inherited the sins of their parents. Leanne Mason even pulled an Old Testament quote from the memory bank of her Christian childhood: "The fathers have eaten sour grapes, and the children's teeth are set on edge."

A week before school ended, Sophie had a bittersweet farewell dinner with John and Karen. The couple had found a small cabin to rent in Ben Lomond, about ten miles up Highway Nine in the upper San Lorenzo Valley. Sophie had moved into a guest cottage behind the Masons' hillside home that they let her have rent-free, including the use of their hot tub and sauna, for as long as she wanted to stay there.

But by then she had realized it was time for her to leave Santa Cruz.

CHAPTER 24

The Real World

1971

Sophie spoke of many things with her mother the summer she moved back home.

They spoke of Steve and his father.

"How could he have kept it from him all these years?" Sophie wondered out loud.

"Artie probably devoted his whole life to keeping it from him," Ruth said. "I'm not at all surprised."

"Why?"

"Artie was a very weak man. Was and still is. He'd told us he planned to non-cooperate, but he caved at the last moment. He enjoyed the good life he'd had as a successful screenwriter, and he wasn't enough of a mensch to do the right thing if it meant giving all that up . . . But then, after he cooperated, he couldn't face the ostracism by his former friends. He begged everyone to forgive him."

"Including you and Dad?"

"Especially us. We'd been their best friends."

"And you wouldn't speak to them."

"No, and it felt very cold, Artie being as pathetic as he was. I was tempted to talk to Rosie, I felt so sorry for her. I didn't put any of the blame on her. She'd probably wanted him to non-cooperate. But there wasn't any point. Anything I could've said to her would only have made it worse."

"He named Dad. I heard it on the recording."

"Yes, he did. He named many people he'd been close to. I can't blame him for not wanting his son to know. Did your father tell you he came up here?"

"He *what*?"

"He called your father and said he wanted to talk. They met at Charles' restaurant, and he begged your father not to tell you or Steve about his having been a stool pigeon."

"When was this?"

"Right after Thanksgiving."

"You mean . . . when we came here after the Mexico trip, you already knew about Steve and me?"

"Yes. And we had to pretend we didn't."

"What did he say to Dad?"

"I don't remember exactly. You'll have to ask him. All I remember is his saying Artie was pitiable and my saying there were others more deserving of my pity."

"Was Dad really the one who recruited him into the Party?"

"No. That was pure crap. They probably told him who they wanted him to name and what they wanted him to say about them. That's what they did—they gave you a script to read."

"You said you and Dad were already turned off to the Party when he was subpoenaed. Was he ever tempted to cooperate?"

"Absolutely not. How we felt about the Communist Party was never the issue. In a democracy, you have the right to be as naïve and misguided as we were. You have the right to change and grow and explore in your political beliefs. But the studios and HUAC were telling us we'd better not explore the wrong beliefs or they'd take away our careers. And when people like Artie stood before them and said, 'Yes, this person was a Communist and that person was a Communist,' they provided the justification for the government to keep up the witch hunts. And for the studios to keep up the blacklisting."

"I know. And I'm so lucky . . . so lucky to be able to say that *my* father did the right thing. I've been so proud of him, ever since I was old enough to understand what he did."

"Do you remember hearing him on the radio the day he testified?"

"No. But I remember your telling me about it."

"You were four years old. I told you that someday you'd be proud of what your daddy had done."

They spoke of many other things. Women's liberation, men, relationships. The complexity and ambiguity of politics and the dangers of simple-minded thinking in a complex world. The joys of working with children and the frightful acceleration of time as one grows older.

In the days and weeks following her arrival, Larry and Ruth told their daughter repeatedly how much they loved having her home again. Nevertheless, Sophie knew it came at the cost of the privacy they'd come to cherish. She had come home needy and vulnerable, her resilience shattered, her self-respect bruised and her heart broken. She needed her parents.

One afternoon, Sophie and her mother discussed her post-university time in Santa Cruz.

"I threw away two years," she said angrily. "Two years of living in a fantasy world."

"You loved it," Ruth said. "And it was an important growing time for you."

"No. It wasn't a growing time at all. It was an escape time. I was in a place that wasn't part of the real world."

The door to Sophie's room was open. "Rainy Days and Mondays," by the Carpenters, was playing on the radio.

"I think all your thinking is distorted now because of Steve," Ruth said. "I think you should take the summer, clear your mind, then go back up there and run that school. Make it even better than it was."

"Mom, that school no longer exists. They disbanded it when I told them I wasn't coming back. There were no teachers left except Joanne, and she couldn't do it alone."

"So get on that phone right now and call up Joanne and tell her you've changed your mind, you *are* coming back. Those people adore you, Sophie. I could see it the night you were here with them. Just tell them you're starting up the school again and they'll rally around you just like they did before. Surely you can find another teacher to replace Steve—"

"Mom, I don't *want* to. I don't want to go back to Santa Cruz."

"Because of the memories? Because of Steve?"

"*Fuck* Steve. I don't want to talk about him, I don't want to think about him, I don't even want to hear his name. No, it's not because of him. It's because that phase of my life is just over. Santa Cruz is over. Being a hippie is over."

"What's the next phase going to be?"

"I don't know. I don't want to think about it. I don't want

to think about anything. I just wanna space out. For a while, at least."

"I worry about you in there on your bed all the time. You're going to get yourself depressed. Why don't you call up some of your old friends and get together with them?"

"I don't feel like socializing. Don't worry about me."

"Maybe you should make an appointment with Harriet Melnick?"

Harriet Melnick was the left-wing psychologist all their friends went to when they needed counseling. Sophie had gone to her as a teenager, when her depressions had first started.

"Harriet Melnick can't help me," Sophie said. "I just have to wait out the bummers till they pass. That's what I've learned to do after many years' experience."

On the radio the Carpenters' song ended. After the KHJ station jingle and a commercial for West Covina Toyota, the disc jockey played a more upbeat song, "Don't Pull Your Love," by Hamilton, Joe Frank and Reynolds.

"Must you listen to that God-awful pop music when you're in your room?" Ruth said.

"That music relaxes me," Sophie said. "It grounds me in reality."

"With all your musical training, all your musicality, and you choose to listen to that crap music. Go play some Bach on the piano. That'll relax you a lot more."

She didn't feel like playing Bach on the piano. She didn't even feel like playing blues on her guitar, which she hadn't taken out of its case since Steve's disappearance.

"I'm going to go take a nap," she said.

"Dinner's in an hour."

"Wake me up."

Sophie closed the door, kicked off her shoes and lay on her bed. Surprisingly, she wasn't depressed. The room was poignant with the memory of the night Tami, Michelle, Susan and Melissa had stood there and asked about her dolls. The chain of events that had triggered . . . Would it have been better if she'd never found the wire recorder? Is ignorance ever bliss?

No. Truth is always best.

Perhaps that was why, instead of getting rid of the wire recorder, she had chosen to put it back on the high garage shelf exactly where she'd found it, the Elwood recording still in place on its spindle.

"Are you going to look for a job?" Larry asked his daughter over dinner.

"Yes, when I get my head together."

"What kind of job are you going to look for?"

"I have no idea."

"Sophie, honey," Ruth said, "if you're going to stay down here instead of going back to Santa Cruz, you really ought to consider becoming a real teacher."

"What do you mean, a 'real teacher'? You mean *public* school?"

"You've been talking about living in the real world. That's the real world."

"I don't think I could handle it."

"Don't be silly. Of course you could."

"You've always hated it."

"I've hated some things about it," Ruth said, "but overall I've loved it. And it's changing for the better. You can do a lot of things now you couldn't do before. They're experimenting with all kinds of new programs, and they're encouraging the teachers to be more creative."

"But the public schools are racist. Public school is where minority kids learn to be ashamed of their culture."

"That's changing, too. You're right, it was horrible. The principals used to tell us to punish the Mexican kids if they spoke Spanish at school. But they don't do that anymore, and you know what they're even talking about now? 'Bilingual education.' It could be the wave of the future—teaching kids in their native tongue until they learn English. Think of what an asset your Spanish would be."

"I'd need a credential, and I don't want to go back to school."

"Nonsense. It wouldn't be that bad. You take a few classes at Valley State, you do your student teaching and in a year or two you've got your credential."

"I don't know, Mom. I just can't even think about it now."

"Take your time."

It didn't take her long to reach a decision.

CHAPTER 25

False Cognates

1971-1975

Sophie's resolve to excise Steve Elwood from her mind and heart the summer after he disappeared lasted a few weeks. Then she began calling his parents once a week to ask if they'd heard from him. It was always Rosemary who answered, and she always said the same thing: "No, we haven't. And please, call us right away if *you* hear from him."

When she realized she was becoming a nuisance to the Elwoods, who were coping with their own pain, she called one last time and said she wouldn't call again but would they please call her if they heard from Steve. Rosemary assured her they would.

On August 14, 1971—just a few weeks after that final call—the Los Angeles Times ran an obituary for "award-winning screen and TV writer" Arthur Elwood, age fifty-five. His wife Rosemary had found him in his study at their Newport Beach home, dead from an overdose of barbiturates combined with alcohol. On the question of accident or suicide, the Orange County coroner's report was inconclusive. Survived by wife, son Steven and two sisters. Plans for a memorial service pending.

Sophie began a ritual. At least once a month, she dialed Information and asked if there was a new listing for an Elwood, Steven. Or Elwood, Steve. Or just Elwood, S. The answer was always the same: "I'm sorry, I find no listing under that name." She also called long-distance Information for the 408 and 714 area codes on the off chance that he'd returned either to Santa Cruz or to Orange County, but some intuition told her he was living somewhere in the Los Angeles area—unless, of course, he'd moved far away, in which case there was no hope of finding him anyway.

In the fall of 1971, Sophie began taking education classes at "Valley State," San Fernando Valley State College (which would acquire university status while she was there and become California State University, Northridge). The following spring, still living with her parents, she was officially admitted to the teacher prep program.

Most of her course work involved educational theory and the politics of education. Much attention was given to issues of minority students, which pleased and motivated her. Many of the students—and a number of faculty members—were militant Chicano activists who strongly advocated bilingual education. Sophie's Spanish fluency and left-wing background stood her in good stead with this group. She got A's in all her classes, but her student teaching, which she began in the fall of 1973, was a comedown.

Mardell Avenue School, where she was assigned, was in a part of Van Nuys that had long been nearly all white but whose once-tiny Spanish-speaking minority had in the past couple of years ballooned to 21 percent.

The teachers didn't like the change. Neither did the principal.

Poverty scared them. It made them feel at first guilty, then resentful at having been made to feel guilty. They didn't know what to do with children who spoke little English and whose parents spoke none. They had no idea how to adjust their tried-and-true lesson plans to accommodate kids who were two or three years behind their grade level in reading and math. They chafed at having to deal with the paperwork and little yellow tickets of the many students who now qualified for free breakfasts and lunches.

Gloria Wetzel, the veteran Mardell teacher who was assigned to be Sophie's student-teaching mentor, was one of those who longed for the good old days when the students looked alike and talked alike, fell neatly into three reading groups and paid cash for their meals at school. She also had a personality, teaching style and manner of relating to kids that rubbed Sophie the wrong way.

Mrs. Wetzel was only in her late thirties, but had a prissy way of dressing and doing up her hair that made her look ten years older. And she had an even worse attitude toward her Hispanic students than most of the other teachers at Mardell. She insisted on anglicizing their given names— María became Mary, Pedro was converted to Peter—and forbade them to speak so much as a word of Spanish in her classroom. She taught her third-graders in what Sophie thought was an uninspired way, and was unsympathetic to those who fell behind or had behavior problems. For most of each school day, Mrs. Wetzel presented a stern, unsmiling face, as if perpetually angry; during her rare good moods, she talked down to the kids in a cloyingly sweet voice so nauseating to Sophie that she preferred the angry demeanor. The principal thought Mrs. Wetzel was the best teacher in the school and repeatedly told Sophie how lucky she was to be doing her student teaching under her.

After two weeks, Sophie asked her university supervisor if she might be reassigned to another teacher. The supervisor told her it wasn't within policy to make such changes and urged her to "make the best" of the situation. Then the supervisor called Mrs. Wetzel to ask if there had "been any problems" between her and Sophie and told her of Sophie's denied request for a change.

Her vanity punctured, Mrs. Wetzel treated Sophie with cold hostility for the duration of their student-teaching partnership. When Sophie came up with creative ideas for lessons, Mrs. Wetzel shot them down and refused to let her implement them, claiming they "strayed too far" from the required curriculum. Undeterred, Sophie went back to the drawing board and, after many hours of work, presented Mrs. Wetzel with a set of lesson plans that would use music as a medium for teaching the required academic standards. Mrs. Wetzel rejected the plans on the spurious grounds that only the music teacher was allowed to teach music, and though Sophie got it on word from the district that this was untrue, the principal sided with Mrs. Wetzel. When Sophie dutifully taught the academic subject matter exactly the way Mrs. Wetzel told her to, the teacher found something to nitpick in every lesson. The wonderful rapport Sophie had with the students was a negative in the eyes of Mrs. Wetzel, who marked her down for weak discipline.

Going by Mrs. Wetzel's report, the student-teacher supervisor gave Sophie an evaluation so poor it virtually ruled out her hiring by any school district, fierce as the competition was for every opening that came up. She had held out hope that the Los Angeles Unified School District, with its mushrooming need for bilingual teachers, might overlook the mediocre student-teaching marks, but it didn't. The District's personnel office assigned her a point score too low to qualify her for a probationary contract, her bilingualism notwithstanding.

"Don't give up," her mother said.

In the fall of 1974, Sophie managed to land an assignment at an elementary school in the barrio of Pacoima where a bilingual program was being established. But due to her ineligibility for a contract, she was placed as a "long-term substitute."

The principal of Rayburn Street School assigned Sophie to a first- and second-grade combination class. It wasn't her preference; she was more comfortable working with older children, and the combination of grades was especially demanding, requiring her to cover the curriculum for both grades and deal with a huge span of reading and math levels. But she adapted. She used her guitar and her singing voice to calm their squirreliness. She drew on the skills she'd learned at SCOS and in her student teaching to develop instructional and classroom-management strategies. The assistant principal who came to observe her gave her an excellent report. The future looked bright.

Until she ran afoul of Connie Ramírez.

Everyone knew that the thirty-two-year-old bilingual-program coordinator had grown up in the area and attended Rayburn Street School as a child. They also knew what her attitude was toward that background. Though she pranced about with affected pride in her Chicano heritage—which had only of late become fashionable— Connie's contempt for the children in the school and the people of the community, try as she might to conceal it, was obvious to all. Seeing herself as the smart Mexican woman who'd clawed her way out of the barrio and learned to survive in the Anglo world, she had little use for those who still lived in the old neighborhood, ate *menudo* for breakfast, placed religious icons in their front yards and were stuck in the culture she'd left far behind even as she pretended to celebrate it. Connie's attitude toward the *mexicano* children was, in Sophie's view, even more poisonous than Gloria Wetzel's, coming as it did from one of their own.

Connie's Mexican-born parents, wanting their children to be good Americans, had discouraged the use of Spanish in their home except when the grandparents were visiting from Mexico. Consequently, there were many gaps in Connie's knowledge of the ancestral tongue in which she feigned such pride, and Sophie heard her make numerous errors in grammar and word usage. The one that most irritated her was Connie's repeated references to the school library as *la librería*.

One day, Sophie committed the grave blunder of calling Connie's attention to the misusage.

"*Library* and *librería* are false cognates," Sophie said.

"False what?"

"False cognates. They're words that sound alike in two languages, and maybe have *related* meanings, but they don't mean the same."

"I have absolutely no idea what you're talking about."

"A *librería* is a bookstore. The word for library is *biblioteca*. Look it up in your dictionary."

When the dictionary bore out Sophie's correction, Connie accepted it with icy politeness. But from that day on, she made careful note of anything Sophie did that could possibly be criticized and called her out for it.

One day after watching Sophie teach a challenging math lesson that the kids were nevertheless following with ease, Connie said: "Your expectations are too high. They're only first-graders."

Another time, while the children were working busily and productively at classroom "learning centers" Sophie had spent many hours setting up, Connie said: "You're being too lenient with them. You should be able to make them work more quietly."

The principal, Mr. Zell, was a kind but ineffectual man. As he and the assistant principal did not get along, he relied on Connie to help him run the school, deal with bilingual issues, translate for parents and—most importantly—keep tabs on all the teachers and report back to him. He had been supportive of Sophie at first, but one day in February he asked her to come and see him after school.

"I'm sorry, Sophie," Mr. Zell said, his fingers tapping nervously on his desk. "You've tried hard, you've been a dedicated teacher, but your performance is just not up to snuff. Your classroom management is weak, you don't have good control, you don't seem to know what type of academic material is appropriate for your students. I'm afraid we're going to have to let you go."

Sophie knew this was Connie's handiwork, but there was nothing she could do. As a long-term substitute without a contract, she had no appeal rights. Not even the union could help her.

How could she have been so stupid? Why couldn't she have kept her mouth shut? Surely she could have endured hearing a library called a *librería* in the interest of keeping her job.

She plunged lower than she could ever remember going, down into a burning hell of self-loathing. In desperation, she called Harriet Melnick. At her appointment she said she felt like killing herself.

"Should I be concerned that you might actually make an attempt on your own life?" Harriet asked her.

"No. But I fantasize."

Satisfied that Sophie was not seriously suicidal, Harriet told her that because she was unlikely to get another classroom assignment without a good recommendation, it was time for her to look at other career options. She also told Sophie that it was time for her to let go of Steve Elwood for good. It had been almost four years now, and still, at least once a month, she had been calling Information.

Harriet's advice so enraged Sophie that she rose up out of her depression with staunch, angry resolve. In Santa Cruz she had discovered who she was, and who she was was a teacher. It was in her blood now, and someday, some way or another, she would teach again.

And she would never, ever stop looking for Steve Elwood.

After being terminated at Rayburn, Sophie began working as a day-to-day substitute. She found it frustrating and unpleasant. Some of the other substitutes she met were young aspiring teachers who had been trying unsuccessfully to get classrooms of their own and would have been able to but for the fact that they didn't speak Spanish. When they learned that Sophie was bilingual—a skill she found difficult to conceal—they expressed amazement that she hadn't been able to land a contract. That put her in the position of having either to lie about having been fired from a long-term assignment or admit it and tell the whole depressing story. To avoid having to make that choice, she began shunning the lunchroom.

Sophie had continued to occupy her childhood bedroom since moving back from Santa Cruz. She'd needed that arrangement while working on her credential, unable to afford a place of her own. But it was no longer tenable. She was twenty-seven; she needed to be on her own again and give her parents back their privacy. While at

Rayburn she'd found an apartment and had been about to put a deposit on it, but her discharge had killed that. Now, with a greatly reduced and irregular income, she faced having to live with her parents indefinitely. The thought of that made her crazy.

Though her self-esteem was stuck at rock bottom, Sophie refused to go back to Harriet Melnick, and Larry and Ruth grasped at straws as they tried to buck their daughter up. They showered her with encouragements and affirmations that rang false to her. She knew her moods were stressful for her parents and wished she could respond to their well-meaning efforts, but they served only to push her deeper into her funk. She found herself getting angry and combative over trivial issues, then afterwards being stricken with guilt.

Then, one afternoon after things had become so strained that Sophie knew her parents were on the verge of evicting her, she came home from a subbing assignment and found an urgent message her father had taken.

The principal of Twenty-Third Street School, in South Los Angeles, needed a bilingual teacher.

Sophie was the one he wanted.

CHAPTER 26

Learning Spanish

1975

Steve had no time for culture shock when he drove into Baja California in the summer of his twenty-seventh year. He was in Mexico on business, and once there, he stayed focused. He couldn't afford not to.

His destination was Ensenada, but not the Ensenada of the touristy little artisans' shops along the waterfront strip where he'd walked with Sophie and the SCOS kids four years earlier. He was signed up for the summer intensive beginning Spanish course at the Centro Internacional para el Estudio de Lenguas y Culturas, Asociación Civil—or CIELCAC.

The little school with the long name was run by a liberal Catholic group that sought to give students an experience with the real Mexico while they studied Spanish. It operated on a subsistence budget out of a rented house on Avenida Abasolo, in the working-class residential district known as Colonia Independencia, far to the east of the beach areas that defined Ensenada for all but

a very few of the *norteamericanos* who came there. Steve had heard
about CIELCAC from a classmate in one of his teacher-prep classes,
and had chosen the bare-bones school instead of one of the more
established language institutes in Cuernavaca or Mexico City
because he could afford it on the meager savings he'd managed to
scrape together from student loans, a teacher's aide job the preced-
ing school year and a camp counselor job the summer before that.

Steve had completed his student teaching and gotten his credential, but he knew his chances of getting a job were slim to none.
The last of the baby boomers had finished their elementary education, causing school enrollments—and the number of teaching
jobs—to plummet nationwide. Meanwhile, many of those same
boomers were now competing for the scarce remaining teacher
openings. In Los Angeles, new teachers lucky enough to land jobs
had to settle for long-term substitute positions from which they
could be terminated at the principal's whim.

Unless they spoke Spanish.

Bilingual education had taken off with a bang. Programs were
being set up at schools throughout Los Angeles as funding poured
in from Washington and Sacramento. But despite the overall glut
of would-be teachers, bilingual candidates who could pass the
District's Spanish fluency exam were in short supply.

"I'm going to do it," Steve had said to his friend Greg as they
sat eating lunch in the Student Union dining hall at Cal State L.A.

"Do what?"

"I'm going to go to Mexico this summer, and I'm going learn
Spanish."

Greg had laughed. "You're not serious, are you?"

"I'm dead serious. I'm going to learn Spanish—and I'm going to
learn it fluently. I know I can do it."

"Not in one summer."

"Yes, in one summer."

"You're fucking crazy. Nobody can learn a language that fast."

"*I* can."

Working with single-minded purpose toward getting his teaching credential, imposing the necessary discipline on himself, had helped distract Steve from the terrible recollections of the past: that day he'd heard the wire recording and learned the truth about his father, compelling his flight from the only woman he had ever loved. His father's death, the guilt he bore for it, his permanent estrangement from his mother—the passage of four years had done little to wear down that mountain of pain, and with the credential accomplished, it was the goal of learning Spanish that now kept his attention away from it—at least part of the time.

Steve's lodging in Ensenada was with a family named Negrete on an unpaved street about a kilometer from the school. He rose every morning at six and went for a brisk half-hour exercise walk along the dusty streets of the *colonia*, leaving himself a half hour to study before breakfast.

At seven o'clock, he sat down to *desayuno* with his host family: María de Socorro Andrade de Negrete, the forty-one-year-old widowed mother whose many sisters addressed her as "Coqui"; Carlos, at seventeen the eldest son and man of the family since his father's sudden death from a heart attack a year earlier; Noemí, a serious girl just shy of fifteen who was excitedly preparing for her *quinceañera*, the Mexican girls' coming-of-age ceremony; Pedro, a twelve-year-old who loved to play practical jokes on his siblings; and Yolanda, at nine the baby of the family, who had declared her intent to marry Steve when she grew up. He assiduously practiced his Spanish conversation each morning at the breakfast table, reminding the family members—who wanted to call him by his English name—to address him as "Esteban."

Dealing with his host family was what Steve had expected to be the most challenging aspect of the summer course. How would he adjust to living in a foreign household where no English was spoken? Would he behave appropriately? But to his own amazement, he seemed to have left his gaucherie and timidity on the other side of the border. Maybe it was that he was too focused on the language challenge to be self-conscious, or perhaps his social ineptitude simply didn't translate across the cultural barrier. Whatever the reason, he felt as if he'd become a different person in Spanish.

There were seven other students in Steve's class at CIELCAC: a priest, a nun, a seminary student, and four ordinary California kids who, like Steve, aspired to teaching or some other vocation where Spanish proficiency was desirable or necessary. The priest and the nun were the two most advanced students, Steve a close third. Their five remaining classmates were well behind them, their participation a struggle, their pronunciation way off the mark.

Steve moved quickly through the beginning, advanced-beginning and intermediate books, studying furiously, utilizing every free moment to practice, study and memorize. He quizzed himself on vocabulary; he perfected his pronunciation; he wrote down and committed to memory colloquialisms and idioms he had picked up in conversation. He engraved in his brain the conjugations of regular and irregular verbs in all their daunting tenses. He paid vigilant attention every minute of the three-hour morning class.

*

Formal classroom instruction at CIELCAC ended at lunchtime. In the afternoon, each student went out walking with a *guía*, a native-speaking guide from the neighborhood. Student and guide would wander about town chatting informally at the student's level, giving the novice a chance to develop conversational ease and pick up vocabulary in a natural way. Steve's *guía*, Rosaura, was a lively fifty-year-old grandmother who continually prodded him to express himself in his new language. Though proud of the rapid progress he was making, she saw him as shy and chided him for it ("*¡Ándale, Esteban! ¡No seas tan tímido! ¡Habla conmigo!*"). Steve didn't think he was being shy at all, but he pushed himself ever harder to make conversation during his daily walks with Rosaura, offering comments on every little thing they saw, pulling out his pocket dictionary whenever he needed help with a word.

One day three weeks into the nine-week session, Steve and Rosaura got back from their afternoon walk early. They arrived at the school at the same time as Barbara Swenk—the weakest student in the group, a plain woman of about Steve's age—and her frustrated-looking *guía*, who left as quickly as she could. Shortly afterward, a young Mexican woman in jeans and a pink blouse walked up to Barbara and said something to her. Steve was some distance away, sitting on the front steps of the school, but could see Barbara's incomprehension—and the exceptional beauty of the young woman attempting to communicate with her.

He walked over and asked if he could be of help. "*Sí*," they both said, almost in unison.

He learned that the young woman, whose name was Ana, was, at twenty, the eldest child of Barbara's host family. She had come to let Barbara know that her mother had had to leave to deal with a family emergency and would not be home to serve *cena* (supper) until late, and that if Barbara wanted to sample the local restaurants, this would be a good night for her to do so.

Steve offered to treat the two of them to dinner.

"You don't have to do that," Barbara said.

"I know," he said. "But I want to."

They piled into Steve's minibus and drove the short distance to the small cinder-block house where Ana's family lived so she could ask her father's permission. She ran in and out, presumably getting a "yes," and it struck Steve once again how different this culture was. A grown woman of twenty having to ask her father's permission to go out to dinner with some friends.

He took them to the tourist strip, to a small seafood restaurant someone had recommended. Over abalone steaks, Steve moderated the conversation, dutifully helping Barbara when he could tell she was lost, proud of having come far enough in his Spanish to play that role. There was a moment when, in the radiance of Ana's presence, he felt the old shyness start to creep over him once again—the first time he'd felt it since coming to Mexico. He pushed it away and asked Ana what her last name was.

"*Iturregui.*"

He could make no sense of the name and asked her to write it on a napkin. It still didn't work for him as a Spanish surname. Ana explained that the name was *vasco*.

Vasco? He looked up the word in his pocket dictionary and found that it meant "Basque." Mystery solved. Steve had learned from his Spanish textbook that the Basque language, spoken in north-central Spain, was unrelated to any other European language. It was, in fact, unrelated to any other language on earth.

He signaled to Ana his understanding of her family name's origin, even drawing a map of Spain on the same napkin on which

she'd written the name, outlining very roughly the boundaries of
the Basque region. She nodded in affirmation and said her great-
grandfather, her *bisabuelo*—he had to look up that word as well—
had immigrated to Mexico from that part of Spain.

She told Steve she was impressed with him. Speaking slowly
to make sure he understood, she said she was impressed with his
knowledge, his intellect, his ability to converse so intelligently in
a language he was still learning. He smiled and felt himself blush.

The following morning, as the CIELCAC students stood around
waiting for class to begin, Barbara thanked him for the dinner.
Then she added sotto voce, "Ana has a huge crush on you."

Steve gave a surprised start. While little girls got crushes on him
all the time, big girls almost always ended up telling him that while
they valued him as a friend, they were unable to reciprocate his
romantic interest. That's what had happened with most of the girls
he'd liked in high school and college. It was also what had happened with the few women he'd gone out with in the year or so
since he'd forced himself at last to stop pining for Sophie Hearn.

It was all he could do to keep his mind on his studies that day.

He confided the situation to Rosaura that afternoon. As he'd
expected, she was delighted at the thought of her shy student's having a romance with a Mexican girl. She offered to serve as modera-
tor if he thought he needed one. He said he did.

At Rosaura's insistence, they walked immediately to Ana's house
to carry out what his guide considered a vital supplement to Steve's
course of study.

"*Esteban tiene algo que decirte,*" Rosaura said to Ana when she
came to the door.

Ana stepped into the grassless front yard, eager to hear what
Esteban had to say to her.

Steve turned to Rosaura, feeling the shyest he'd felt since his arrival in Ensenada, and asked her in a whisper what to say first. He'd asked her that question repeatedly during their walk over, but she had coyly talked around the answer, telling him to decide for himself. Now, however, Rosaura suggested he initiate courtship by saying simply, *Tú me gustas*—I like you. It felt to him both too naïve and too direct, but he said it anyway, the blood rushing to his face as he softly enunciated the words.

"*Tú también me gustas a mí,*" Ana said, smiling sweetly as she matter-of-factly echoed his sentiment.

He turned to Rosaura again. "*¿Qué digo ahora?*"

She prompted him to ask for a dinner date that night, to which Ana responded, in a very serious tone, that this time—since it was to be just the two of them—he would have to formally ask her father for permission. She invited him in. His nerves trembling, Steve approached the family patriarch, who sat watching TV and drinking a beer in the tiny living room. He was amazed at how boldly and easily the words slid out: "*Señor Iturregui . . . le pido permiso . . . para llevar a su hija . . . a cenar conmigo esta noche.*"

Dad gruffly gave his consent with the proviso that his daughter be brought home no later than nine o'clock.

Steve took Ana to El Rey Sol, a restaurant much fancier than the one they'd gone to the night before. She remarked at the prices and asked if he was sure he could afford it, at the same time reassuring him that it didn't matter to her if they went to a cheap *taquería* as long as they could be together. She told him that the price of the cheapest dinner on the menu was a week's salary for her father. He assured her that while it wasn't something he could manage on a regular basis, she needn't worry.

Steve was touched by her concern for his finances, even more so by her unabashed statement of wanting to be with him—a declaration that would have been uncool for an American girl on a first date.

He was smitten.

She asked him about his family. He told her he had no siblings, his father was dead and he hadn't spoken to his mother in four years. Why? He answered vaguely: *motivos personales.* Then she asked him about his previous experiences with women. Had he ever been married? Had he had many *novias* (girlfriends)?

He told her about Sophie, and Ana wanted to know all there was to know about the only serious *novia* he'd ever had. He told her they had lived in the same house and run a school together. Why had it ended? Once again he was vague: things just hadn't worked out. Had there been any contact in the four years since? No. Was he still in love with her? No. It had taken a long time, but he'd finally gotten over her.

Ana said she'd had many *pretendientes*, or suitors, including some who had claimed to be in love with her, but hadn't gotten serious with any of them. Then, about midway through the meal, she began talking about marriage in a charmingly innocent way. She told Steve that she hoped he would quickly agree to formalize their relationship so she could tell everyone that Esteban was her *novio* and that then, after perhaps a year of formal courtship, they would set a wedding date. She told him she had only one more year to go in the *escuela comercial*, where she was studying to be a secretary, and would then be ready to take a husband.

He got her home at exactly nine o'clock and walked her to the door. She kissed him lightly, barely grazing his lips with hers, and darted into the house.

After that first date, Steve and Ana saw each other as often as propriety allowed, most often in the company of others. They met at the end of each class day and sat and talked on the steps of the school for an hour or so until it was time for *cena*. Normally she would go home and he would return to the Negretes', but a couple of times she invited him for supper with her family. Saturday nights—the only time they were alone—he would take her out for dinner and a movie. They would hold hands in the theater and then kiss and caress gently in the front seat of Steve's bus for five or ten minutes before he drove her home. That was the extent of their physical relationship. She'd told him early on that while it was not for her to judge other young women who chose to have *relaciones íntimas* with their boyfriends, she was proud of being a virgin and intended to remain one until she was married.

Steve had told her that was fine.

As the summer wore on and Steve's facility with the language continued to improve, he and Ana talked over their future plans and herein the road began to get rocky. A church wedding? That would be problematic seeing as how Steve was not only a non-Catholic but a non-believer in any religion. Ana's family was not strongly religious, attending Mass only a few times a year, but she said she knew her parents would still want her to be married in the church—and *not* the First Unitarian Church of Los Angeles, as he had at one point suggested. They tabled that issue for later discussion.

A more serious question was that of which country the young couple, once married, would reside in. Steve envisioned himself bringing Ana to live with him in Los Angeles, where he would get a teaching position and she would take ESL classes in night school until she was proficient enough in English to get a job as a bilingual secretary. It seemed to him an ideal plan, but she rejected it each time he brought it up.

Ana made it increasingly clear that she did not wish to leave Mexico. She had no desire to uproot herself and move to a country whose language she didn't know, a country where she knew Mexicans were looked down on and subjected to discrimination. She wanted to remain in Ensenada, live near her family and have Steve teach English at the local *escuela preparatoria*. But her flustered *novio* was no readier than she to transplant himself permanently to a land in which he would always be a stranger.

As the summer waned, their discussions became more emotional. Ana became upset several times and let loose with tirades of words that Steve had to look up in his dictionary. By summer's end, he had come to realize what folly the whole notion of marriage had been. She, too, had come to see that there was no realistic future for the relationship, and they were able to end it on a sad but mutually agreeable note. Steve realized now how dishonest he'd been with both himself and Ana, the reality being that he would never again love a woman the way he had loved Sophie—still loved her—whom, wherever she might be, he could never be with again.

Though he had denied it, Ana had obviously sensed, when Steve first told her about Sophie, that he still had feelings for her. When they parted, she predicted that someday he and Sophie would find each other again and marry.

"*Te vas a casar con ella,*" she said.

"*No*," Steve said softly but with finality. "*No es posible.*"

"*Sí*," Ana said with equal assurance. "*Con ella te vas a casar.*"

The six-week courtship had, if nothing else, fostered a dramatic expansion of Steve's Spanish proficiency. When he got back to Los Angeles in early September, he took the school district's fluency exam and passed it handily at the "A" level, making it a near-certainty he would be contracted as a bilingual teacher.

CHAPTER 27

Twenty-Third Street School

1975-1977

Sophie's new assignment was in a depressing part of South L.A. that had been all black until a year or so before she arrived, when a sudden and wholly unexpected influx of Mexican and Central American immigrants had shaken up the local schools and caught them unprepared.

She was an instant success.

The principal of Twenty-Third Street School, Mr. Patterson, had been desperate to find a Spanish-proficient teacher for the class in which the limited- and non-English-speaking third-graders had been placed. There had been several promising candidates, but he hadn't been able to hire any of them. The reason: they were all Hispanic.

As part of a court-ordered integration program, the Los Angeles school district had ordered all principals to racially balance their staffs, reversing the long-standing tradition of matching the ethnicity of the teacher with that of the school. Schools in white-majority, suburban neighborhoods would be required to fill any vacancies they had with minority teachers, while inner-city schools of color could recruit only Caucasians. The district had made no distinction between black and Hispanic, lumping both together as "minorities"; it had compounded that stupidity by failing to exempt bilingual teachers from the rule, with the result that Spanish-speaking teacher candidates could not be placed at the schools where they were most needed unless they were "non-minority." Teachers like Sophie—white but proficient in Spanish—were suddenly worth their weight in gold. "Little" issues like poor evaluations and even dismissal from another position could be overlooked.

Sophie was left to her own devices at Twenty-Third Street School. If there were any problems with her performance, Mr. Patterson didn't want to know about them. She was one of only two bilingual teachers in the school, and as the more fluent of the two, she was repeatedly called on to help develop strategies for dealing with their growing numbers of Spanish-monolingual kids; though there was no funding yet for a bilingual coordinator, Sophie became the de facto expert. She put her other talents to work as well, using music in her teaching and putting on full-scale bilingual musical productions for the whole school, upstaging the regular music teacher who came to the school twice a week. Though still technically a long-term substitute, she knew her position there was secure. At long last, she felt valued and appreciated.

Being left alone was what Sophie had needed in order to grow as a teacher. Her creativity kicked into high gear and her teaching skills blossomed. She moved out of her parents' house and into a cute apartment in Silver Lake. She was happier than she could ever remember being, and her mood stayed up.

She liked herself. The future was bright.

At the end of the 1974-75 school year, Mr. Patterson gave Sophie a glowing evaluation. In the fall she was awarded a probationary contract.

Two years later she had tenure.

Sophie felt guilty about having rebuffed Greg Durcan's romantic overtures. He was such a nice guy. Greg was a fourth-grade teacher; his classroom was two doors down from hers. He'd been hired the year after her.

She felt sorry for him. She knew why so many women rejected him: he was too eager and too needy. Over time, however, the two of them became good friends. They ate together in the teachers' cafeteria every day and confided nearly every detail of their personal lives. Greg told Sophie every time he found a potential new flame, and she coached him on how to make a good impression. When a promising relationship didn't work out, it was on Sophie's shoulder that he cried.

Greg, in turn, knew all there was to know about Sophie's love life: nothing. While she occasionally went out on a date and had had a couple of brief relationships since moving back to Los Angeles, there was really only one man in her life, a man she hadn't seen or heard from in over six years now. She admitted to Greg, with some embarrassment, that she still called Information every few months to see if there was a listing for Steve.

Greg had strong advice for Sophie: Give up. Stop chasing a phantom. Leave Steve's memory behind and go out with other guys. He even tried to fix her up on a couple of blind dates, which she declined.

Then, one day, Greg happened to be in the teachers workroom running off copies of a math worksheet on the old spirit-ink duplicator (the new Xerox machine in the main office was for office staff only) while Sophie made her periodic call on the workroom phone, the only one teachers were allowed to use.

"Hello . . . Could you please tell me if you have a listing for the last name Elwood, first name Steven, or Steve, or just the initial *S*? It might be a new listing . . . No? Are you sure? Well . . . thanks anyway."

She didn't notice Greg's ears perk up.

"Sophie," he asked her in the cafeteria as soon as they were seated with their lunch trays, "this Steve guy you've been telling me about all this time—the one you've been trying to track down—is Steve *Elwood?*" He laughed.

"*What?*" She suspended her fork in midair. "You *know* him?"

"Yeah," he said with a big grin, "I knew him. We were in the credential program at Cal State L.A. together." As Sophie set down her fork, he began to laugh again. "All this time you've been telling me about this guy you can't get over . . . and it was *Steve Elwood* you were talking about! I don't believe it! This is just too weird!"

Sophie didn't laugh.

"What do you know about him?" she said frantically. "Do you know where he is?"

"No. I haven't heard from him in—let's see—at least two or three years. But I do remember him talking about this girl *he* had never gotten over . . . and I seem to recall his mentioning Santa Cruz. Isn't that where you were with him?"

"Yes."

"I should've made the connection sooner."

"Tell me more. Tell me everything you know."

"All I remember is that he wanted to be a teacher real bad . . .

and he wanted to learn Spanish real bad, too. Yeah, he was gonna take a summer class in Mexico. He figured he could get fluent in one summer, and I told him he was nuts. I never saw him again . . . never knew if he went ahead with that plan."

"Do you think he could be teaching in L.A. Unified?"

"Very possibly. He was real passionate about wanting to be a teacher. Of course, that doesn't necessarily mean that—"

"Is there a way to find out? You think Personnel would tell me?"

"I dunno."

"Are you *sure* you don't remember anything else about him? Any names of friends? Anybody he was dating?"

"No . . . he was kind of a loner. Never mentioned any dates. I don't think he went out on any. He was still too hung up on this woman he kept talking about—who, I now presume, was you. Holy shit! Talk about coincidences!" He laughed again.

Sophie sneaked to the parking lot immediately after dismissing her kids at 2:10 (teachers were supposed to stay until 2:40) and sped downtown in her Honda Civic. At 2:25 she arrived at the Los Angeles Unified School District administrative complex on North Grand Avenue. She could have just called, but she figured that her chances would be better face-to-face.

The young woman at the counter in the personnel office was friendly and sympathetic, seeming to understand intuitively that Sophie's need to find out about Steven Elwood was a matter of the heart.

"We're not allowed to give out any information about District employees . . . but wait just a minute."

The woman came back after six minutes.

"Yes, he is employed in the District. But I can't give you any more information than that."

"You can't tell me what school he's at?"

"No. I could get in trouble even for what I just told you."

"Okay. Thanks for that."

"Good luck."

From there Sophie drove to Cal State L.A. and walked all the way across campus to the administration building. But the clerk at the student-records office wouldn't tell her anything, either—except that, yes, Steven Elwood had been a student there at one time.

Unbearably frustrated, she drove home to Silver Lake and ate dinner alone.

"*El . . . pirata . . . Peralo . . . con . . . su . . . pata . . . de . . . palo.*" Verónica Padilla struggled through the story in her Spanish pre-primer while Sophie listened patiently. "*Y . . . su . . . pícaro . . . loro . . . busca . . . un . . . tesoro.*" Verónica was a third-grader on the border between "NES" (non-English-speaking) and "LES" (limited-English-speaking), and her Spanish reading was at first-grade level. She brushed her long hair out of her eyes as she plodded through the passage about Peralo the peg-legged pirate and his mischievous parrot searching for treasure.

"*Muy bien, Verónica,*" Sophie said. "*Estás mejorando.*" Verónica's reading had improved very little, but the girl needed encouragement. Sophie was about to move on to the next child in the reading circle when the door opened and María Cornejo, the bilingual coordinator, entered the room. She walked slowly and stepped softly, trying not to distract the more advanced kids who were at their seats working on written assignments while Sophie conducted the reading lesson with the lower-level group.

"Excuse me, Ms. Hearn," María said almost in a whisper. "I'm sorry to interrupt your lesson. Could you please come and see me in my office after school?"

"Yes, Ms. Cornejo."

María Cornejo had been at Twenty-Third Street School for only two months. Sophie had been leery of María when she'd first arrived, her only experience with a bilingual coordinator having been a bad one, but they had warmed up to each other quickly. María was a native of Madrid and spoke pure Castilian; she was impressed with Sophie's Spanish—even though it was Mexican Spanish, which sounded comical to many Spaniards—and they had many long discussions in Spanish about language, kids, educational philosophy and the dysfunctionality of the Los Angeles Unified School District. Whenever María asked her to come to her office, Sophie knew it was nothing to worry about. On this occasion, as it turned out, their school was to host a conference the following month for all the bilingual teachers in their area, and María wanted Sophie to help her develop a presentation.

As they brainstormed ideas, a thought slowly crept into Sophie's mind.

"María," she said, "do you have a list of all the bilingual teachers at all the schools in Area C?"

"Yes, I do."

"May I see it?"

María handed her a mimeographed list. Sophie scanned it slowly. The name she sought was not on it.

"Is there a list of all the bilingual teachers in the entire *district*?" she said.

"I'm sure there is," María said, "but I've never seen it."

"Is it possible one of your supervisors might have it?"

"Yes. The Area bilingual people . . . I'm sure they do."

"Would there be any way you could get a look at it?"

"Why? Are you trying to find somebody?"

"Yes."

Up until that moment they hadn't shared any personal confidences, but Sophie proceeded to tell María the entire story of her and Steve. María was enthralled. They talked until after four o'clock.

"The supervisor I know best is Juan Reyes," María said. "I don't know him well enough to call him, but I'm going to see him at a meeting next Tuesday. I'll ask him then."

"Thank you, María," Sophie said. "Thank you, thank you, thank you."

Sophie could hardly pull herself through Monday and Tuesday, so great was her excitement. As she drove home Tuesday afternoon she could think of nothing but the phone call she expected to receive from María that evening, and she whipped herself into a frenzied high. After six years, she could be on the verge of finding Steve! But by the time she got home, the mania had evaporated as she realized what a long shot it was. What if his name wasn't on that list? She would have worked herself up for nothing. And the overwhelming probability was that he wasn't on it. It was highly unlikely he'd become fluent in Spanish—certainly not in one summer. But in two or three summers, perhaps? No, as hard as she tried, she just couldn't imagine Steve Elwood speaking Spanish at all, let alone well enough to be a bilingual teacher. And if he was just an ordinary teacher, he wouldn't be on the list María had promised to look at for her. He wouldn't be on any list that María or anyone else she knew had access to. He'd be just one of fifty-thousand-plus teachers at any one of the more than five hundred schools in America's second-largest school district. He might be teaching any grade from kindergarten to high school, anywhere in the district from San Pedro to Sylmar, from Watts to Woodland Hills.

But maybe he *had* become fluent by now, incredible as it seemed, and was working as a bilingual teacher at some school in the District—where she would be able to contact him!

No, it wasn't likely at all. And even if he *was* on that list, how could she assume he would want to see her? It had been six years now; he'd probably found someone else. He might be married and have kids. For that matter, even if he was still single and unattached, might he not still be so freaked out about what had happened with his father that he wouldn't want to see the woman he associated with those events? He had, after all, run away from her once. Her number was listed, and if he'd wanted to contact her, all he would have had to do was thumb through the telephone directory.

But even if he didn't want to see her, it would be nice at least to know he was okay.

She resolved that if Steve wasn't on the list, she would finally let go and give up her search. She would make no more calls to Information. And, yes, she might even let Greg fix her up on some blind dates.

The call from María came at 5:43.

CHAPTER 28

Lost and Found

1977

Steve's first few years of teaching had been hard. Learning to oversee a classroom, organize his lessons and manage his students' behavior had been severe tests for him, and many times he'd been on the verge of giving up. Luckily, both his student-teaching mentor and the principal at his first job had seen his potential and nurtured his strengths while helping him overcome his weaknesses. He had improved so much that he was now considered one of the better teachers at Hames Avenue School.

Today, however, it was taking extra effort to govern his third-graders. It was one of those days when they were antsy for no particular reason.

It was the end of the school day, one minute before the 2:10 dismissal. Steve had the children lined up at the door ready to walk down the hall and outside to the gate. He was in a hurry to leave; he was going to an in-service training at Fifth Street School, a half-hour's drive away in East L.A., and he hated being late. If he left right after dismissing the kids, he could make it with time to spare.

"Come on, Michael and Antonio," he said to two boys, one black and one Hispanic, who were clowning in line. "Show me you know how to line up. Come on, Marcos, come on, Rubén, you can do better than that. *Dos filas rectas.* We'll leave as soon as I see two straight lines." His tone was gentle but firm. "I like the way Sharie is standing," he said of a tall black girl at the head of the line. "Come on, the rest of you, you can do better than that. How fast can you make two straight, quiet lines? *Es un reto.* That's a challenge. We won't leave until the lines are straight and quiet."

They shaped up. Steve led them through the hall and down the stairs in two silent lines, glancing back at them every few seconds, while other classes followed less quietly behind their teachers. He led his children out, released them at the main entrance and darted into the main office to initial his sign-out card.

He was on his way out the side door leading to the teachers' parking lot when he heard a woman's voice call out.

"Oh, Mr. Elwood."

His heart sank. It was Penny Grado, a second-year probationary teacher who was, for some reason, always turning to Steve for guidance even though he himself was only in his third year. She taught fourth grade and had some of the students he'd had the year before. He wished he could bring himself to say "Excuse me, Ms. Grado, but I'm in a hurry," but she was the kind of person whose feelings you were always afraid of hurting. Steve had lost a lot of his shyness through his success as a teacher, and it vanished completely when he was with kids, but certain types of social situations with adults still vexed him. He still had trouble being assertive.

"Mr. Elwood, you had Mario Estrada last year, didn't you?"

"Yes, I did."

"How was his behavior with you?"

"Terrible."

"Good, I'm glad it isn't just me. Did you find anything that worked with him?"

"Well, he sometimes responds to positive reinforcement. Little rewards, gold stars, things like that. Also, he likes having responsibilities in the classroom."

Ms. Grado didn't let it go at that. She asked him about two other problem children Steve had had the previous year, then wanted to chitchat about the adorable and well-behaved ones. Finally, he managed to say, "Well, guess I'd better be going, I have an in-service," but by that time he'd lost ten minutes, the time advantage he had counted on.

He race-walked to the lot where his aging VW bus was parked. As he backed out of the space, he suddenly saw in his rearview mirror a woman standing in his path, frantically waving her arms.

Who was this woman? Another of the new teachers wanting advice? Now there was no way he could get to the in-service on time. He would have to be firmer with this one than he'd been with Penny.

He rolled down the window. "Look, I'm in a really big hurry—"

Why was this woman smiling? Who the hell was she?

When he realized who she was, he stopped halfway out of the parking space and switched off the ignition.

At first they just gazed at each other, neither knowing what to say.

"Come on," Steve finally said. "Get in."

After Sophie got in, he pulled back into the parking space, forgetting about the in-service and the one salary-advancement point it would have earned him. As he sat there staring at the woman who for six years had scarcely for a moment been out of his thoughts, he kept repeating to himself, *This isn't a dream.*

He finally broke the silence in Spanish. "*Qué sorpresa es, después de tantos años.*"

Sophie's jaw dropped. Considering that he was on a list of bilingual teachers, she had expected him to speak Spanish reasonably well—but not this well. His fluidity and pronunciation were nearly as good as hers.

"*¡Qué bien hablas!*" she said. "*¿Cómo aprendiste?*"

Steve proceeded to tell her—in Spanish—how he had embarked on his study of the language. He told her about his time at CIELCAC, about Rosaura and the Negrete family, about how he had, to everyone's disbelief, attained fluency in just one summer. He did not mention Ana.

"I knew I had a gift for languages," he said, switching back to English. "I was the top student in my high-school French class."

They talked for a while about their respective schools, an easy topic. Finally, he said, "Wanna go have an early dinner?"

"Sure. Where?"

"I know a good Chinese restaurant on San Pedro Street. It's not that far. You can leave your car here and I'll bring you back."

"So how did you find me?" Steve said on the way to the restaurant.

"Perseverance."

"How did you know I was at Hames?"

"My wonderful bilingual coordinator used her connections."

"How did you know I was teaching in the district?"

"Your old friend Greg Durcan. He teaches at my school."

"Greg Durcan! How did *he* lead you to me?"

"He didn't, really. All he could tell me was that you *might* have learned Spanish and *might* be teaching somewhere in L.A. The rest took a lot of persistence and research."

"You went to that much trouble?"

"Yes, I did. I've been looking for you for six years."

"Not continuously, of course."

"Yes. Continuously."

"You're joking."

"No. I'm not."

"Jesus Christ."

"My dad died a couple of months after I last saw you," Steve said as they sat waiting for their food. "He OD'd on Nembutal and vodka. They never knew if it was accidental or intentional."

"I know. We read about it in the paper. I'm sorry."

"It was my fault."

"No. Don't say that."

"I'm not just saying it. It's an absolute fact."

"How can you possibly know that?"

"Even if it was an accident, it was my fault. I was the reason he got drunk and forgot how many pills he was popping." Steve paused. "That day I split from Santa Cruz, I drove straight down there and confronted him."

"I knew about that, too. I called your house and your mom told me."

"I just let loose and screamed at him. I called him a coward and a hypocrite and a liar, and I said that I would never love or respect him again. I left him sobbing and begging me to forgive him. I just walked out and never saw him again. I went to see my mother a few days after he died and she wouldn't let me in. She yelled at me and blamed me and said she would never forgive me. I went to the memorial service, and she yelled at me again—in front of everybody—and told me to leave. So I left and never saw *her* again. I was definitely to blame—whether it was accident or suicide doesn't matter. It tore me apart . . . still tears me apart today. But then at the same time, I still hate him for what he did and I hate myself for being his son. Jesus fucking Christ—*he named your father!*"

"I know he did. But you're not responsible for that."

"Doesn't matter. It still sticks to me because I *benefited* from what he did. Everything I ever had—the pampered upbringing, the nice houses, the toys when I was a kid . . . the cars, the allowance, the film equipment—even my education! Every penny they ever spent on me was dirty money, made possible through the efforts of Arthur J. Elwood, cooperative witness, informer, stool pigeon. You and your parents went through the hell of the blacklist so that I could grow up in heaven."

"But that's all way in the past now."

"Not to me it isn't."

The waiter came with their food. They ignored it. Steve kept talking, sniffling back tears.

"Don't blame yourself for the wire recorder. If I hadn't found out that way, I would've found out some other way. I mean, what did he think? I was going to live out my entire life in blissful ignorance? So anyway . . . I've been living in torment ever since, wrestling with those two contradictory emotions that keep tearing at me." He dabbed at his eyes with his cloth napkin. "Every single day of my life . . . without exception . . . I relive the whole thing over and over again. I've tried to live normally, and I have to a large degree . . . I mean, I did learn Spanish, and I did become a successful teacher . . . but the pain never stopped. It's still there, and it'll always be there. I've been seeing a shrink."

"Has he—or she—helped you?"

"She's great. Very smart, very empathetic. She tries hard, but there's a limit to what she can do. She can't take away the pain and remorse, she can't take away the shame over what my father did . . . or the guilt over what *I* did. She's tried to teach me some strategies for coping, like writing imaginary letters to my dad, but that doesn't help much, because it's pure fantasy. No amount of psychotherapy can turn back time, and it doesn't seem like there's anything I can do . . . or that any shrink can help me do . . . to face up to the realities of what happened, other than to say that my dad was a piece of shit for doing what he did and that I'm a piece of shit for being his son . . . and for what I did to him, even if he deserved it."

"What a terrible way to live," Sophie said, touching his arm softly. She picked up the serving spoon and gave each of them a little bit from each of the platters.

"It's the pits," Steve said. "But there's another thing I haven't been able to stop obsessing about, either."

"What's that?"

"You. I've never once stopped thinking about you."

Now Sophie's eyes welled with tears. "Why did you run away like that, Steven? Why didn't you stay and let me help you with it?"

"I just . . . I just couldn't face you. It was such a huge part of my identity, being the son of a blacklisted writer . . . or, rather, *thinking*

I was the son of a blacklisted writer. I was so proud of it. It was part of the deep connection you and I had . . . or thought we had. With that carved out of me, I didn't feel like I had much left to offer you. I knew how you and your parents must have felt about my dad, and I couldn't face that. So I went crazy. And I ran."

"Yes, and we had to figure out what to do with all the stuff you left behind. I was distraught, too. I was devastated to lose you. I've never stopped thinking about you, either. I never gave up trying to find you . . . I've already told you that."

"I'm so sorry I did that to you. I guess that's one more thing I'm guilty of. I managed to hurt all the people I loved."

"No . . . don't feel guilty about me. I'm just glad I finally found you. Even if it took six years."

"I'm glad you found me, too." Steve hesitated. "Are you seeing anyone now?"

"No."

"Have you had any serious relationships?"

"No. How about you?"

"Nothing either, except . . . No, not really."

"Nothing except what? Oh . . . I'm sorry. Never mind. You don't have to tell me."

"No, that's okay. There was just this one girl in Mexico . . . it wasn't that important. It didn't amount to anything. Except to make me realize that I was still in love with you."

Now they were both crying softly. They stared at each other, without words, until she asked him, "Where did you go after you confronted your father?"

"I came up here. To L.A."

"That's what I'd figured. Where did you stay?"

"I crashed with friends, mostly. Sometimes I slept in my bus.

I started working at a bunch of different odd jobs, and I got a crummy little apartment in the Wilshire district, where I still live. Eventually I got a teacher's aide job, and then I started working on my credential."

"I kept calling Information, but they never had a listing for you."

"I wasn't listed. My mom called me several times while I was staying with a friend and screamed at me again . . . as if I weren't already having enough trouble coping with my guilt . . . so by the time I got a place of my own, I'd decided I wanted no further contact. So I got an unlisted number. I feel guilty as hell about her, too . . . However much she hated me and blamed me, I should have tried harder to reconcile. But I just couldn't bring myself to call her. And I still can't. We haven't spoken in six years."

"Why not write her? Wouldn't that be easier?"

"Do you have any idea how many letters I've started and then crumpled up?"

Though they spoke with the intimacy of former lovers, it wasn't easy or comfortable. It was strained. Nothing was assured.

They talked for almost two hours. When the waiter came to check on them, their serving bowls were still full. Steve asked for the check. The waiter asked if they wanted to take their food home. They said no.

Steve drove them back to his school, where Sophie's Honda was still parked in the lot.

"So where do we go from here?" she said as they sat in the bus.

"May I see you again?"

"Are you serious? Why else have I been looking for you all these years? Come over to my place Saturday afternoon. We can talk, and I'll make dinner for you, or we can go out."

"Okay."

On Saturday it took Steve twelve minutes to drive from his little studio apartment off Wilshire to Sophie's bungalow in Silver Lake. Just three miles, via Normandie Avenue and Beverly Boulevard. They'd lived that close to each other for two years without knowing it.

When he arrived, they fell into each other's arms as if it were still 1971 and they were still back in Santa Cruz, before that terrible day.

They had much to share.

They discussed in detail how each had come to the decision to teach in the public schools, how their views had evolved and their lifestyles changed, how far they'd both come since Santa Cruz. They discussed the major news events that had happened since they'd last seen each other: Watergate and the fall of Nixon; the end of the Vietnam War; the election of Jimmy Carter. They exchanged opinions on the politics of bilingual education (they were both for it but critical of the fanatics) and talked about their shared loathing of the school district administration. They compared stories about the jerk principals they'd suffered under and the good ones who'd helped them thrive, the wonderful and challenging students they'd had and the intricate travails of classroom management.

They talked all through the night and into Sunday. Sporadically, they fell into each other's arms to sleep, only to wake a few hours later and start talking again.

Monday they both called in sick.

*

Things moved quickly after that weekend.

Their renewed commitment exceeded what they'd had in the Santa Cruz days. They were older, wiser and more settled from the years apart. Yet, paradoxically, those years seemed to have vanished. It was as if, for both of them, there had never been anything or anyone else.

But the pain of what his father had done, and of what he had done to his father, stayed with Steve—two raw spots in his psyche that could never heal completely, even as years and more years passed. His mother died of cancer in 1986 without their having reconciled; he learned of her death a year later from a friend of a friend. For the first few years, he spoke regularly of the pain, often breaking into tears.

Then he stopped talking about it.

Sophie could still tell when he was weighted down with hurt. Sometimes she found him crying, but when she tried to talk to him and comfort him, he turned away. So she stopped trying.

She went alone to Steve's former therapist for more than a year after Steve stopped going. The counselor—with whom she developed a better rapport than she'd ever had with Harriet Melnick—helped her learn to accept some things as they were, to be aware of and respect the boundaries. She had to avoid any mention of the Hollywood blacklist, and her parents had to do the same in Steve's presence. When occasionally she got together with the sons and daughters of her parents' blacklistee friends—usually when a parent died—she went alone.

Yet they were able to build a beautiful life together, and a happy home. They hiked in the mountains and jogged on the beach. They explored new restaurants and shopped flea markets. They were passionate, playful, tender, joyous, unswervingly devoted lovers whose love deepened day by day.

Steve's agony was the dark underside of what was wonderful between them and a burden Sophie was willing to bear.

She never regretted it.

CHAPTER 29

Celebrating Life

LOS ANGELES TIMES OBITUARY
SEPTEMBER 8, 2005

Lawrence H. Hearn, 88; Blacklisted Screenwriter

Lawrence Henry Hearn, whose once-promising career as a Hollywood scribe was cut short by the McCarthy-era black-list of suspected Communists in the film industry, has died. He was 88.

Hearn, who had been in failing health for several years and earlier this year suffered a debilitating stroke that left him paralyzed and unable to speak, died Sept. 2 of heart and kidney failure at Encino Hospital, according to his daughter, Sophie Hearn-Elwood.

A World War II veteran, Hearn was born in Chicago in 1917. In 1928 he moved with his family to Los Angeles, where his father, Henry Hearn Jr., worked as a reporter for the

Los Angeles Daily News and later for the Times. Originally planning to follow in his father's footsteps, Hearn graduated from the Columbia School of Journalism in 1939 and began his career as a screenwriter the following year. After co-authoring three scripts—only one of which made it to the screen—Hearn found himself blacklisted when he refused to answer questions about his political affiliations before the House Committee on Un-American Activities in 1951.

Hearn and his wife, Ruth Katz Hearn, joined the Communist Party as college students during the Depression but had already begun to feel alienated from its rigid ideology by the onset of the McCarthy red scare. They remained inactively in the party because, said Hearn-Elwood, "they didn't want to feel like they'd been intimidated into leaving."

The Hearns' disenchantment with Communism came to a head in 1956, with the Soviet invasion of Hungary and the revelation of atrocities committed during Josef Stalin's three-decade reign of terror. They formally quit the party that year, denouncing Russian Communism for its betrayal of the humanist and pacifist ideals that had attracted them to the movement in the 1930s. They nevertheless remained committed to progressive and liberal causes for the remainder of their lives, and Lawrence Hearn never repented of, and continued to defend on principle, his refusal to cooperate in the HUAC hearings.

Though Hearn invoked the Fifth Amendment in the hearings to avoid being compelled to identify other suspected Communists, "he actually considered it a First Amendment issue, a free-speech issue," said Hearn-Elwood. "My parents considered themselves patriots. They loved America and believed in its ideals. They believed that the right to hold unpopular opinions was part of the American fabric, and they thought it was un-American to attack that right with intimidation, with the threat of your livelihood being taken away."

Unable to get writing assignments after his HUAC appearance, Hearn moved his family to Mexico City in 1956, following the lead of other blacklisted writers who had hoped to find work in the Mexican film industry. Hearn was unsuccessful in his Mexican venture and after two years returned to Los Angeles. He found sporadic work writing television scripts using the pseudonym Hank Lawrence, penning episodes for a variety of shows as well as several documentary scripts and some short children's plays that aired on local TV in Los Angeles. Though he wrote several original screenplays, Hearn was unable to make the leap back to the big screen even after the blacklist dissipated in the 1960s, and he continued to write for television under the Hank Lawrence *nom de plume*.

Hearn remained active in the Writers Guild in his later years, teaching writing classes and conducting numerous seminars about the blacklist period. Ruth Hearn, an accomplished pianist and Juilliard graduate who for years taught music in the Los Angeles public schools, died in 1997. The Hearns were longtime Van Nuys residents.

In addition to his daughter, Hearn is survived by a brother. Plans for a memorial service are pending.

This time he said yes, he would go.

He had refused to go to her mother's service eight years before. He hadn't said why, but she knew. All the old ones who would be there. The old ones who would know who he was, who would remember who his father was. He amazed her by saying yes this time. She knew how hard it was going to be for him.

The service was held at Writers Guild West headquarters, at Third and Fairfax. As she had expected, he kept to himself. While people were arriving, milling about, coming up and hugging her, he sat in the back and talked with the videographer.

She could see he was interested in the man's video camera, a high-definition professional model he was probably wishing he could afford. Though his filmmaking days were in the remote past, he had recently bought an inexpensive camcorder and was having fun playing around with it. It reminded him, he said, of the passion he'd had for recording events in motion so long ago.

"Thank you all for coming here today to help celebrate my father's life," Sophie said, concluding the service.

At fifty-eight, she had a youthful face and long, flowing, unapologetically gray hair.

As soon as she stepped down from the podium, a gaggle of old folks surrounded her and fussed over her. Some were robust despite their years; others, frail and shaky of gait, moved with canes or walkers. A few sat in the front row in wheelchairs, caregivers at their sides.

"That was a lovely service, Sophie dear," Aunt Marie said as they hugged.

"A wonderful tribute to your father," Uncle Tim, her father's brother, said.

"Thank you," she said to each of them.

"Not many of us left now," a stooped-over but energetic old screenwriter said. "Our numbers are dwindling apace."

"I know," she said sadly.

The group began to drift toward the adjoining lounge, where a buffet of steaming-hot food sat ready. Steve hung behind, still chatting with the cameraman. As Sophie wound up her conversations with the elders, a woman of about her age stepped into her field of view, patiently awaiting her turn.

"Sophie?" she said.

"Laura!"

Though they'd been best friends as children, they had seen little of each other since high school. Their lives had taken very different paths. Laura had graduated from UCLA and gone on to law school; she was now a superior court judge.

"I'm so sorry about your dad," Laura said as they embraced.

"It was for the better," Sophie said. "There wasn't much quality to his life after he had the stroke."

Another elderly lady, a writer's widow, approached Sophie.

"That was lovely, dear," she said.

"Thanks, Hannah. Thanks for coming."

"I loved that collage you made. You put a lot of work into it."

"Thank you."

"It's so sad," Laura said after Hannah was gone. "We never see each other anymore except when one of our parents dies."

"And now they're all gone," Sophie said. "I hope that doesn't mean we don't see each other again."

"We mustn't let that happen. Are you guys still living in Silver Lake?"

"No. We're in my parents' old house now."

"That house in Van Nuys? Where you lived when we were kids?"

"Yes. That's the one. You used to come over . . . and you'd bring your dolls, and we'd join our doll collections together and act out epic movies with them."

A fortyish black woman came over and interrupted them. "Sophie?" she said. "I'm Jessica Drayer. I was in that workshop your dad did about ten years ago for young African American writers. I just wanted to tell you how sorry I am."

"Thank you. It's nice to meet you."

"I'm very indebted to your father. He helped me launch my career. By the way, I loved looking at all those old pictures of him in your collage . . . I assume you made that collage. He was really handsome when he was young."

"Yes, he was."

"So nice to meet you," Jessica said as she walked away.

"Yes," Laura said, resuming their conversation. "I remember us playing together at your house. I remember other things, too . . . like that little folk-song gathering you had. Where I met Dave Mandell."

"Yes. I remember that, too."

"That's so awesome! Living in the house where you grew up. I sold our old house when Mom died, and the new owner tore it down and built one of those godawful McMansions."

"We might have to do the same with ours. It's in *really* bad shape. Needs a lot of work we can't afford to do. The roof is sagging, the foundation still has cracks from the '94 quake . . . my parents didn't keep up with maintenance. And they were terrible packrats. They *never* threw anything away. There was a lifetime's worth of junk in that house. And the garage? You wouldn't believe it. We're still having to go through it little by little, one box at a time, and either donate or throw stuff out. We rented a great big dumpster and filled it in a few days."

"How long have you been living there?"

"Almost a year. Since Dad went into assisted living."

"How is Steve?"

"Steve's fine. He's here."

"He's here?"

"That's him over there." She motioned toward where he was sitting, still talking to the videographer.

"How wonderful that he came!"

"It was really hard for him."

"Still?"

"Nothing's changed."

"That's great that he's here. I'll get to meet him, finally . . . for the first time since we were four years old. I wonder if he'll remember me."

"He might. Just don't mention that you're a blacklisted writer's daughter."

"I won't. But it's such a shame he's had to hide like that. I mean . . . nobody here has anything against him."

"He knows that. But he's still carrying his father's baggage. You know that's the main reason we never had kids?"

"Really?"

"He didn't think he could be a good father after . . . you know. He's just never been able to get over it."

"Even after all these years?"

"Yes."

"How sad . . . that it's affected yours and his life so much."

"I know. If he were a normal person, he would've gotten over it long ago. But he's just so obsessive."

"Does he have OCD?"

"No, he hasn't been diagnosed with anything. He just can't let anything go. He used to have all kinds of theories about it. Once he said he thought it was from his parents' overprotecting him out of guilt. But that was back when he still talked about it."

"Wow."

"I've done a lot of thinking and wondering over the years about what makes him tick. I think it's possible he might have Asperger's."

"Asperger's. Isn't that what Bill Gates has?"

"Yeah, they say he has it. Einstein and Beethoven supposedly had it, too. Steve has a lot of the characteristics—poor social skills, highly focused intellect, the obsessiveness—but then maybe it's just something unique to him. Steve's Disorder."

"It probably is unique to him. And I'd be willing to bet his father's guilt did have a lot to do with it."

"Who knows?"

"You've certainly had a lot to deal with."

"Yeah. But so has he. He's had to cope with me being bipolar."

"You have bipolar disorder?"

"Since my teens. But I was only officially diagnosed about five years ago. My psychiatrist is still experimenting with different meds."

"I don't mean to change the subject, but . . . do you think it would be okay if I said something to him? Like, I know how hard it was for him to come, and—"

"No, please don't. Any mention of it would freak him out. He hasn't even talked to *me* about it for at least twenty years—it's kind of an unspoken understanding that we don't go there. But I know for sure that he still thinks and suffers about it as much as ever, and I can always tell when he's thinking and suffering about it."

"That's so sad."

"Remember, now—*nothing* about the blacklist."

"Not to worry."

"Let's go get some food before the line gets long. I'm *starving*. I was up most of the night working on that collage and I skipped breakfast."

They joined the group in the other room and served themselves from the buffet table. Several other people offered Sophie their condolences while she held her plate of food. Finally, she and Laura made it to a couch and sat down.

While they were talking and eating, Sophie saw Steve come in. The videographer was gone. Steve got his food and sat down alone in a plush chair in the middle of the room, from where he could watch Sophie and make eye contact with her as he ate in silence.

Then she saw a tall, stately blond woman in her forties approaching them. Sophie broke off her conversation with Laura and stared at the woman, trying to identify her, as she came closer.

"Hi, Sophie," she said. "Do you know who I am?"

Sophie looked her up and down. She didn't look even vaguely familiar.

"I'm Susan Vaughn. Remember me? From the Santa Cruz Open School?"

"Oh, my God!" Sophie stood and pulled Susan into her arms. "What are you doing here?"

"I'm living down here now, in Glendale. My husband got a job as a prop manager at Disney, and I'm teaching high-school Spanish at a charter school in Pasadena. We've been down here almost three years now."

"But how did you find your way here?"

"I kept meaning to look you up, but I never got around to it. Then I read in the paper that your father had passed away, so I called the Writers Guild and found out when the service was going to be. I'm really sorry about your dad. I remember him really well from that night we camped out in your backyard, on the way back from Mexico. He was so nice."

"Thanks, Susan. It's so wonderful to see you! I can't believe this! How's your mother? And Michelle? And Geoffrey?"

"They're all doing fine. My mom's still in Santa Cruz. She met a guy and remarried not too long after you left, and my stepdad was a real father to the three of us."

"That's wonderful."

"Geoffrey and Michelle are both married, both with kids. I have a sixteen-year-old son."

"That's fantastic. I'll bet your mom loves being a grandma."

"She does. She just wishes we all lived closer."

"Are you in touch with any of the other kids from SCOS?"

"I'm not personally, but Michelle's kept in touch with several of them. She and Melissa Zweickert exchange emails regularly. And you remember Tami Hagar?"

"Of course. How's she doing?"

"She's doing pretty well now, but she had a really rough time of it. Her mom's boyfriend tried to molest her, and she ran away. She got put in foster care for a while. Then she moved in with an aunt in Sacramento, and I guess she still lives somewhere up in that area. She has a really nice husband, she's working as some kind of medical assistant, I think, and she has a kid. I forget if it's a boy or a girl."

"I'm *so* glad to hear that. I've thought about her and worried about her a lot over the years."

"Listen, I have to tell you this. It was on account of your Spanish lessons, and that trip to Mexico, that I got really heavily into Spanish. I ended up majoring in it in college, and now I'm teaching it."

"That's wonderful. That really makes me feel good. Oh . . . Susan . . . you remember Steve Elwood?"

"Of course. How could I not?"

"We're married. We just had our twenty-fourth anniversary."

"I figured you were married, from your hyphenated name in the obituary. So he came back to you."

"No, I came back to him."

"And you worked everything out?"

"Not everything. But enough to make a happy life together."

"I'm so glad."

"He's right over there. He won't believe it when he sees you. Oh . . . I'm sorry. Susan, this is Laura. We grew up together. She and I and Steve used to play dolls together when we were little."

"The dolls you were going to look for that night?"

"Yes . . . and I didn't find them. Instead, I found something I wish I hadn't. But that's a long story I can't tell you right now."

The three of them talked for about ten minutes, exchanging phone numbers and email addresses. Sophie wrote her information on each of two slips of paper torn from a copy of the memorial service program and gave one to each of the two women, each from a distinct epoch of her life. For a moment she contemplated the vast expanse of time they represented, and the waning numbers of her parents' generation, and it made her feel old and slightly melancholy. Her generation would be the next to die. But then she looked lovingly at Laura, at Susan, and the sadness gave way to warmth and the wisdom of years.

The crowd in the room grew smaller until there were fewer than a dozen people left. Steve finally came over and sat in a chair facing the couch where Sophie, Laura and Susan were sitting.

"Hi, honey," Sophie said. She nodded toward Susan. "Do you know who this is? Do you recognize her?"

"Hi, Steve," Susan said. She got up and walked over to him. "I'm Susan Vaughn. Remember? From Santa Cruz?"

"Oh, my God," Steve said, jumping up. "Susan. Little Susan." He grabbed her in a tight embrace.

"And you remember Laura? The three of us used to play together."

"Yes . . . I do." He held out his hand to her. "I do remember you, Laura. Even after all these years. It's nice to see you again."

"It's wonderful to see you, Steve."

"I need to get going," Susan said.

Hugs were exchanged, along with promises to keep in touch. Susan departed, leaving only Sophie, Steve and Laura. They made small talk for a while.

Then Steve said: "I don't remember your parents, Laura. What were their names?"

"Edward and Georgia Gelman."

"Are they still alive?"

"No, unfortunately. My dad died in 2000, and my mom passed in '03."

"Was your dad a screenwriter?"

"Yes, he was."

"Was he blacklisted?"

Laura gave a start. "Uh . . . yes—" she said timidly. "He was."

"I guess my parents were friends with both your parents and Sophie's."

"Yes."

"But then my dad did something very bad." He paused for a moment. "Has Sophie told you that whole story? And about how we met again?"

"Uh . . . a little bit," Laura said, neither she nor Steve noticing the stunned look on Sophie's face.

"Yeah," Steve said, "my father was one of the bad guys. A 'stool pigeon,' as you folks say. But he was so ashamed of what he'd done that he tricked me into thinking he'd done the opposite." As he said this he smiled, almost mischievously, as if he were saying, *My daddy was a very naughty boy.*

"Well . . ." Laura said, clearly at a loss for words.

"But then . . . you know what happened? It was the craziest thing—"

"Laura knows the whole story," Sophie said.

"I know, but let me tell it anyway. Sophie's dad had this old wire recorder—"

Sophie rose from the couch. "Don't anybody stop talking," she said. "I'll be right back."

She went out into the hall and found her way to the ladies' room. Grateful that no one was inside, she stumbled into a stall and cried soft, joyful tears.

EPILOGUE

2006

Sean Davidson hefted a big box of clothes from the back of his Ford Explorer and carried it across the parking lot to the back entrance of the Out of the Closet thrift store in North Hollywood.

"Yo, Sean," Doug Aiken, the store manager, called to him from the back entrance. "Got something to donate?"

"Yes," Sean said, setting the box down. "First batch of Charlie's clothes. I've finally begun to face getting rid of his things, *poco a poco.*"

"Hey, I'm really sorry about Charlie."

"Thanks. He held on a lot longer than anybody expected. Almost twelve years."

"Speaking of that . . . are you sure *you're* okay? You know we do free testing here."

"Thanks, I've been tested twice. I'm clean."

"Well, thank God for that. Got anything else to donate today?"

"No, but for sure I'll be back. You wouldn't believe the amount of clothes he had."

"Wanna take a look around the store? We got a whole buncha new stuff the past few weeks."

"What kind of stuff?"

"Well, we've got some—ah, I know what I wanna show you."

"What's that?"

"Follow me. You're a sound engineer, right?"

"Yes, I am."

"And you collect old things? Old sound equipment?"

"Yes, I do."

"Well, I got something right over here you might be interested in." Doug led Sean to shelves loaded with old, mostly worthless stereo components, TVs and computer monitors. Nestled among these things was something much older.

"This here's a real antique. Fifty, sixty years old would be my guess. Some kinda recorder."

Sean raised his eyebrows and examined the machine with interest. "Wow," he said. "This *is* an antique. It's an old wire recorder."

"It still works. Took some doing, but we managed to figure out how to thread the damn thing. There's some interesting stuff on this reel. Sounds like some kinda courtroom drama . . . or maybe even a real courtroom. I couldn't tell."

"This thing was made just after World War II. They only made them for a short time, until tape recorders replaced them. I remember Charlie talking about these . . . I think he said his dad had one. But this is the first one I've seen. Look how thin this wire is!"

"It's marked at ten bucks, but I'll let you have it for five."

"I'll take it."

Sean walked out of the store with the twenty-eight-pound machine swinging at his side, momentarily forgetting his grief in the excitement of a boy with a new toy.

The End

NOTE FROM THE AUTHOR

Dear Reader,

I welcome honest feedback on this book, and strongly encourage you to share your opinion at Goodreads, Amazon, or wherever you browse for books. If you liked *The Wire Recorder*, please tell a friend who might also enjoy it.

I invite you to visit my website, **www.thomasalevitt.com**, for information you might find interesting, including background material about the Hollywood blacklist and the story of how *The Wire Recorder* came to be written.

Sincerely,
Thomas A. Levitt

ABOUT THE AUTHOR

Thomas A. Levitt is a Los Angeles native whose parents were blacklisted in the 1950s. He attended UC Santa Cruz and taught in the Los Angeles public schools for thirty-three years. *The Wire Recorder* is his first published novel.

Made in the USA
San Bernardino, CA
08 August 2018